PLUMMET

PATRICK YON

ABSOLUTELY AMA⚡ING e BOOKS

ABSOLUTELY AMAZING eBOOKS

1.

I was in a room again. Familiar but not personal. This time, I was on the bed, waking. The room was bare except for the bed. The walls were off-white in color, a washed-out tan. The carpet was the same drab color and there was one window, covered with closed, plastic blinds illuminated by the light outside. The room was dark except for the weak light from the window and I didn't know what time it was. I didn't know what day it was. I didn't know where I was, what city I was in. I knew it was me. The room was clean, but why was I here, alone? Where was I? Then there was the feeling that I was a boy or a younger man at someone's home. No. It wasn't a home. Something else and something wasn't right. There was a darkness. Doom. Why did the room look so plain? Poverty? Depression? It faded away.

Then a voice in the dream. A woman's voice. She's annoyed. I woke and there was pain from the back of my head to the front. I tried to open my eyes but they were dry and everything was out of focus. My mouth was dry. I blinked several times and looked straight ahead and tried to focus on a rectangular box outlined in yellow illumination. There was someone in the room. A woman. Everything was blurry and the pain in my head throbbed with each heartbeat. I closed my eyes.

"Three hundred and twelve dollars?"

The woman's voice. I was in a bed. I turned over slowly towards the voice and my cheek fell on cool sheets. I opened my eyes again and saw a woman holding money in one hand and pants in the other.

"Whah?" The noise came from me but it didn't sound like me.

"Wake up, lover. It's time to settle up."

I closed my eyes again. I didn't want conversation. I didn't want thought. I didn't want this woman here. I rolled away from the voice and drifted away.

"Hey, fuck head. You can deal with me or my man. Believe me, you'd rather deal with me."

Broken images flashed in my mind and dread filled blank places in me. There was a club. A strip club. And a woman. This woman? How'd I get here? Where is here?

"You owe me $500. You said you had it. I'm giving you credit for half the drugs. So it's $500."

Drugs? Did she say drugs? Fuck. No wonder I can't wake up. What did I put in my body? I rolled over again onto my stomach and pushed myself up on to my hands and knees. Drool pooled in my lower lip and I closed my mouth thankful for the moisture. A siren from outside. It blared louder then faded, with what? Distance. Time. I turned my head and looked at her. She's young, short cutoff jeans, large fake tits under a black spaghetti strap top. Her hair looks like it was spray-painted with a pinkish-purple nail polish. I picked up a stripper. It came back to me in a series of regrettable images. I got a hotel, she called someone, drugs were brought. We fucked. Were there others?

"Tell me you've got the money."

I turned from her and crawled to the edge of the bed. The cool air on my ass told me I was naked except for a T-shirt. Unintentionally, I farted.

"That's nice. Look if you think this is a joke I'll call Cody."

I slid off the bed, half stood and held out my hand, silently commanding – or pleading? – that she stop talking.

Each throb of pain in my head yanked a string that jostled a stomach full of filth. I closed my eyes as I pondered vomiting. Don't call. Don't talk. Just give me a few moments. I half-opened my eyes and stiffly walked to the bathroom, turned on the light and closed the door. The brightness blinded me and I fell to my knees in the direction of the toilet groping for the cool ceramic where I rested my cheek. My heart was pounding and I breathed deep breaths trying to fend off the nausea. I don't want to puke. If I puke, I'll shit. Who cares? It's a motel. But I can't do that. Why not? I can do all of what I did last night but not that? No, I can't. I pushed myself up, sat on the toilet and grabbed a small trash can in front of me. I heard the sound of a door shutting in the room. Did someone come in or leave? What did she say his name was? Carl? The thought of a confrontation opened the gates and I hurled into the trashcan. Shit poured out at the same time. I hurled again. When I was sure I was finished, I spat and put the trashcan on the floor and cradled my head in my hands. I need to shower. No. I need to get out of here. I cleaned up. When I reached for the door I stopped and listened for the sound of anyone in the room. Nothing. I opened the door and walked back into the room. The girl was gone and I looked for the rest of my clothes. Those are gone too. An empty liquor bottle was laying on the table with three plastic cups and a mound of cigarette butts in an ashtray by a lamp. All I had was the T-shirt I was wearing. I went to the window and held back the blinds. A shaft of sunlight punched me in the face. When my eyes adjusted, I saw a parking lot with a few cars. Seagulls squatted motionless on the pavement. Beyond was a bank, a convenience store and a fast food restaurant. I recognized the four-lane street beyond. I was in North Charleston. How in the hell did I end up in a motel in North Charleston? I dropped the blinds and went back to the bathroom where I was confronted with my image in the mirror. Black, graying hair stuck up in comical array all over my head. Dark, puffy semi-circles hung under bloodshot eyes. The skin of my face looked dull and sagged as if wanting to slide off my skull. I splashed cold water on my face, grabbed the largest towel I could find and wrapped it around my naked waist.

Walking across the parking lot to the motel office, I tried to ignore the click-drag-click sound behind me. I looked up at the motel sign. See. The motel sign. It's here. I'm here. Other people can see it too ...

"Sarge?"

I kept walking. A little faster even.

"Can you hold up, Sarge? I'm havin' a little trouble keepin' up."

I stopped but didn't turn around. He's not going away. You know it. Talk to him. What could it hurt?

The sun was rising higher in the sky and with it the heat. The nausea intensified. Just the heat but I knew the return of Corporal Billy Shores to my life could also trigger vomiting from the raw fear of what it meant. I turned and looked at him, or my mind's manifestation of him anyway. It wasn't a pleasant sight. He leaned on a crutch under his right arm. The left arm was a stump, torn off above the elbow, bone, tissue and blood exposed. The left leg was missing below the knee. He was shirtless but wore government issue pants that were stained at the waist and left leg with blood. The left side of his face was crushed and his eye was missing along with a chunk of his skull, exposing the brain. At least he had a head. There have been times when that was missing too but he still talked, which can be disconcerting.

"Billy."

"Where are your pants, Sarge?"

I turned and started walking. Another wave of nausea, more intense this time. I considered throwing up again but it passed. My grip on the towel was so tight my hand was cramping.

"Who was that girl? Did she take your pants? Is she your girlfriend? Is she mad at you or somethin'? You sure know how to piss off a woman, Sarge ..."

I reached the door to the motel office, opened it and walked in, hopefully leaving Billy Shores outside. There was no one in the small lobby but an employee at the desk. He looked up at me, then to my waist and back to my eyes.

"7 B?"

"Excuse me?"

He reached down and handed me a brown paper bag, saying nothing else, just looking at me with an expression that said he knew more than he cared to know. I took the bag with my free hand and dumped the contents on the desk. My phone and debit card spilled out. I opened the texts on my phone. U owe me $500. Txt me when u have it. I'll bring your wallet clothes gun.

My gun. She has my fucking gun. How did my fucking gun get in the hotel room? I curse and walk out the door.

~ ~ ~

Outside the motel office there was no sign of Billy Shores. I walked up the sidewalk to the bank holding my towel and ignoring the faces in the cars driving past. One asshole honked his horn. I stood behind a car at the ATM in the shade of the drive through. The bank was closed and I wondered what day it was. When the car pulled away, I walked up to the ATM, pulled up my account, checked my balance and withdrew $700 leaving $34.18. As I was standing there a car pulls up behind me. I looked over and saw a young woman staring with her mouth open. Two children in the back seat were straining to see me. She calmly backed up and drove off through the drive through lane. I took my receipt and money, went to the McDonalds next door and called a cab. Then I sent a text: where?

Plummet

Seconds later, I got my answer.

I bought a large coke, hash browns and an egg, bacon, and cheese biscuit and waited. When the cab arrived, I gave him the address then filled my gut with cold caffeine and warm grease as he drove us down Highway 52 towards Charleston. I wiped my hands on the towel when I finished and fought off more nausea. The idea that this girl's pimp boyfriend would be waiting for me churned my stomach and I wondered if I might lose my bowels in the cab. I farted to let off some pressure and that seemed to help. I rolled the window down and caught the cabbie looking at me in the rear-view mirror. What can I say brother: It stinks. At a minimum, there was beer, tequila, probably jager, some kind of barbiturate, pot, cigarettes, bacon-egg-and-cheese biscuit, Coca-Cola and hash browns all mixed together inside of me, triggering a chemical reaction that would certainly produce foul odors. Add anxiety, shame, regret and a dose of fear and he should have been thankful I didn't add liquid shit to all the other putridity that soiled the back seat of his cab.

~ ~ ~

The cab turned onto Greenleaf Road, a straight strip of sun-bleached asphalt penetrating a dusty industrial area on the bank of the Cooper River. We may have turned off what eventually becomes Meeting Street, but there was nothing of the Charleston charm out here, a few miles up the river from the city. We drove past rusty storage tanks, warehouses, empty loading docks and sandy lots filled with container boxes. The cabbie pulled over and stopped the car when I told him this was the place. Facing us on the other side of the road was an 80's era, piece of shit black Mustang convertible with the top up. Except for the cab and the Mustang, the road was empty and quiet. I handed the driver some cash and asked him to wait. I clutched the towel, got out, tucked my phone inside the towel at my waist and walked across the hot, sandy asphalt to the Mustang. The window was down and a young, muscular bald guy covered in tattoos was in the driver's seat. My girlfriend from last night was next to him smiling as she wedged a long, pink fingernail between her teeth. Carl's muscular arm was draped casually over the steering wheel. Faint music filled the inside of the car. Beyoncé maybe. Or Rihanna. Carl was looking straight ahead through sunglasses. Several thick gold chains hung around his neck.

"Five hundred?" I started thumbing through the bills with my free hand wondering how I was going to get the right change without dropping the money or the towel. Carl looked in the direction of the girl and she reached into the back seat and pulled out a white garbage bag. She held it in her lap. I had to bend over slightly to see in the car.

"Should I give it to him, Cody?" I tried to think if I called him Carl. Cody turned to me.

"It's seven fifty."

"She said five hundred."

"She ain't management. She's a cunt and a pair of tits. I'm management. Seven fifty. Call it a late fee."

I stared through the window at Cody and the girl. She was looking straight ahead and not smiling anymore. In the back seat the head of a metal baseball bat was visible. The sun seemed to shine hotter, the air grow thicker.

"I don't have that much."

Cody reached down and turned off the car. Although he didn't say anything else, the look on his face told me he was unhappy. I have developed over the years the ability to sense when physical violence was imminent and, when it wasn't. It's a useful skill. At times, I can stand my ground in the face of cursing, threats and posturing, looking like a tough guy, confident all the while that no punches would be thrown. Conversely, there have been times when I knew what's about to go down and I could prepare myself for what had to be done. Standing there on the road in the hot sun, naked but for a towel and T-shirt, I knew Cody was going to get out of the car and beat my ass, then take all the money I had. I couldn't run. Flight wasn't an option. Given the situation, I made my decision. I gripped the towel tight in my right hand and when Cody turned his face in my direction, I punched through the open window with my left and hit him just below the middle of his sunglasses. Blood splattered over his face and both of his hands flew to his nose. Dropping the towel, phone and money, I jerked open the car door and with my right hand reached behind Cody's neck. I grabbed a fistful of tank top and gold chains and dragged him out of the car. From down the road I heard the engine of the cab revving and the wheels spinning on the sandy shoulder as the cabbie made a wild U-turn and drove off in my only ride out of the place. A cold bolt of desperation sent a charge through me and I stomped Cody's head into the pavement with my heel, my balls and dick flapping with every stomp. The girl was screaming in the car, cursing me and crying out for her pimp. When I was sure he wouldn't get up I walked around to the passenger side of the car.

"You fucking asshole!"

She was trying to roll up the window but it was a manual so I had time to reach into the car and unlock the door. I opened it, grabbed her by her pink-purple hair and pulled her into a parking lot. She fell to the ground with a screech and more profanities. She threw a handful of sand towards my face that caused me to turn away from her. She scuffled back towards the Mustang and by the time I reached her she had a hand on the baseball bat. I pulled her back out of the car and fell backward landing hard on my bare ass with her crashing down into my crotch.

"Goddammit!"

Tiny bits of shell, sand and rock tore into my ass. The

bat clanged across the ground behind me. The girl turned around on top of me, grabbed my hair with one hand and began punching me in the face with the other. I grabbed her by the throat with my left hand and squeezed. She let go of my hair and pulled at my fingers with both hands. A thought flashed in my mind: End this bullshit before Cody gets up or the cops get here. I let go of her throat and when she dropped her hands I swung a fist that landed in her jaw. There was a loud crack and she fell off me onto the parking lot moaning. I scrambled off the ground and limped around to the driver's side of the car. Cody was trying to get off the ground and looked up at me as I picked up my phone, towel and money laying near where I dropped them and got in the car. The keys had been left in the ignition. The white bag that I hoped contained my clothes and gun lay in the floor in front of the passenger seat. As soon as I had the car in drive, Cody's body slammed into the door and window next to me. I hit the accelerator and the car spun out on the loose sand and dirt. Cody slid off the side of the car as it pulled away. I gunned the engine and as the car tore down the road, I could see Cody in the rear-view mirror, struggling to stand up in a cloud of dust. He was holding up an arm, giving me the finger. At the end of the road I turned in the direction of downtown Charleston. I knew if I passed a cop anywhere near Greenleaf I would get pulled. But I didn't see any and soon I was in heavier traffic filing into downtown. I guess the cabbie didn't want to get involved.

2.

The public garage off St. Phillip Street wasn't full and I found a spot on the second level. After turning the ignition off I sat back and breathed deeply, staring, without thought, straight ahead past a concrete wall to the building across the street. For a few moments I just stared at the building thinking about it and nothing else, the nearest I could get to thinking of nothing at all. Then I looked down. I was still naked except for the t shirt and I began to take mental note of all the areas where I felt pain: my ass, my knees, my right elbow and the back of my head. Both of my feet were throbbing. I did notice that my hangover was all but gone, flushed from my system by the adrenaline. " new cure. I'll have to remember that one.

"You whipped his ass, Sarge."

I looked up into the rearview mirror and saw Billy's reflection, smiling back at me. He was uninjured this time, and I could see he was wearing his khaki, Marine -issued shirt, probably the uniform known as Charlie, but I could only see part of him in the mirror. At least he had a face.

"And hers. Although for a moment, I thought she had you ..." He laughed a little and looked out the window.

I watched him in the mirror but said nothing. Don't talk to him. Maybe he'll go away. But what I didn't ask myself is why is he back? I hadn't seen him in months but I guess a drug-fueled sex party was enough to resurrect him. I'd been doing good, not completely sober but none of the hard stuff. Just booze and pot but mostly just booze. The thought of going back on medication flashed in my mind trailed by a brief sensation of panic. No. I'm not doing that. I don't need it. Billy will go away. I just need to rest. But the worry was there and telling myself that I'd be okay wasn't as reassuring as I wanted it to be. Seeing dead people isn't normal. Carrying on conversations with dead people is psychotic. Even after I was "cured" I knew I wasn't far removed from relapsing into major mental health problems. I don't think Billy ever went away. He's just been hanging back waiting for his time. But I had been doing better and the thought of being sucked back down into all of that was, well, terrifying. My former life was gone but I had worked to find another one, a life that was simpler, that didn't have as many "moving parts" which is what I called anything in my life that could change on me at any time. People, for the most part. My law license had been indefinitely suspended which eliminated a lot of moving parts for me: clients, other lawyers including partners in the firm, staff, witnesses, judges, probation officers – a lot of people that depended on me or expected a certain level of professional competence that I was no longer able to deliver. But I had been able to integrate a few moving parts back into my life at my own pace. My job as a freelancing paralegal allowed me to control my workload. If I felt the load growing heavy, I didn't have a boss throwing more on top of me. I could just decline the work. A nice problem to have, too much work. Not something that bothered me at the moment.

I reached over, grabbed the garbage bag and pulled out a pair of smoky jeans, a wallet and flip flops. I smashed the bag together in my hands to make sure that was it. No gun.

"Fuck!"

"Hey, don't worry there, Sarge. We'll get your gun back."

There was no sign of anyone on my floor of the garage

so I got out and gently slid the jeans on over the cuts and road rash. The flip flops hurt even worse. The bottoms of my feet were toasted and torn. I leaned back in the car searching it good for the gun. Billy was gone, which helped, but there was no gun. I even checked the trunk and glove box knowing it wasn't there. I grabbed my phone and money and started to leave but stopped, leaned back in and grabbed the towel. I shut the door and threw the keys into the driver seat. I considered wiping the car down but threw the towel over my shoulder and limped to the exit. They don't want the cops in their life any more than I do.

As I walked down St. Phillip Street, I fought the urge to go home and go to sleep. I checked my phone for messages. The first was from Wendy, my ex. Just two words: child support? The next was from "the office" call. The Office wasn't really an office, it was a bar called The Post Office that I visited, well, every day. If anyone wanted to find me, they would either call or go to the Post Office. If I wasn't there, they'd leave a message. It was called the Post Office because the building where it was located used to be a post office a hundred years ago. Whoever named the place didn't care to put much effort in the process. But it was a good bar and a short walk from where I lived. It was mostly a hangout for locals. Waiters, waitresses, cooks and other staff from the restaurants downtown would go there in the early morning hours to have a few drinks after work. So the place never got cranked up until after midnight and I was usually gone by then. Except for last night.

Depending on who took the message, I would either get a call or a text from whoever was working at the time. A one-word text from the Office at 10:15 am was a message from Sam. Sam thought that by sending me a text he had involved himself enough to get all the dirty details of a case. Usually he just texted a number. Since he wanted me to call, experience told me the potential client was an attractive woman. I called and Sam answered.

"You couldn't just text me the number?" I couldn't resist taking a shot at him, but his return shot was better.

"What happened to you last night?"

Dread opened a bottomless pit in my stomach. I stopped walking, moved away from the street to a shaded area under a tree.

"Why?"

"You and Todd were partying pretty hard with a couple of women. Then, all of a sudden, poof, you were gone."

Todd Burley. I was with slimy Todd Burley last night. Things were making as much sense as they probably ever would. Burley was busted once for spiking a woman's drink with Rohypnol then having his way with her once she was out of it. He beat the charges and stayed out of sight for a while but started making an appearance now and again at the Office and other places not found on tourist brochures. I had been trying to stay away from him. Why was I with Todd Burley?

"What? You don't remember?"

"Sam, when it comes to last night, I remember too much. Before you tell me about the girl who's looking for me, tell me what day it is."

"Saturday. How do you know it's a woman?"

"Are you sure it's not Sunday?"

"Saturday. How'd you know it's a woman looking for you?"

"Because I know you. I also know you took a picture of her with your phone telling her you would send it to me along with her number so I would recognize her."

"You're good."

"You're predictable."

"Well, I don't think she bought it."

"You didn't get the picture?"

"Oh, I got the picture, but she was posing for it. Her eyes

are half closed and she's licking her lips. She totally busted me. You ought to see her tits."

"Give me the number and maybe I will. And send me the pic. It'll help me find her in a crowd."

"Like I said."

I called the number. She wanted to meet ASAP so I told her I'd be at the coffee shop on the corner of Calhoun and King in fifteen minutes. I was only two minutes away but I wanted to wash up in the bathroom, get some coffee and take a few minutes for myself. I had shared more of my day so far than I normally like to do.

~ ~ ~

After getting as much of the dirt and dust that I could off my face, arms and head in the bathroom sink, I got in line. Looking at the people around me, I realized how filthy I still was. I looked like a homeless person and probably smelled like one too. Two girls ahead of me in line glanced my way then moved a little further away. I was mildly amused by it actually. It's been a while since I gave a shit about that.

I sat at a table for two with my coffee next to the window facing Calhoun Street. Looking around at the other customers I realized how oddly normal the scene was despite my presence. Not far from me two young mothers sat, talking over coffee, their babies laying quietly in their carriers. How would they react if they knew that not one hour ago and five miles from here I was half naked beating up a pimp and his whore? Not to mention last night. And what do I know of these people and what they have done? None of us know. We walk past each other, drink coffee next to each other, our secret selves hidden from view. One look at me should give them a notion of my history. But children don't cry, mothers don't scream. Tables aren't knocked over by people rushing for the exits. Not knowing, not looking, we each go on with our private lives, taking in the small parts of the world we want but otherwise living oblivious to what is happening outside of ourselves. How often and in what places do we unknowingly come within the sphere of danger? I had learned to live with the knowledge – no, the fear – that at any moment I could lose it again. For the most part I felt good, but last night and the reappearance of Billy had me worried. Staying out, partying, sharing my waking moments with hookers, derelicts and a dead Marine, that was my life just before I went off the edge. I was still walking over trap doors. Maybe all of us do. But the problem with trap doors is the trap part. You can't see them. But I knew they were there because I had fallen through before. I lived with the fear that with one wrong step the world would open and swallow me again and the worst part was, I didn't know if I could avoid it. Not knowing how the night before had happened proved as much.

Through the door and around the tables and customers walked Staci Turner into my world. Looking like a Kardashian with black hair pulled back in a ponytail and sunglasses that covered half of her head, she wore a tight, tan dress that fit all of her curves, swooping low below her neck and revealing a long, straight, arresting line of cleavage. I would have recognized her without Sam's picture. I raised my hand a little above my head and waited for her to look in my direction. She was scanning the room as she walked. When she saw me, she hesitated a moment – incredulity? – her sunglasses hiding the truth in her eyes as she took in her first sight of me. She walked over.

"Mr. Peale?"

"Jack."

"I'm Staci Turner."

"Grab a chair."

For a moment she didn't move, just stood there with her mouth a little open, still reluctant to accept what she was seeing. Then something like resignation swept over her

16

body and she hopped onto the tall bar stool chair at the table. I watched her tits bounce as she settled in and placed a small black purse on the table.

"Coffee?"

"No. This shouldn't take long."

She took off her glasses and looked at me with almond-shaped eyes that were from another place.

"You caught me at an ... awkward time, Ms. Turner." It sounded lame but she was clearly uncomfortable with my appearance. "What can I do for you?"

"Simply put, I need you to find someone. That's what you do, isn't it? Find people?"

I had taken a drink of coffee when she said "That's what you do, isn't it?" and it went down wrong. I started coughing and couldn't talk. A guy at the next table folded his paper down and looked at me, then at Staci, then back at his paper. Then back at Staci.

"Sorry."

"Did I say something wrong?"

"No. Just ironic I think."

"I never really knew what that meant."

"I'm not sure I do either. So, Ms. Turner, who do you want found." She hadn't asked me to call her Staci.

"His name is Mahmoud Khalil. I need you to find him as soon as possible."

"Okay. Let's start with where he lives."

"If I knew that I wouldn't need you."

I paused, attempting to convey my irritation. At her or myself I wasn't sure. I was tired. I needed a shower, a shave and a change of clothes. It was a dumb question but she could have handled it in a less bitchy way. But what did I expect, deference? I looked like I had climbed out of a dumpster.

"Last lived."

"Oh, I don't remember, some condo at Wild Dunes I

think."

"Is he a personal acquaintance?"

For a moment she looked away towards the line of people at the counter as if thinking how to respond.

"We met in college. Chapel Hill. That's been about ten years ago. We became close in school, drifted apart after graduation but stayed in touch over the years. About seven months ago he showed up here in Charleston. We saw each other often. I introduced him to my friends and he seemed to be settling in. Then, all of a sudden, he's gone. I haven't heard from him in over three weeks.

"Why do you think he's in Charleston?"

"I don't know if he is. It just seemed like the place to start. Mr. Peele, we were close in college but a lot of time has passed. I don't know what he was involved in or who he was with other than the time he was with me."

"Any reason to think he was involved with the wrong kind of people."

"No reason but like I said, I didn't really know him anymore. I just can't help but think something bad has happened. The police think he probably just decided to leave town, kind of the way he showed up. Unannounced. On a whim."

"But you don't think so."

"No."

"Why so sure?"

She looked to her right then moved to the edge of her chair and leaned across the table to shorten the distance between us. Reflexively, my eyes fell to her chest and bounced back to her face as her tits mashed against the smooth wood surface, causing cleavage to bulge out of her top. I swallowed hard. For some reason she lowered her voice as if telling a secret.

"We dated in college for a while but I broke it off after a few months. When he showed up here after all those years, well ..."

"Okay. So, things were going well between the two of you when he disappeared. No fights, no old boyfriends coming on the scene, no talk of dating other people?"

"No. No. None of that."

"Where did he work?"

"I honestly don't think he did. He said he worked for an investment bank but he seemed to have a lot of free time."

"Which one?"

"He never mentioned a name."

"Okay, Facebook, Twitter, Instagram?"

"Nothing recently. He has – or had – accounts but there hasn't been anything new for a while."

"How long is that?"

"The same. Three weeks. Maybe longer."

There was something wrong with what I was hearing, with this gorgeous person telling it.

"I'm sorry, but this isn't adding up for me. Why not let it go? This guy swoops in from nowhere out of your past, with no apparent job or reason to be here other than you, then disappears again. Why bother?"

She sat back in her seat and clasped her hands on the table. "I must not have been clear about how I feel about him."

"Oh. Well, if that ..."

"I want to know if he is okay. That is very important to me."

"That's understandable."

She picked the purse up from the table, opened it and pulled out an envelope that she slid across the table to me. Her demeanor changed.

"That's five thousand. I don't know what you charge. If you find him by Thursday, I'll give you another ten grand. If you haven't found him by then, just tell me what I owe. If this goes beyond Thursday I won't be needing your services any longer."

The relief that only a substantial amount of money can bring poured over me. I was so stunned that the strangeness of the Thursday deadline didn't register with me. I fought the urge to rip open the envelope and count the money. Hell, I wanted to bathe in it.

"Email?"

"Just text me or call."

"Well, you aren't giving me much time so I'd better get going."

"Mr. Peele. I'm giving you that money with the expectation that I will be your only client for the next few days, agreed?"

I smiled. "I'm all yours."

The smile wasn't returned.

She got out of the chair and put on the ridiculously large glasses that only she and women like her could pull off.

"Call me tonight and let me know what you've found out."

Before I could say anything she had turned and was leaving for the door. I watched her ass and her ponytail swishing back and forth. I caught the guy with the paper watching her too. He then looked at me. I gingerly slid off the tall chair and grimaced when my feet and weight hit the floor.

"Ex-wifey." I gave him a wink and limped out, leaving him to ponder the improbability of that union.

3.

*L*ucky for me, I was an undesired inhabitant of a garage apartment on a small street South of Broad. Lucky because my home was in walking distance and I had no idea where my car was. Undesired because the other inhabitants of the haughty homes South of Broad did not accept the existence of tenants in their neighborhood. Technically, I wasn't a tenant because I had no lease and didn't pay rent. The garage and apartment was on a lot with a two-story home owned by my aunt Martha who now barely lived in a nursing home, dying alone in a bed from a stroke and COPD. Five years ago, when the wax melted and I crashed to earth in a heap, it was Martha who took me in when everyone else shut me out. And there I have lived, even after I found Martha lying in the garden eight months ago, her face contorted, making guttural sounds, her eyes full of fear. So, I had some vague authority to live at 117 B Whitsett Lane, indefinitely it would seem. But since I did not own the property and my sullied reputation was known by most if not all of my immediate neighbors, I was unwelcome, a fact which made my home that much more appealing to me.

During my gimpy walk to Broad Street I decided to call my real ex-wife Wendy to let her know I would be sending her the child support she had inquired about so succinctly in her text earlier.

"Can I drop by and get it?"

"Sure. When?"

"You mean you got it? All of it?"

We were married ten years and I still couldn't tell if she meant to piss me off or if it was just an irritating, unintended aspect of her personality. Whenever we talked, it didn't take long for me to become sarcastic.

"Right, like I would I have called if I didn't have it." I felt like an ass as soon as the words came out of my mouth.

"I like to think you would have. Maybe I'm wrong."

"How much?"

"$630. You're behind two weeks. That'll get you caught up."

"Come by the apartment in about an hour."

"Why? Do you need time to get it? I'm not coming over there unless you have it right now. My lawyer told me I ought to make you pay through the court."

"Wendy. Two things. First, you know I don't have a steady cash flow. Making me pay through the court will be a pain in the ass for both of us. I may miss a payment or two, but I always catch it up."

"Well, I've got bills too, and they don't let me miss payments. Plus, your daughter is getting older. She's started her period which means tampons and -"

"She's only twelve-years-old!"

"So?"

"So! Isn't she too young for that?"

The darkness again. A purplish brown gloominess dimmed what had been a better mood. Wendy was talking again but I had zoned out.

"... her age so it's perfectly normal. What was the second thing?"

"What?"

Wendy paused. "You were going to lecture me on two things. What was the second?"

I didn't feel like talking anymore. I had meant to tell her that her lawyer was a cocksucker but that was gone now.

"Oh. Nothing. I forgot."

Another pause. "Are you okay?"

"Yeah. So, I'll see you in an hour?"

"I'll be there but meet me outside. I don't want to get out and I won't dare blow the horn."

"You got a phone. So do I. Call when you get there."

I hung up with the realization that once again, in the drama of my broken life as father and ex-husband, I was the ass hole, my ex-wife the grown up and my daughter the all but fatherless child.

~ ~ ~

After limping three blocks I caved and flagged a rickshaw. And why not? I was flush with cash and hurting like hell. When we arrived at Whitsett Street, I was easing my body from the rickshaw's seat to the sidewalk when I heard one of my neighbors squawking down the street. It was old, squatty Mrs. Thomason standing next to a dark sedan, raising hell at the closed, driver side window. She was beating on the top of the car – that she could barely reach – with a rolled-up paper. I had never seen the car before and it was apparently illegally parked on one-way Whitsett Street, the transgression that invited the wrath of old Mrs. Thomason. I crossed the street into the pea gravel drive of 117 B and stiffly walked up the wrought-iron steps to my apartment.

~ ~ ~

The cool inside of my apartment was an oasis. Maybe a bit of moldiness in the air but it was home and I was the only one there. Well, the only real person anyway. Billy Shores entered the den from the bedroom, hobbling on the crutch again but this time I could only see one injury. His entire mouth was ripped away, a piece of his jaw hanging to his skull by a strand of connective tissue. He stood there, slightly swaying and staring at me with exhausted, pleading eyes. As irritating as his talking could be, the silence was more disturbing, because it laid the sinister question of his presence bare before me. And I didn't dare consider it, walking instead into the kitchen and looking in the refrigerator for some tangible assurance that comes from something routine. What's for lunch? There's ham, cheese, what about lettuce? Yep, no that's got too much brown on it, maybe tomato.... I looked up, telling myself it was necessary to look for a tomato on the counter but of course I glanced back to the den. Billy was gone and relief swept over me. I closed the refrigerator and stood there listening and waiting. When I was sure he was no longer there, I went for a shower and shave.

My phone vibrated on the table next to the bed as I put my shirt on. I walked over close enough to see Wendy's face on the screen. I grabbed the envelope given to me by Ms. Turner, pulled out seven hundred-dollar bills and opened the door. Wendy's minivan was parked in the driveway. As soon as I reached the bottom of the steps I could see my daughter Megan in the front passenger seat, head down, looking at her phone or a magazine or her nails, anything but me. Wendy opened the door.

"Here ya go. That's seven hundred." Wendy took the money and started to count. "Hey sweetie."

Megan gave me a plastic smile and toss of her hand.

"Can we talk for a second?"

"Sure."

We walked far enough away from the van so Megan couldn't hear. I prepared myself for another scorching assault on my shortcomings as a father. "I thought you didn't want to get out of the car." My lame attempt to lighten the mood. Wendy ignored it.

"I need a favor."

"Fire away."

"Can you keep Megan this week?"

Why was my initial response to any request that I keep

my daughter always "No"? Because I was a selfish prick and a crappy father. Over time I had trained myself not to blurt out an answer, but to pause and think about a response. I wanted to spend time with Megan, but I always doubted she wanted to stay with me. And this time I had a good reason for her to stay away. "Let's see ..." I pretended to ponder my schedule but was actually considering whether or not Megan should be with me since Billy Shores had reappeared. If Wendy knew, would she even consider it? No, she wouldn't, but I wasn't going to discuss my hallucinations with Wendy in my driveway. Sensing my hesitation, Wendy pushed harder. In a quiet but emphatic voice she said "Please. I need this."

I didn't want the details but I believed her, whatever it was. Telling myself again that Billy would soon disappear and that Megan's presence would probably help, I relented. I also think I wanted to prove to Wendy that I was there for Megan when she couldn't or chose not to be. Whatever the reason, it was a mistake.

"Sure. I'd love to."

Back inside my apartment above the empty garage, I just stood in the quiet and tried to get a handle on everything I was suddenly feeling inside: this morning's events and the reappearance of Billy Shores, the upcoming week with my daughter and the nagging knowledge of my lost car and gun. Then there was the client and her... what was he to her anyway? Something wasn't right with her. There was something she wasn't revealing. Wouldn't reveal. I knew she wasn't telling me the truth but that's not uncommon with clients. They usually don't tell the truth or just tell their version of it, whether they believe it or not. No, she's withholding facts, important facts and that's what I want. Not truth. She's not in love with him, but that's what she was selling. And she was selling it and selling it hard. She came to me with a purse full of cash and a chest full of cleavage. A package deal no man like me or what she guessed me to be would turn down. And she was right. She knew me before she met me. But why the hard sell? Then there's the time constraint. She needs the job done quick but what else? I went to the fridge and pulled out a beer, grabbed my phone and sat on the couch. Ms. Turner wanted me to see things her way or at least be convinced of her lie. I looked at the time on the phone. One thirty. The numbers made me tired. It felt like 5:30 after all I'd been through. I went to my contacts and scrolled down to the name I was looking for and hit the speed dial. I thought of Staci Turner again, but this time it wasn't what she had asked me to do that I was thinking about. An image of her leaning over the table at the coffee shop appeared in my mind, she was smiling and I was letting her take me away when a voice on the phone interrupted.

"You white, carless motherfucka." The fake, Jamaican accent was almost laughing.

"Batista."

"You can't leave cars like that on the street."

"It's a piece of shit."

"Exactly, mon. Visual pollution."

"Where is it?"

"Where you left it.'

"If I knew that, we wouldn't be talking." I thought about my gun. No, I'd still be calling him.

"The Paradise. You had a party last night?"

"You heard?"

"Who would I be if I didn't know?"

"You are the man, Batista."

"I also heard about dis morning."

"Who was he?"

"Lucky for you, nothin' to worry 'bout. Small timer. Small fishy."

That was a relief. I didn't think they were connected but

there's always the chance. If they had been, well, I was glad I didn't have to deal with that.

"I've got to leave it there a while. I'll get it later today."

"Is that all you got for me?"

Quid pro fuck me. Ju Ju Batista extracted some benefit from every human contact he made, 24-7. I admired him for that. And I knew it when I called. What I gave him was information. Flotsam and jetsam that might be worth something to him now or later.

"The county has a new CI. Don't have the name yet but he's young, green. That's all I know right now."

"Weak, white mon, weak."

"That's all I got."

"I guess dat's enough to keep some piece ah shit from bein' stripped to its axles in the parking lot of a nudie club."

"You are the man, Batista."

"Anything else, Peele? "The Jamaican accent was heavier now. The Ju Ju Batista myth has him a native of Haiti, landing in Charleston by way of New York City. My information has him born and raised in Goose Creek, not twenty minutes from Charleston. Batista was a pastiche of confusing bits of cultural misinformation and bullshit. I'm sure he didn't know the difference between Jamaica and Haiti.

But did he know about my gun? He knew about the fight so it's possible, even probable. I didn't want to get into that with him yet. If he thought I was desperate, the price would be high.

"Nope. Just the car. Why?" Here it comes.

"This is for free."

Doubt made me pause. "What is it?"

"Lissen. I've heard there are some bad people in town."

"I know. You and me right?"

"I'm not fuckin' around, Peale."

"Okay. What's that got to do with me?"

"Maybe nuthin'. It's just your name was brought up."

Unexpectedly, fear shot through my body, freezing me for a moment. There was no reason any of what Batista was saying should cause me immediate concern. But when you've fucked up as much as I have in your life, a vague, ominous feeling follows you that makes you think – or feel – that somewhere there is someone that wants to do something bad to you. And it's just a matter of time. What Batista said gave credence to what had been just a crazy notion, not too different from seeing a ghost.

"Thanks for the head's up. You'll let me know if you hear more?"

"Of course I will, mon. I want you healthy so you can keep feeding me useless information like your nameless, faceless, whereabouts-unknown CI that you told me about."

"Later, Batista."

"Live long and pross-paahh."

It came across as a bad joke.

~ ~ ~

I threw the phone on the couch next to me, took a swig of beer and thought about the gun. My Sig nine-millimeter was stolen, hopefully in the possession of Cody the small fry pimp. But who knows? I hadn't thought about it because there wasn't anything I could do but wait. Yeah, I got the girl's number but after this morning I'm not expecting favors. Those fucking morons trying to shake me down. Nope. There's nothing to do but wait for the call. They'll need money soon. They could sell it to someone else but I'm sure to pay more. Patience was the best move at the moment. It wasn't like I could report it stolen. The police would surely want to know why someone who had lost his right to own and possess a gun still owned and was trying to regain possession of a gun. I looked at the TV and considered getting off my feet for a while. No time. Got to get on this missing person. Another ten grand would be very welcome right now. I looked in the fridge again for food but there wasn't much there. I had to go to Martha's house anyway to take in the mail, check on things and use her computer. I drained the beer, got two more from the fridge and walked over to house.

The old homes in Charleston fall into one of two categories: Pre-War and Post-War. And by war I don't mean either of the World Wars or the Vietnam War. I mean The War. The war upon which Charleston culture seems to pivot. Martha's home is post war but not by much. It's nineteenth century, white with wrap around porches on both floors. There is a live oak tree that shades the small front yard between Martha's house and the neighbor's, its branches bending and reaching in response to what time has brought to bear upon it. The house has remained more stoic over the years, helped here with a coat of paint, there with a new board or brick. I walk up the steps, feeling for loose boards with my foot. I look up at the ceiling of the porch, painted light blue to resemble the sky so that spirits will be drawn out of the house. But I wasn't look for spirits, only peeling paint or mold. I felt obligated to look after the place until … until when? Inside the house was stuffy with the air of old, lifeless things. I left the front door open and walked through to the rear of the house to the kitchen and opened the back door. A breeze of fresh air from the harbor blew into the kitchen. I opened a beer and put the other in the fridge where I saw a pizza box from two days ago. Very edible. I took it to the place where Martha's computer was kept, a small room at the back of the house overlooking the garden in the back yard.

According to the tax assessor's website Mahmoud Kahlil didn't own a car or real estate in Charleston County. I didn't think I'd find anything different but I had to check. Facebook was more helpful. Pictures showed a boyish, good-looking face on a middle eastern man who was about thirty-five. He had four hundred twenty-nine friends. There were pictures of him at a Chicago Cubs game, at restaurants, various places outdoors in or near a large city (Chicago?), always with three or four people. I didn't see anything that looked like Charleston and none of the pictures identified the location as anywhere close to Charleston. There were no pictures of Staci Turner. There was nothing under birthplace, relationships, education or employment. The last post was almost one year ago and was a picture of Kahlil in what looked like a street in Italy or Greece or the Middle East. Nothing unusual except that he was alone in the picture and he was growing a beard. The post was dated August 7.

Twitter was more interesting, not for anything he had tweeted but for who he was following. The feed consisted mostly of tweets from what appeared to be people from the Middle East based on the names and subject matter. There were journalists, individuals, self-described Ahuman rights observers" and news agencies. Kahlil had tweeted nothing. Not even a retweet. I couldn't tell when he had last visited the account. But where Facebook looked like the account of a typical American guy in his thirties, the Twitter account could have belonged to someone who had never been to the U.S. Then I noticed something. When I scrolled through the groups and individuals he was following, there were two mosques, one in Chicago and one in Columbia, here in South Carolina. I Googled the address on my phone and saved the location.

After finishing the pizza and beer I closed up Martha's house and walked the three blocks over to the Post Office for my afternoon check-in. It was a clear day with gusty breezes that made the tops of the oaks and palmettos sway against the sky. Sort of unusual for mid-October. Feels like a storm. I looked around stupidly as if I could see a storm coming but there was nothing but blue sky and white clouds. I walked down an alley that led to the back door of the bar. " thin man leaned against a wall next to a pile of flattened cardboard boxes, smoking a cigarette in the shade. He was a frequent appearance near garbage cans and dumpsters.

"What's happenin', Rodney?"

"Storm comin'."

"Yeah? Metaphorically or literally?"

"Don't know nothin' bout any of that."

"I'm just messin' with you, Rodney. Is Sam here?"

"Yeah. He's in there. Soze Jess."

"Don't work too hard."

Jess was behind the bar and Sam was looking at a TV mounted in the corner near the ceiling. Jess saw me walk in and grabbed a glass as I reached the bar.

"Any messages?"

"Yeah. One from me." Jess held up her middle finger with her right hand and placed a pint of pale ale in front of me with her left. "Why do I feel like your fucking wife, Peale? Taking your calls, pouring your beer – beer that I usually pay for, by the way – meanwhile you're out all night fucking who knows what."

"Ya'll shut the hell up."

"Any messages, dear?"

"I can't hear the fucking TV!"

I look up at the TV. An attractive woman in a skin-tight dress stood in front of a weather map of the Caribbean. Below Puerto Rico a ragged circle of green, yellow and red formed the familiar radar image of a tropical storm.

"That thing isn't coming here. It'll turn before it hits us. Sam freaks out every time thunderstorms gather in the Atlantic."

"Hugo didn't."

"Statistics, Sam. Not going to hit us. The Gulf, Florida, maybe the Outer Banks. Not us. We might get rain and wind. Big deal."

"Seriously, any messages?"

"A Social Security called. Her name and number are on the board." Sam's eyes hadn't left the TV. Then he remembered Staci Turner. "Hey. What about the one from earlier? Did you talk to her?"

"Talked to her and met her. She hired me to look for a guy. Here's your finder's fee." I pulled out a hundred and laid it on the bar in front of Sam.

"Hold on, ass wipes. Where's my tip?"

"Jess, Sam put me on a paying client. You flipped me off and gave me a beer." I dug out my cash and put a one dollar bill on the bar. "There you go." She stared at me, then moved down the bar pretending to work.

"So what's her deal?"

As I said, Sam was faithful about getting me clients but he expected to be kept informed. He didn't have much of a social life outside of his job at the bar. That's not right. He didn't have any social life outside of the bar that I knew of. Sam was large and pudgy with a soft, friendly face and little concern for personal hygiene. What beard he had wasn't shaved often and he usually smelled of body odor. But he seemed happy and that's the only reason I didn't feel sorry for him.

"Missing person case. An ex-boyfriend that came back into her life suddenly disappeared. She's concerned. Wants me to find him by Thursday."

"You're looking for a corpse. Dude is dead."

"Why's that?"

Sam reached for his phone in his pocket. "Are you serious? Look at her." He held up his phone. On it was Staci Turner and her lascivious pose, all tits and pouty lips. "Some guy is banging this and he just leaves town without a good bye? Bull shit. Dude is dead."

"That's not the picture you sent me."

Sam smiled. "She let me take two."

"He's been looking at his phone all day." Jess said from down the bar. "I thought it was the weather report on that storm. Now I know the truth. You disgusting pig."

"What storm?"

"Hey, she's going to be my date tonight. I've been thinking about it all day."

"Peale, give me her name and number. I'm going to call her and let her know that her image is a victim of sex crimes."

"I'm beginning to feel an obligation to let her know myself. What storm?"

"Come on now. Are you telling me that those poses don't give me the implied permission to ... to do ..."

"To do what, Sam?"

"Whatever I want? I mean, with the picture."

"That's it. Peale, give me her name and number."

Jess was holding up her phone, just waiting on the number to dial.

"Go ahead. I know what she'd say."

"Alright, Jess, it's Staci Turner. Her number is ..."

"Staci Turner?" Jess lowered the phone.

"Yeah. That's the client. Staci Turner."

"The Chief of Police's stepdaughter?"

It hit me all at once, like the light coming in the window this morning when I pulled back the blinds in the motel room. Staci Turner is the daughter of Rasha Carlton, the wife of Charles Davis Carlton, Chief of Police for the City of Charleston. The almond shaped eyes, black hair, olive-brown skin come from her mother who is from Syria or Iran or someplace near there. Before marrying the Chief of Police, Rasha Carlton was Rasha Turner, widow of the late billionaire Christian Wilcox Turner who was a very prominent figure in Charleston prior to his death in an airplane crash several years ago. The widow's marriage last year to the younger, handsome police chief had tongues wagging for months in Charleston.

"Uh, yeah."

"You didn't know she was the stepdaughter of the chief of police, did you?" Jess had a smart ass look on her face. "What kind of private detective are you?"

"I'm not a private detective. I'm a paralegal."

"Right. I forgot. And the difference is ... what?"

"Not important." I drained the beer and put the glass on the bar. "Sam, can you run me up to North Charleston?"

Sam passed the question to Jess with a look.

"Go ahead. You aren't doing anything anyway. Just be back by three. I want you here when we open. For paying customers."

Sam dropped me off next to my car in the Paradise parking lot. I checked out the interior for contraband and cranked the car before waving to Sam that everything was okay. He left in the direction of Charleston and I headed for the airport to have a talk with a TSA employee I knew. Maggie Felton was a large, unattractive, course woman with no scruples. She had a personality and lifestyle that spawned sexual legends. One had her sexually assaulting a guy that had knocked on her door to inquire whether she knew Jesus as her Lord and Savior. Maggie, wearing nothing but a house coat, invited the gullible missionary in, where – rumor has it – she tore of the robe, threw the stunned fellow to the ground and lowered her genitalia onto his face and started to grind. Meanwhile, she opens the poor guy's fly and starts munching on his package, in kind of a sixty-nine position except the missionary was more like a squiggly 'one,' flattened out and struggling the way he was. I didn't believe that one or any of the others that I'd heard. But each story was believable to anyone that knew her. I wasn't looking forward to the conversation.

Inside the terminal I went to the Delta desk and asked

a ticket agent where I could find Maggie. The guy gave me a look that bounced between bewilderment and disgust.

"Hold on." He walked through a door behind the desk and was gone for several minutes. I leaned against the desk watching the people drift through, pulling suitcases, holding hands, pushing strollers, but there was no sign of Billy Shores. That should have made me feel better but it didn't. Somehow, if I saw him when I looked for him, his reappearance wouldn't be so menacing. I had convinced myself that seeing him again was just a result of the drugs and partying I had done, the drugs having lit up some dormant cluster of neurons that was home to the ghost of Billy Shores. As soon as it was out of my system Billy would go back to sleep and leave me alone. This theory came with a bonus feature: if the drugs brought Billy back, any drug might do the same, including the pharmaceuticals the psychiatrist would give me if I went back to her. I didn't want to go back on those because I couldn't function when I took them. But not being sure about how Friday night had happened and seeing Billy again scared me. I didn't like to admit it to myself but I had been through hell, put others around me through hell. But I was in a good place now, probably better than I deserved and I didn't want to lose what I had. So I told myself that the temporary resurrection of Billy Shores was what I could expect if I chose to party with Ted Burly. After a couple of days, the poison would leave my system and Billy would disappear again. It sounded good. Then I would hear the voice of my ex-wife, the voice of reason, responsibility, maturity: What if he doesn't disappear in a couple of days? What then? An unpleasant voice saved me from answering.

"Peale! You come all the way out here to ask me on a date? You coulda called."

I turned and forced a smile. A small cap of brownish-gray curls covered a head above a pink, sweaty, porcine face.

I forced myself to keep eye contact.

"How are you, Maggie?"

"Horney!" She laughed and I tried to. The Delta agent next to her grimaced.

"Maggie. Can we talk somewhere in private?"

"What's wrong with here?"

I looked at Delta and she turns to see what I'm looking at.

"Mike. Take a smoke break."

Delta started to say something but stopped, quickly turned and disappeared again through the door.

"All right, Peale, what do you want? Information?"

"I need to know if someone came through here in the last year."

"And I want Johnny Depp as a personal carpet muncher."

This was going in a direction I didn't want it to go.

"I'll pay you for the information."

"No shit. How much is the question and ..." Here she smiled and let her eyes grope my body – "what with."

I felt like the victim of an assault but knew I had to play along with her.

"Come on Maggie, I'm not near enough man for you."

A reptilian smile spread across her face. "So you say. What's the name?"

"Mahmoud Kahlil."

"A raghead?"

"He's American."

"Not with a name like that."

"It's the twenty-first century, Maggie."

"Do you know what kind of bells and whistles this could set off?"

"I have an idea. That's why I'm talking to you. Can it be done?"

"Somebody can do it. Question is, can I do it? I'm not

exactly upper management."

We both stood there a moment. Maggie, hands on her hips, twisted her mouth in thought, as if pondering competing schemes to infiltrate TSA's data banks without detection, although I knew that wasn't likely. I knew she could do it. She wasn't considering whether or not it could be done, she was deciding what to charge. She looked at me with a serious expression.

"Okay. I'll do it. But this is what I want ..."

I drove back to Charleston almost hoping Maggie couldn't come through with anything on Khalil. I squirmed in my seat thinking about it. She didn't want money. She wanted a man. Any man. She said it could be me or someone else, she didn't care, but she wanted him for a night. There was only one condition: he couldn't be a pro. That told me she wanted it to be me and there was no way in hell that would happen. What I had trouble understanding was the trust she put in me. She was going to let me have the information on Khalil and take "payment" afterwards, hanging the obligation over my head. Maybe it wasn't trust after all. Maybe she knows where I live. I put that thought away immediately. My home is my refuge. I can't live with the thought of Maggie, in a house coat, pounding on my door in the middle of the night, forcing her way in and ... It couldn't be me. I've done a lot of things in my life, but that ... no way. It would have to be someone else and I knew that my man lived somewhere among the passel of derelicts, drug users, fornicators, criminals and sub-humans I know that live in the Holy City.

When I arrived home, Whitsett Street looked like a crime scene. In front of Martha's house, a police cruiser was parked, left side tires on the sidewalk. Another cruiser, further down and parked the same way, crowded the other side of the narrow street. Before pulling into the driveway, I could see faces of neighbors, anxiously surveying the scene from their porches. My heart sputtered, then quickened when I saw another black and white cruiser parked in my driveway behind a black, late-model Tahoe with dark windows. I'd seen the Tahoe before and my heart rate slowed when my mind started making sense of the scene. I parked the Taurus next to the Tahoe. As soon as I opened my door the two front doors of the Tahoe opened. I got out and stood in the pea gravel drive as two men in dark suits stepped out of the SUV. One stood next to the back door on the far side while the other asked me to follow him around to the other side. The hair on their heads was shaved down close and they had ear pieces with wires that disappeared into their collars. If I didn't know better, I'd think the president was paying me a visit. But I knew better.

The pea gravel was making a lot of noise crunching under all those feet and it annoyed me. This intrusion annoyed me. But, as one of the men opened the door and motioned me into the back seat, I told myself, this should have been expected and what the hell, this little meeting might even clear up some of the cloudy mystery encircling Mahmoud Khalil.

Charles Davis Carlton sat in the backseat talking on his phone as I slid into the empty seat beside him. He said his goodbyes and put the phone in his coat pocket, turned to me and smiled a big smile that showed lots of teeth.

"Jack Peale. How are you my man?" He stuck out his hand for an awkward handshake.

"Chief Carlton."

"Oh hell no. It's Charles. None of that Chief shit."

"What can I do for you, Charles? Did you find a body in my garden?"

"What? Shit no!" Then he faked a serious expression and leaned closer. "Why? Should we look?" He leaned back, smiling silently, his eyes fixed on mine. The smile faded. "No Jack, I'm here ... unofficially."

"I don't think my neighbors will see it that way."

"Oh. The escort. Yeah ..." He shook his head as if trying to dislodge an unwanted thought. "I hate that shit. But ... it's required."

We exchanged silent looks, mine quizzical his cautious and searching.

"You met with Staci this morning."

"What of it?"

A serious look came over his face, looking as if he was struggling with what to say. I didn't know the man personally, but the public image he projected was loquacious and confident. This was someone else.

"My wife asked me to talk to you."

"Okay." I was growing tired of this and it must have shown in my voice because he face flashed with irritation.

"Staci is a beautiful, strong-willed woman ..." He stopped as if he'd forgotten his lines. His head dropped and a faint smile creased his face again. It was easy for him to smile. It was his default expression. "Ah hell. Let's say it how it is. She's a spoiled, pain in the ass. There. My stepdaughter is a spoiled, pain in the ass." He was looking at me again, like the statement explained why he and his entourage were in my driveway and blocking the street.

"If you say so. I've only spent a few minutes with her."

"Her father lived a lifestyle – no, he provided a lifestyle – very different from my own."

"Billions of dollars can do that. So what's the problem? Now that her daddy's dead and her mother has married a civil servant, Staci isn't a happy debutante?"

"Money isn't the issue, Jack. There is a family trust that is … well, let's just say it is sufficiently funded."

"So what is the problem? Why are you here?" The conversation was going in circles. That told me he really didn't know what to say which meant it wasn't his idea to come here. Now the smile was gone, replaced by an expression that exceeded humbleness and approached vulnerability. I was truly impressed.

"It's a poorly kept secret that I have political ambitions." He glanced at me for my reaction. I was stoic. He continued. "Rasha supports me one hundred fifty percent but Staci..." He grimaced slightly. "Staci doesn't care about all of that." The smile came back. "But hey, she's an adult. She has her own life and she's free to live it, right?"

"Only, you don't want events in her life to be an issue for you, a public issue." I decided to make a guess at the point of all this in the hope of getting him out of my driveway sometime soon.

"Thank you. Well put. I don't know why that was so hard for me to say." His phone was vibrating and glowing inside his pocket. He leaned over and pulled it out, glanced at the caller and returned it to his pocket.

"So, what can I do for you Charles?"

"I'm concerned about the guy she wants you to find. He's not the kind of person her mother or I want her associating with."

"Ignoring the fact she's probably close to thirty years

old, why not?"

"Jack, you and I both know that money has the tendency to attract the wrong people. Staci's past is a repetition of her life intersecting with the lives of the wrong people. For a while it seemed she had grown out of that. But her meeting with you proves we were wrong."

"Again, what can I do for you?"

Irritation flashed across his face. He wasn't enjoying his role in this. "Keep me informed. I know she has you looking for someone. Just let me know if you find him."

He was uncomfortable. He was crossing a line and he knew it. But why would that bother a man like him? "You know I can't do that."

"No. I know you can. And my life consists almost entirely of repaying favors. How would you like your law license back?"

The offer stunned me and I wondered at first if I had heard him right. I mumbled something and reached for the door handle.

"Jack, it's a serious offer. If that doesn't interest you, think of something else." I slid out of the door onto the pea gravel and turned to face him. "But the offer stands. Just keep me informed." I reached and took the card he was holding out. "I take care of my friends, Jack. Our friendship can be worth more to you than what Staci is paying. Think about it." He rolled down the window on his side of the car. "Okay, Dave, let's go." All at once, there was movement. First the guys with wires in their ears moving around the SUV, doors shutting, then the SUV and cruiser backing out of the drive into tiny, cramped Whitsett Street. And after a moment, all was quiet again except the birds and the sound of a neighbor's door shutting down the street. Then another. And another. I walked up the steps to my apartment wondering what Staci Turner had brought to my life and who this Khalil could be to garner so much attention. I entered the apartment and let go of the screen door, sending the slapping sound through the still trees, across the silent rooftops south of Broad.

I opened a bottle of beer in the kitchen and went to the sofa, thinking about the offer. Everything I had achieved as an adult had been taken from me three years ago and I had reconciled myself to who I had become. I didn't have a choice. I had become who I was. All that had been taken away – the wife, daughter, home, job, law license, friends – were the aspects of a temporary existence I was destined to lose. I wasn't meant to be a husband, much less a father. I shouldn't have tried to be a lawyer or be the member of a country club or owner of a nice home in an upscale neighborhood. I was a person that shouldn't extend his responsibilities much further than himself. And since I had dared venture beyond myself, that life was taken away by God or justice or karma or fate. Something.

That's what I told myself. And that's what I kept telling myself so I could live with what I'd become. The new me. No, the true me. Then comes Charles Davis Carlton, down from Olympus, offering a mortal the divine gift of rebirth, causing me to doubt the story of me that I was telling myself. Even if I told myself that same bullshit story every day for the rest of my life, I knew, deep down, it wouldn't matter. I wanted it back.

5.

She could see Fort Sumter from the window where she stood, the American Flag, fluttering and small in the distance.

Rasha liked her home on the Battery. It was old, but still beautiful. Just like me. Tourist passed by all day, every day, just to look it.

Her eyes shifted from the water to the street below. A horse drawn carriage was stopped on East Battery, its costumed driver talking and gesticulating while the occupants craned their necks and took pictures with their phones.

She hated it at first. Hated the whole city. When her first husband had bought the house in 1983, she threatened to stay at their place in Manhattan whenever they were in the States. She was a city girl after all. London. New York. Rome. Not Charleston. You couldn't call the place a city. More like a village. A stage lot where tourists came to take in a post card version of the Old South and dine on fried seafood.

That's how most of Charleston made a living. The tourist trade. But not her. And not most of her neighbors on the Battery either. Their homes weren't paid for or maintained by restaurants, dress shops or tour guide services. Shrimp cocktails and mimosas wouldn't have covered the monthly utilities and taxes, even in the eighties. No, the money on the Battery had to come from other places. Trust funds, tax- sheltered off shore companies, other large corporate holdings, the places where you could find the fortune she had inherited from Christian Wilcox Turner when he died in that plane crash.

Then came Hugo. 1989. The storm had left the live oaks and palmettos torn, uprooted, stripped and bent and the bottom floor of her home flooded by the tidal surge. But the place didn't go down. None of the other homes on the Battery did either. Following the storm, the media had referred to the multi-million-dollar homes on the Battery as "sturdy", "proud" and "time-tested." Rasha saw them as defiant and began to feel a connection to the place.

She learned that the City had survived not only hurricanes over the years but an earthquake, fire and of course, The War. From what she could tell, the War was still being fought by some. Not an actual war of course, but an attitude of "us vs. them". She recognized that too. Racism lurked in the dark corners of this attitude and she knew she was a "them." The dark skin, dark hair, the accent. "Not from around here." No problem there. After all, she came from the Middle East. She understood tribalism. Skepticism of others, an intolerance of their ways. But there was also generosity, friendliness.

The South. The Middle East. Both rooted in the Old Testament. Lots of blood in the Old Testament.

She turned away from the window. There will be more blood.

~ ~ ~

Almost two weeks had passed since Charles Carlton had come home early after speaking at a luncheon to find Rasha and Staci talking with an older, middle-eastern man on the second floor of their home. He wore a grey suit with no tie and a blue shirt unbuttoned at the top. They must have heard him climbing the stairs because all three were standing when he entered the room. Rasha and the visitor were

46

looking in his direction. Staci was looking down, holding a glass of ice tea. He would have thought nothing of the meeting had both women not been wearing a hajib. Rarely had he seen his wife wear the head covering. He had never seen Staci wear one and at first didn't recognize his stepdaughter, thinking instead that she was a visitor also. The look on his face had concerned Rasha and she quickly introduced him to the guest.

There were three types of people in Charles Carlton's world: those that could help him, those that couldn't and those that could hurt him. The first he wooed, coddled and cajoled; the second he ignored; the third kept him awake at night and occupied his thoughts during the day as he schemed of ways to minimize the damage they could inflict. After the brief introduction, Chief Carlton had excused himself and returned to his office, worried that the man in his home was the third kind. Later, after running a background check, he knew the man could be trouble. That night, before going to bed, he confronted Rasha about the visitor. She was sitting up in bed, in her nightgown, reading something on her phone.

"Are you going to tell me why an arms merchant was in our home this afternoon?"

Rasha put down the phone and closed her eyes. When she opened them again she asked "Do you trust me?"

Carlton let the question hang in the lamp lit air of the bedroom long enough to imply the opposite of what he was going to say.

"Yes."

"I'm trying to control a situation."

Electric pain shot through Carlton's gut and he gritted his teeth. "A situation?" was all he could manage to ask.

Now Rasha paused, considering how much to tell.

"I didn't think you would come home so early."

"But I did. Part of me wishes I hadn't."

"And the other part?"

He looked her in the eyes. "Wants to know everything."

Everything? She almost smiled at the devastation that would cause him. Instead she looked away, watching her hands smooth the comforter over her lap. I'm not telling everything.

"He has information about William's death."

To Carlton information was a commodity. It could be bought, sold or bartered with. There was extortion too, of course, but that was just forcing someone to buy information under unpleasant circumstances. "And what is he planning to do with this information?"

"Nothing. He is concerned about us."

Carlton's eyes narrowed. "This involves Staci. doesn't it?"

"It involves all of us."

"All of us?" He walked over and sat on the side of the bed and looked his wife in the eyes. "Is there something I should know?"

She leaned forward and kissed him on the side of his mouth then whispered on his cheek, "Yes. Know that I love you and you can trust me."

Carlton put his hands on her shoulders and gently moved her far enough away to look in her eyes once more. Nothing was said and she moved close to him again and kissed him on the mouth. Her night gown slid off her shoulder.

The doubt and suspicion could wait until the morning. For a reason he did not want to think about at the moment, his beautiful wife wanted to make love. He stood up, undressed, turned out the light and got into bed.

~ ~ ~

They lay in the near-dark of the bedroom, the only light coming from the half -opened door of the bathroom. She was turned away from him but he knew she was awake. They didn't make love often and after three years of marriage it was clear to him that his wife used sex to manipulate him. He understood manipulation and didn't begrudge her for it. Rasha was older than him but still beautiful, still able to capture the attention of younger men walking down King Street. She seemed to enjoy it when they made love which made him admire her even more. But whether she enjoyed it or not didn't matter. It was obvious to Carlton she knew its value and wouldn't dilute its purchasing power through over supply.

"So, is there something new about William's death?" His voice sounded strange in the dark room and he wondered if she might pretend to be sleeping when she didn't answer right away.

She turned over and faced him. He was looking at the ceiling but he could feel her eyes on him.

Just as I thought. Sex was Plan A. Since that didn't work, she'll move on to Plan B.

"Are you sure you want to know?"

As much as he loved the sex, Plan B was much more effective. With one question she both threatened him and positioned herself as his protector. But if what he knew about the visitor was correct, Rasha couldn't protect him, or more specifically, his career.

Now he turned on his side and looked at her, the long dark lashes closed over her almond shaped eyes.

"I always want to know everything."

Her eyes didn't open but she smiled, weakly. Not a smile of joy but one acknowledging the dark humor of a joke that wasn't funny. She opened her eyes and looked at him, looked at him staring at her with something he probably thought looked like an unyielding will. Something she could turn in any direction she wished.

"Staci owes a debt to the man you saw us with. Or more accurately, to some men that he represents."

"Not a financial debt." A faint hope persisted that this could be handled with money. Rasha's and Staci's money.

"No. There are no financial obligations. Nothing direct anyway."

It may have been three o'clock in the morning but he was awake now and ready to go into action. "Go on."

Rasha then explained everything to him, feeling as if each sentence was a punch landing on something vital in her husband, watching him crumble before her eyes as she laid there, her head on her pillow. She didn't enjoy it, but knew he needed to know. There was no way she could keep what was coming from him. He needed to make plans. Protect himself.

Carlton had thrown the sheets off and begun pacing the room before she had finished, his mind racing with thoughts, fears, schemes and extrapolations. When she had finished, she raised up on an elbow and looked at him. He stopped walking.

"When is this supposed to happen?"

"I don't know."

"Where?"

She told him. "But the details have been kept from me."

He then asked a question he didn't want to hear the answer to. "Why haven't you done anything to stop it?"

She looked at him in silence and he knew if she didn't say anything she would be telling him what he didn't want to hear. She supports this.

On the floor below the bedroom he took his cup of coffee and walked out onto the balcony from his office that overlooked the back yard. It was dark and quiet. A cool breeze brought the smell of salt marsh from the harbor. He could hear the leaves of the trees shimmering as the breeze pushed through the branches. His mind left his surroundings and focused again on what he had to do.

First, he could go public. Notify the press, have Staci arrested and let things go from there. Rasha would be implicated too. Probably divorce him. Even if she didn't leave him he'd have to divorce her. And her fortune. Even if he exposed the plan, there was a good chance it would stick to him and ruin him politically.

Second, don't go public but notify the feds. And state law enforcement. Let them handle it. He would be seen as dealing with the situation properly. But that would place the outcome in the hands of others. People with their own agendas who would protect their own interests. He would be a weak player in it all, exposed and expendable. In the end, he and Rasha would divorce. His political career damaged if not destroyed.

Third, he could handle it himself. Privately. This had the most appeal. It kept alive the hope that his marriage wouldn't end and his political ambitions wouldn't suffer. And how hard could it be? Staci, for all her charms and abilities, was a novice in the world of crime. He had spent most of his career in law enforcement and had all of the tools afforded a law enforcement agency at his command. All he needed to know was who, when and where and he could stop this and there would be no one that would care to bring it to the attention of law enforcement or the media. And once Rasha and Staci realized he wouldn't let anything like that happen, they wouldn't try it again. Or wouldn't be asked to try again. The people that had approached his wife and stepdaughter would be picked up and spend the remainder of their days at Guantanamo or wherever the US government took terrorists these days. He would make sure Staci and Rasha understood that.

Carlton saw that he was no longer thinking strategically but musing. His reasoning was breaking apart and morphing into fantasy. He wasn't going to intimidate

Rasha, Staci or the people they were beholden to with whatever authority he possessed as the police chief of Charleston. But it was clear that the only option that gave him a chance of saving his career and his marriage was the third option. And why not? It was the only option that offered the possibility of keeping matters under his control. It might even result in Rasha and Staci living at his mercy once it was over. He told himself he was fantasizing again. He didn't have that kind of control over them and they knew it. There was nothing he had that either of them needed and that fact had always shaped the dynamics of the family. He was dependent on them because of the money. He had never seen an opportunity to change the way things were until now. If I can stay clear of this while stopping it from happening, they will both live with the knowledge that with one call I could end their way of life. He placed both hands on the balcony railing and leaned forward and looked out into the darkness with a smile. Yes. That was the way to handle it. Out in the darkness he could see that place in the future where Staci behaved herself because she feared what he could do to her and Rasha respected him even if she didn't love him anymore. He would never have to worry about Rasha refusing him money. Her fortune would be as good as his. All of the potential for power that resided in him would then be realized in that place, somewhere out there. He just had to get to it.

His smile faded as an uneasiness returned. He had first felt it when he had asked Rasha why she hadn't stopped Staci and she hadn't responded.. She supports this. He didn't want to believe it but he knew it was true. Rasha was a forceful woman and nothing within her influence happened without her blessing or a fight. And from what he could tell, Rasha had put up no resistance to what was being planned. When she had revealed the target to him, there was nothing in her voice or her eyes that told him she opposed the bombing of a synagogue in downtown Charleston. Hearing it had made him feel sick but Rasha had spoken the words as calmly and with no more emotion as she would in discussing a shopping trip. We've been instructed to bomb a synagogue.. And then a truth came to him, one he could not ignore, had to accept. I may not be able to stop them. I need help. He would still be in charge, but he would have to bring others in, people he could trust. Walking back into his office from the balcony, he knew who to call.

6.

It wasn't that Charles Carlton doubted his wife loved him. Why marry a poor public servant if she didn't? But Carlton was a realist. If made to choose between him or her daughter, Rasha would choose Staci every time. The love she had for Staci came from another place. It was older and stronger.. And that was the problem. Rasha wouldn't do anything that would hurt him if she could help it. But Staci? She never gave him or his career a second thought. After learning his wife and Staci had involved themselves with a possible terrorist attack in Charleston, Carlton knew he had to be proactive and had called a friend in Washington for help. Not official help. He was still convinced he should – and could – handle this on his own. But he needed someone with a certain skill set that would be discreet. So, he had called a friend with the intention of making the request in the vaguest possible way,

"Chief." The voice on the phone was deep, melodic, familiar. Welcoming.

"Congressman."

"It's good to know I'm not the only politician awake, working for the people of South Carolina."

Carlton knew Congressman Clarence Davis well enough to know he was awake every day by 4:00 am., no matter when he went to bed. The man was sixty-eight years old, seemingly tireless and the only black member of Congress from the State of South Carolina, He was Carlton's political mentor and a crucial friend.

"I sleep when I can."

"And right now, you can't."

"I guess not."

"I think I know why."

Pain shot through Carlton's gut. Did he somehow know about Rasha's and Staci's contact, what they'd agreed to do? If he did, it came from a government agency so others know too. There would be no way to control it …

What do you mean?"

Some information came to me that will be of interest to you."

"What would that be?"

"Your stepdaughter has been spending time with a guy named Khalil. " lot of time."

"Okay. Why would you be interested in who she spends time with?"

"I can't give out details. Let's just say that he's being watched. He's in Charleston. His contacts are being checked out. When Staci's name came up, I was told."

Carlton was immediately making a connection between this Khalil and what Rasha had told him about the people they owed a debt to. How much does he know?

"Why were you told?"

"As you know, Rasha has contributed a lot of money to me over the years. Thank her again for me, by the way. When Staci was being looked into, my name came up, I was told. As a courtesy, in case anything needed to be done to prevent an embarrassing situation. I said there was nothing to worry about when it came to Staci Turner. I was correct in saying that, wasn't I?"

Carlton's throat had become dry while the congressman talked, the edge of a hot knife slicing the inside his gut. Whoever was watching this Khalil wasn't going to stop just because the congressman said everything was okay. This damn thing was already getting out of control.

"Of course."

"Good. Now what did you want to talk with me about?"

Carlton hesitated. How much can he say without Clarence Davis making a connection?

"I need to add someone to my security team."

"Oh really? From what I hear, it's almost the size of a platoon already."

"This is different."

"What do you need?"

"Let's call it a freelancing bodyguard. One that's more proactive than the typical version."

The congressman made a sound on the phone that indicated he was putting this all together.

"I'll ask around. Tell you what Chief, I'm going to be in Charleston Thursday. Let's get together. It's been too long."

Two nights later, the congressman was on the deck, looking over the back yard of the Carlton home on the Battery, holding a bourbon drink. He shook his head, smiling.

"Charles, why in the hell would you want to bother yourself with politics when you have this." He walked away from the railing towards the bar and added ice cubes to his drink.

"My dreams were formed when I was young and poor. They were dreams of power and influence. Not expensive homes and vacations."

"Well, when I see wealth like this, I see power. I see influence."

"Bought with a dead man's money."

The congressman nodded his understanding of the sentiment and tossed peanuts in his mouth. "So, what's on your mind, Chief, other than power and influence?"

"I didn't want to discuss it over the phone the other night. Thanks for meeting with me."

"Shut the hell up. You don't have to kiss my ass. It's just

you and me. Talk."

"I didn't tell you the truth the other night. I am concerned about Khalil. About Staci."

"You already knew?"

"I didn't know the name, but I knew of the contact."

"Any idea who he is?"

Carlton didn't like lying to his friend but told himself he didn't know if Khalil was connected to the terrorists or not. "No. Probably nobody, but Staci has a habit or attracting the wrong type."

"Chief, I can assure you, he is not a nobody. The people that contacted me wouldn't be interested unless he was somebody."

"Who told you? The FBI?"

"No. They aren't government. I can't reveal who told me. Now, I'm sure they have government contacts, employ former government ... let's say, operatives. But they are not government. No, they are very much >for profit'. "

Carlton didn't like what he was hearing. A private group, powerful enough to have the ear and confidence of a congressman knows who his stepdaughter is hanging out with? Is watching that person? What else do they know?

"I can't say I like the idea of some shadowy group surveilling Staci."

The congressman smiled. "Worried about blackmail? Don't. Not their style. This isn't about you Chief. Not to them anyway. Like I said on the phone. They were looking out for me."

"Can I ask why?"

"Sure. They're like any other corporation or special interest in this country. They want to buy politicians. They want friends that can cast votes. Like you, they have plans. Plans that can benefit from legislation. Or be killed by it."

That made sense and would have been more convincing if none of this had come to his attention on the heels of his conversation with Rasha. Carlton had the disconcerting feeling of being a pawn in someone else's game.

"Okay. So, have you given any thought to what I said about a bodyguard?"

"Didn't you say a 'special kind of bodyguard'? A bodyguard with special skills?"

"Something like that."

"Well, Chief, twenty-five years of war in the Middle East has created an oversupply of bad dudes for hire. I know of someone that can help with what you need. A private security contractor. I'll have them contact you."

"Do you trust them?"

"Of course. They have the best kind of loyalty. The kind that can be bought."

Carlton didn't like it, but he trusted Clarence Davis. He didn't just trust that the congressman would look out for his best interest, he trusted his judgement.

"Ok."

"One other thing, Chief. They don't come cheap. But they are expensive for a reason. Remember, part of what you will be paying for is confidentiality." The congressman chuckled. "You'll have to tap into Rasha's money. A police chief can't afford these people." He laughed some more.

The reminder that his ambitions were probably wholly dependent on his wife's willingness to fund them irritated Carlton. He suspected the congressman knew how much it irritated him.

"When will I hear from them?

"I don't know. It depends on how they contact you. I'll get in touch with them tonight."

~ ~ ~

The next morning, Carlton was contacted by a man who said he was a private security contractor. He gave Carlton the terms and a brief background of his experience and training. He did not reveal the name of an employer or if he had one. He gave the impression he was an independent contractor. Carlton hadn't like it. The arrangement had been too informal, too loose. He even suspected the name the man had given him – Thursday – was fake. But Carlton told himself that this was where he was and it had to be done. He had agreed to the terms and told Thursday about Staci and Khalil but said nothing of terrorists. But that didn't matter. Thursday already knew about the terrorists. His employer had briefed him on Rasha's and Staci's involvement with a terrorist group before he had left for Charleston. But Thursday's employer hadn't told him everything. Resolute Corporation had plans for Charles Carlton's future, his career. But Thursday didn't need to know anything about those plans. He just had to stop the terrorists from blowing up those plans along with whatever it was they were planning to blow up in the beautiful city of Charleston.

7.

The Islamic Center was a two-story converted office building secluded behind tall trees not fifty yards off a busy road feeding into downtown Columbia. There were three other cars among the many empty spaces in the lot next to the building. I parked and noticed the quiet as I walked to the typical double doors you would find as an entrance to any office building. It then struck me that this was my first time in a building devoted to Islam. Once inside, I looked around. Frankly, I was disappointed. There was a bulletin board advertising an upcoming supper, a summer camp for kids, a car wash to raise money and a list of local businesses run by Muslims. What was I expecting? Death to the USA? Death to Israel? A soft voice behind me broke the silence:

"May I help you?"

I turned around. I must have jumped a little too. "Oh, yeah ... uhm ..."

"Forgive me for startling you. Assalamu alaikum."

Now that was more like it. But what do I say in response? "Thank you."

"What can I do for you."

He was a small man with glasses, mirthful eyes and a beard. He wore what looked like a religious cap on his head and matching, loose fitting clothes. The shirt came down below his knees.

"I was hoping you could help me find someone." I watched his eyes behind the glasses. They seemed to lose some of the mirth but he continued an easy smile.

"What is your name?"

"Jackson Peale. I'm a paralegal from Charleston."

"Mr. Peale, I am Kasim. Let's go into my office."

His office was located in a small room, bare except for a desk, two chairs and a few books on a credenza against the wall.

"May I get you anything? Tea?"

"Oh, no thank you." I caught myself feeling like ... what? An intruder? No, it was something else ...

"Well, who is it you are looking for, Mr. Peale?"

I pulled out my phone and brought up a picture of Khalil I had downloaded from Facebook and passed it to S. "His name is Mahmoud Khalil. A friend of his is worried about him. He has been missing for several months."

Kasim Looked at the picture and returned the phone to me.

"Mr. Peele, while Columbia is the capital city of a southern state, there are many Muslims in this community. Many people pass through this center, especially when you consider the university not four blocks from here."

"It doesn't seem very busy today."

"It is Sunday. Today is the Christian holy day, but our holy day begins Friday and ends Saturday. And, this isn't a mosque. It is a community center. Tomorrow will be much busier when the children are here for school."

"I knew this would be a long shot," I immediately questioned in my mind the use of a firearm metaphor – "but Mr. Khalil had 'liked' a post from this center on his Facebook page. It's one of the few bits of evidence I have linking him to South Carolina."

"And this friend of his, he cannot provide more information?"

"Not much more."

He sat back in his chair. "Relationships can be so transitory these days."

"Transitory ... right."

"Is there anything else I can do for you?"

"Do you have an email list or, better yet, a mailing list that I could look at? You know, like a contact list, of your members."

"We do maintain such a list but I'm sorry to say I cannot reveal it to you. Our members do not want this information disseminated to others. You understand, of course?"

"Oh yeah, I understand." The mirthful look in his eye had returned. What brought it back? Comfort? Control? "Could you at least look at your list and let me know if Khalil is on it? You wouldn't be providing me with contact information, just the knowledge that he has some affiliation here." Again, I questioned my choice of words and watched him as the mirth left his eyes again and his face contracted into a serious expression.

"Yes. I think that would be okay. But I will not be able to research this for you until later. If you leave me your number, I will let you know what I find out."

"Thanks. That would be great."

We looked at each other for a moment, both knowing what the outcome of his research would be. He slowly stood from his chair.

"Mr. Peale, I hope this person you are looking for is not in any trouble. Despite what you see and hear in the media, Islam is a peaceful religion."

"Well, I don't watch much TV."

He didn't smile and the serious expression returned.

"I grew up here, in Columbia. My name was Freddie Jones. My grandmother used to take me to

Tabernacle Baptist Church not three miles from here. But I didn't listen. When I was a teenager I became a drug user and fell into crime to support my habit. If asked I would say I was a Christian but that was a lie. There was nothing in my heart. My life didn't have meaning until I was introduced to Islam while serving a sentence in prison for armed robbery. Islam not only saved me, it transformed me. I want that same transformative power to work on the lives of those that seek it. That is why I am here. Every life should have meaning."

What is it about people that makes them preach sermons? Are they trying to convince me or themselves? Maybe both. "Well, my life had meaning once. Too much meaning. A few years ago, I decided to try meaninglessness for a while. It seemed less ironic." I had no idea if that was the correct use of the word but I've found that if you use the word >irony' or >ironic' with preachy people or other posers, it throws them off and allows you to leave the conversation with the feeling you had, in some way, won. It had its intended effect. All he said was "Well then ..." and I thanked him and left, but not before leaving my mobile number on a post it note. Wasted effort, I thought.

Leaving Columbia eastbound, I-26 rises and falls with the eastern edge of the sand hills before settling at last onto the coastal plain and the flat, straight stretch of interstate highway that leads eventually to the bridge over the Cooper River. My 1998 Taurus hummed along at 60 mph in the right lane, cars whizzing by on my left, my right arm draped over the wheel. I was in two parts: one was driving, more or less minding the road while the other was thinking, bouncing from one fragment to another. Meaninglessness? I told the guy I was trying meaninglessness? What does that even mean? Why be the ass hole, Peale? The guy opens up a little, tries explaining something about himself to a total stranger and you respond with sarcasm. Why is that? What's the point? Because he wasn't being honest, that's why. About his life, maybe he was, but he wasn't being honest about Khalil. He knows something, maybe not a lot be he knows more than I do. That was nothing but a dance I went through back there and that's why I was an asshole. Khalil. Hell. Khalil's a ghost. Billy Shores is more real. I've got a name, a few pictures and a few lines of bullshit from Staci Turner about her lost love. And what about Turner? Why not come clean about who she was? Why come to me at all? She claims she went to the police but that was a lie. Until the chief's visit yesterday, I had wondered why Staci hadn't flashed her tits at some investigator down at police headquarters and got him to look for Khalil for free. But it was obvious now why she hadn't. As I was running this through my mind I came up on the back of a slow-moving tractor trailer. Before changing lanes, I glanced in the rear-view mirror and saw a Crown Vic hanging about fifteen car lengths behind me. Something about it looked familiar. I slowed down and it closed in by several car lengths before matching my speed. We drove along like that for a mile or so until he pulled off at an exit. Settle down, Peale. You're getting paranoid. I was, it's true. Ever since talking to Batista I felt like I should be looking over my shoulder. What he said was getting to me and why shouldn't it? Batista was no alarmist. He wouldn't have said anything if he didn't think there was truth in it. But who? What did he call them? Bad people? Was that it? I had come up with two possibilities and one was a stretch. No, both were stretches but nothing else I could think of made sense. Plus, he said they were foreigners. What was the saying, the simplest explanation is usually the correct one, or something like that? Great. What if there isn't a simple explanation? I couldn't let it paralyze me, not now. I'm behind schedule already. Last night when Staci Turner called I told her what I had which wasn't much. The short conversation told me she wasn't impressed. Not that I expected her to be. I need more information. No, that isn't right. I need more facts. I've been getting information but most of it was just noise. I'm not getting anywhere with information. I was reminded of a time I went to the emergency room with chest pains. I spent almost two days at the hospital undergoing tests. After the doctors had eliminated every possible cause they could think of that would have caused chest pains, I was discharged without knowing what had caused my chest pains. Fifteen thousand dollars later I only knew what hadn't caused the chest pains. Nothing I had learned so far was telling me where Khalil might be. But then I realized that I hadn't been trying to find Khalil, I'd been trying to find out why Staci was looking for him. And why would you be doing that? I answered out loud. "Because I don't believe her." I was distracted and wasn't focusing. It doesn't matter why she wants him found, just find him. That's the job. 'Why' isn't important. But my mind couldn't make sense of this job from the beginning and Carlton's visit only confirmed that Staci was bullshitting me. But again, who cares? It doesn't matter. Find the guy. I shut down the discussion and focused on the road in front of me.

Later that night, back in my apartment, I started cooking a late supper. I put some rice on the stove and got some shrimp out of the refrigerator. I turned the heat down on the rice to a simmer after it began to boil, opened a beer and pulled up a play-list of music on my phone. As the music began playing, there was a knock on my door. I froze with the immediate thought that it was Maggie. I told myself the knock was too light for her. I looked at the clock: 10:36 p.m.. Unless she's serving papers, a woman that shows up at your place at 10:36 p.m. is looking for sex, which made me worry it might be Maggie after all. The knock came again and I realized it may just be a neighbor, wanting to discuss the scene from yesterday. I walked to the door knowing none of my neighbors would knock on my door at 10:30 at night. I opened the door expecting just about anyone but the person standing in front of me. Staci Turner's black hair hung down around her face that was smiling at me. Her white blouse was unbuttoned far enough to suggest just about anything I cared to think of.

"Can I come in?"

"Yeah, yeah, I'm sorry. You surprised me."

She walked in looking around as I shut the door. I watched her brown calves flex with each step she took in her heels. Her black skirt stopped at mid-thigh. She tossed her small black purse onto the couch.

"You live here alone?"

"Uh, yeah. My daughter will be staying with me this week but, yeah, I live alone." She hadn't been here a minute but was taking control of me. Get a grip, Peale. Hot thirty-year-olds don't drop in on you for sex. She's here for a reason. Find out what it is. She turned to face me and slightly lost her balance. "Whoops." She gave one of those smiles that imply a shared knowledge. But of what? Why is she here?

"I have to confess something to you."

"Don't hold back."

"Moody is not my boyfriend. He never was." She just stood there as if she'd made a delivery and was waiting on a tip.

"So why the big rush to find him."

"He owes me money." She tilted forward slightly as if wanting to whisper a secret. "Laahhtz of money." Her eyes were mostly closed when she said this and she stumbled a little before regaining her balance.

"Why not go to the police?" I knew the answer but wanted her reaction. "You've got connections."

A dismissive sound came out of her, part sarcastic laugh, part something else. Her eyes weren't laughing. "My stepdaddy." This time the sarcastic laugh was more audible. "There's something I can't decide about my stepdaddy. Does he want to control me or does he want me out of the picture?" I guessed she knew about the police chief's visit.

"Okay."

"It's my money. It's my life. I don't need some ambitious, small time politician to protect me. What I need are people I can rely on. She walked closer to me. "I came here tonight to find out if I can rely on you."

Again, more control shifted from me to her. I mumbled a weak response: "You can."

"I think I can too." We eyed each other for a second or two. "Bathroom?"

My mind scanned recent memory. What does the bathroom look like? There was nothing I could do. If she had to wipe the seat, so be it.

"Right through there to the left."

She smiled inscrutably and disappeared around the corner. The door shut and I walked into the kitchen and turned off the stove. What in the hell is going on? Every vibe in my body told me I was about to have sex with this beautiful woman. But why? She may be a little drunk but even if she was blasted, why me? Vibes don't worry with Why? They don't explain. Vibes deal only with what is. I pulled a bottle of vodka from the freezer. The toilet flushed and the door opened. When I could hear her in the den again I asked "How about a drink?"

"That would be perfect."

"Vodka?"

"Sure. Straight. Well, with lemon if you have it."

I brought her the drink. "Sorry. No lemon." She took it from my hand and drank it all at once. She closed her eyes and let her tongue trace along her lips. I stood there holding my beer. Her eyes opened and I reached for her glass. When I pulled it toward me she didn't let go and came with it. She looked into my eyes then away, a slight smile curling the edges of her mouth. I rested my hand that held the beer just above her ass and pulled her closer until her tits were pressing against my chest. She tilted her head back with closed eyes and I kissed her. She made faint sounds of pleasure and the glass and beer bottle fell from my hands onto the carpet. We fumbled with the buttons on our clothes while trying to kiss. With her blouse opened she reached behind her back and unsnapped her bra. "Let's go in there." As she walked into the bedroom her blouse and bra fell to the floor and she kicked off her shoes. At the bed she turned around wearing nothing but the skirt. Her brown skin and dark eyes were dimly lit by what little light there was from the den. I walked up to her and we kissed again, my hands running up the back of her skirt, each grabbing a cheek. She unzipped the skirt and I pulled it so it fell to the floor, revealing a black G-string. My pants and underwear hit the floor and we fell into bed.

When it was over, I didn't want it to be over. We lay next to each other breathing deeply. Usually this was when I got out of bed and went to the bathroom, cleaned up and left. But this was my home so I couldn't leave, not that I would have if it wasn't. My right arm rested on her thigh and I thought about how close my hand was to the small patch of hair between her legs. I closed my eyes and spread my fingers, lightly squeezing her inner thigh. She rolled over to me and I looked down as she laid almost on top of me. She pulled her hair back from her face and looked at me.

"Hi."

Her voice was playful, flirtatious.

I ran my middle finger down her spine until I reached the hump of her butt then lightly cupped her cheek with my hand.

"Hi."

My voice sounded winded. She smiled and her eyes roamed around my face.

"You could be from the Middle East."

"What?"

"The black hair. Brown eyes" She looked down to my chest and ran a fingernail down to my stomach. "The dark skin ..." She looked back at me, then laid her head on my chest, slowly running the palm of her hand as far down my thigh as she could reach and back again.

At fifty-one I wasn't inclined to ponder why this young, beautiful woman just made love to me or why she was still lying in bed with me, apparently enjoying the after moments of sex. I knew enough to enjoy it while it lasted. You can deal with the reasons and motivations later. But the small, faint voice of the little man in my head could be heard through the blood thudding in my ears: "It's a trap! You're not that good looking! You're old!"

"Sorry. Nothing that exotic."

"Oh, so I'm exotic am I?" She looked at my face again smiling.

"Yes. And beautiful. But you know that."

Her face became serious and she kissed me, lightly at first then harder, her tongue probing my mouth. I rolled over on top of her and grabbed a tit and her legs spread apart. To my surprise, my dick somehow came to life and I went into her again. A moan of pleasure came out of her and she reached behind me, grabbing my butt and pulling me inside her. I got on my knees and put her legs over my shoulders and gripped the bedsheets on either side of her head, thrusting deeper insider her. Her hands still gripped my butt and her arms pressed her tits together, bouncing with every thrust. And with every thrust she panted commands "Don't stop! ... Fuck – me ... Fuck – me! ... Hard -der!" until the commands became screams and a shudder went through her body.

"wait ... wait ..." Her hands released my butt and her arms fell to her sides. I pulled out of her and fell over onto the bed, breathing heavily. I had no idea if I came or not. I don't see how it was possible if I did and didn't care at the moment. I was more concerned that I might have a heart attack. Isn't that when they happen, during sex? We just laid there like that, diagonally, our heads at opposite ends of the bed, not saying a word. Finally, I slid off the bed. As I walked past her to the bathroom I ran my fingertips down her arm. Her eyes were closed but she smiled.

I wasn't in the bathroom more than a few minutes but when I came out she was gone. I went to the window by the door and parted the blinds. A black Mercedes convertible was backing out of my drive into Whitsett Street. It was too dark at the end of my driveway to see who was in the car.

When I turned off the lights and locked the door I could hear the music streaming from my phone. Until then, I hadn't been aware of it and smiled at the thought. I turned off the music and walked through the silence of the bedroom and fell face first on the sheets, breathing in the smells she had left behind, until I was asleep.

8.

When I woke up Monday morning it was past nine o'clock. I had less than four days to find Khalil and was no closer than when I began. Yet, the thought of ten grand was far from my mind. All I could think about was last night. I told myself that it had been a long time since I had been with a woman as beautiful as Staci but that wasn't true. I had never been with a woman as beautiful as Staci. But when I thought about being twenty years older than her, the corny thoughts and feelings drifted away. What the hell was last night? Where did that come from? I tried to find an explanation that didn't preclude the possibility of Staci actually being attracted to me, but I couldn't. Yeah, she was drunk, but it was a calculated move to counter whatever she thought Carlton was up to. "You're out of your league, Peale."

The coffee maker gurgled and spit and sighed while I cleaned a cup in the sink wondering where to go from here. Sunday had been a bust as far as the investigation went, bringing me more questions than answers. It was only then that a dark notion wormed its way into my thoughts. She's not going to pay me the ten grand. It came from wherever the knowledge gained from life's experiences resided within me. I call it my gut and I don't have to ask it for advice. It usually tells me what I don't want to hear, overriding my brain, my emotions, my dick. But she's loaded. Ten grand is nothing to her, said my brain and my dick. My emotions liked this explanation also and my mood improved. I poured a cup of coffee and my gut withdrew from the conversation.

I had all morning and the early afternoon before I picked up Megan from school. Despite the Thursday deadline I was facing, another matter had forced itself to the top of my to-do list. As good as last night had been, I couldn't shake the feeling I'd had when Staci first knocked on my door and I had thought it was Maggie. I had to find her someone and I had decided on who it would be.

As it turned out, finding Todd Burley wasn't as difficult as I thought it would be. He had been keeping his head low until the other night, not drawing attention to himself and certainly not advertising where he lived. My first stop was a long shot but I had to check it out. I stopped by the Office to find out if Sam or Jess knew anything. Sam knew nothing and offered several useless suggestions. Jess huffed at me with a look that said she should cut me with broken glass for suggesting she would know anything about what Todd Burley did outside of the bar. I moved on. Driving around I remembered Todd talking about playing poker machines at a store on Hwy. 17 South that paid off winners. I couldn't remember the name so I drove South on 17 checking out the name of every store hoping one of them would jog my memory. After driving several miles, I passed a convenience store with a familiar sounding name, the In & Out. I went inside and asked the clerk if he knew Todd Burley. He did but didn't know where Todd lived so I walked to the back of the store and into a dark room that was lined with video poker machines. There was one guy playing. My only chance. He didn't respond when I leaned against the machine he was playing and asked him if he knew Burley.

"How often does he come here?"

No response. The guy was thin and bald and stank of body odor. He sat on the stool, curved and bent over, with one large thin hand under his chin and the other on the machine, slapping buttons.

I dug in my pocket and pulled out a twenty and held it up. The button slapping hand reached up and slid the twenty out of my hand.

"Comes in every day around three and stays a couple of hours." Slap. Slap. Slapslap.

"Any idea where he lives?"

No response. Slapslapslap. Slap. Slap. I reached in my pocket and pulled out my last twenty.

"Foxrun Apartments. #23. Actually went there last week."

I started to ask why but realized I didn't care and left. I drove back to Charleston. Now that I knew where Burley lived, I just had to figure out how to get him and Maggie together.

Although I didn't see her much, I still cared about my daughter. That sounds lame coming from an absentee father but, I did care. Thinking about her could make me feel happy or sad or worried or any other emotion, depending on what I was thinking at the time. I also kept in mind what I thought was best for her. For a long time that meant not being in her life, not exposing her to who I had become. But since I'd been doing better, I'd decided to become more involved. Not all at once, but gradually. I wanted to be careful and not screw it up. This week with her gave me a chance to do that. The timing wasn't great, with needing to find Khalil by Thursday. But I couldn't use work as an excuse, not if I wanted her in my life. Billy Shores showing up again was more of a problem. But I had convinced myself he would be going away soon so I put that concern away, too. I was determined to prove to Wendy, Megan and myself that I could do this. So, later that day at 2 p.m. I drove to her school to sign her out early instead of waiting in the car line at the normal dismissal time. I did this so she could avoid the embarrassment of climbing into the Taurus in front of the other kids. She had never said anything to me about the car but I wanted our week together to go well. Starting it off by embarrassing her didn't seem smart.

However, as we walked to the car in the parking lot, she barely noticed the POS, throwing her bag in the back seat and plopping down beside me in the front without saying anything.

"I thought we'd get pizza tonight, after homework."

I looked over at her. A nod was the only acknowledgment as she stared out the window. I decided to leave it alone. I wasn't going to figure out the mind of an adolescent girl on the ride home from school. After riding in silence several blocks she turned to me.

"Weren't you in the Army?"

I had been worried about what she would say to me first. Out of everything I had imagined, from "I hate you!" to "I've missed you", – I never thought it would be the words that actually came out of her mouth. The question brought both relief and pain and I had difficulty getting a response out of my suddenly dry throat.

"Marines."

"Oh yeah. Mom had mentioned it."

"Why?"

"We are supposed to interview a veteran for a paper in history class. You know, for Veteran's Day and I was wondering if ..."

"You want to interview me?"

I looked over at her. She was smiling and nodding her head. For some reason the sight of her smile crushed me and I looked back at the road ahead. I couldn't recall her ever smiling at me before and the guilt and remorse for not being around all those years emerged from some hidden place. Add to that the emotions stirred by my experience in the Marines and I was fighting back tears. I had decided over the years that what happened to me in the Marines probably ruined my life. I kept it buried. The few times it was ever unearthed I was fucked up and either sobbing or raging. Now she wanted me to talk about it. I would have to create a PG-13 version. No cursing, no emotions, minimize the gore. It was history after all, something malleable. Cleanse it and relate it to a twelve-year-old so she can box it in with four corners and turn it in to the teacher for a grade.

"Okay. When is it due?"

"Friday."

"Cutting it close aren't you?"

"We just found out about it. I think the teacher decided to do this at the last minute. "All right. We can get started tonight over pizza."

Megan finished her homework on the couch and we walked down King Street to a pizza restaurant she liked. After we ordered I took a drink of water and watched as she pulled out a note pad and her phone.

"Should I record it?"

"That's up to you."

It was odd. This was the first time I had been alone with Megan and instead of catching up, she was interviewing me. Except for not knowing how I was going to talk about my time in the Marine Corps, I was thankful that we were talking. I had feared sitting down with her, feared the awkwardness that comes with having nothing to talk about. That wouldn't be a problem now and I saw the tradeoff. I didn't want to talk about the Marines but I didn't want to spend an hour eating pizza over failed attempts to talk with my daughter.

"Okay, I'm ready. I'll ask questions and you answer them."

"Fire away."

"When were you in the Marines?"

"I enlisted in 1981 when I was eighteen years old, right out of high school."

"Before college?"

"Yes."

"Why?"

"I wanted to be on my own. I needed to be financially independent from my parents, your grandparents. Back then, we weren't involved in Iraq or Afghanistan or anywhere else. If there was going to be a war it would have been with the Soviet Union and nobody wanted that. So, the chances of seeing any combat seemed slim. I thought I would enlist, serve my time and then go to college."

"Where did you serve or what do you call it?"

"Stationed?"

"Yeah. Where were you stationed."

"Camp LeJeune, North Carolina. I was with the 1st Battalion, 8th Marines of the 24th Marine Amphibious Unit."

"What does that mean?"

"That was just the name of the group I was assigned to. It was what you call infantry. I was trained to carry out ground combat operations."

"Were you an officer?"

"No, not quite. I started out as a private and reached the rank of sergeant."

"Did you go anywhere other than North Carolina?"

"Was I deployed anywhere? That's what you call it when a Marine or soldier is sent somewhere."

"Right. Were you deployed anywhere?"

I felt my throat getting dry. I gulped down more water.. If the pizza was here I would eat a slice, anything to delay putting the first words to the memories I had long kept silent. I looked around for our waiter but no luck. I put down the water along with all of my cards.

"Megan, I haven't talked about this before. Well, I have

but …"

"About being in the Marines?"

"Yeah, but what I mean is that I haven't talked about what I'm about to tell you."

"Are you not supposed to?"

"It's not anything like that. Something bad happened and I haven't wanted to talk about it. For years I tried to live as if it didn't happen but it was always there. It's hard to explain."

She was quiet for a moment, looking at her note pad and scribbling with her pen.

"If you don't want to talk about it, it's okay."

"I want to, but there are things I can't tell you. Do you understand?"

"Yes."

"You've heard of Israel?"

"Of course."

"Right beside Israel is a country called Lebanon."

"I've heard of that too."

"Good. In 1982 Israel invaded Lebanon because terrorists were operating there and attacking Israel. The government of Lebanon more or less supported Israel but there were many Lebanese who didn't and were unhappy with their government and Israel. These people actually supported the terrorists. Anyway, I was sent, along with the 24th Marine Amphibious Unit, to Beirut, which is the capital of Lebanon, as part of an international peace-keeping force. Are you not going to write this down?"

"No, I'll get it off the recording. I just want to listen."

"Our barracks, the place where we stayed, was a four-story building at the Beirut airport. On October 23, 1982, just after six o'clock in the morning, a suicide bomber drove a truck full of explosives into the lobby of the barracks. I was on the far side of the building on the second floor. My roommate and I had just returned to the room after breakfast. He was a corporal, Billy Shores from Texas. I remember I was looking out the window, over the runway at a plane landing when the floor beneath my feet rose, lifting me up and tilting me. Then, in an instant, all sound was sucked from the room then returned in the same moment as a concussive blast of air, heat and parts of everything that was around me. That's all I remember. I sometimes think I remember falling but it's not a real memory, just my mind trying to fill in the gaps. I woke up days later in a hospital aboard a US Navy ship off the coast of Israel in the Mediterranean Sea. Both legs were broken, my right arm was too. I had a severe concussion and a lacerated liver. I lost two teeth. My colonel, who wasn't in the building at the time of the explosion, told me the entire building had collapsed from the explosion. They found me a day later under a large slab of concrete that had landed at just the right angle to shelter my body from the falling debris..."

The waiter arrived with the pizza and we cleared a place on the table without saying anything.

"You folks need refills?"

"Maybe in a few minutes." Neither of us had drank much of what we had.

I shoveled a piece of the pizza on to the spatula in an effort to return to Charleston from Beirut. I had told Megan all I thought she should know about the explosion but she might have questions.

"Hold your plate over here."

I served myself and cut into my slice with a fork. Megan just quietly stared at her plate, picking at her pizza with her fork.

"What happened to Billy Shores?"

I stopped eating and looked at her. Her eyes met mine and I could see how much she looked like me with her dark hair and brown eyes.

"He died." I didn't tell her they found four pieces of him and never found the fifth. He had been behind me on the other side of the beds, just feet away yet I was here talking to my daughter thirty years later and he had been ripped apart. I can't count the number of times my mind has tried to recreate what happened to explain that result. My survival had been a miracle, the colonel said. God had plans for me he said. At the time I could believe it. There had to be some reason I had survived. Why not God?

"Daddy?"

"Yes?"

"Mama said you couldn't be a husband and father because of something that happened to you. Is that what she meant?"

"She told you that?"

Megan looked down at her plate. "No. I heard her talking one night when she thought I was asleep."

Inexplicably shame crept over me as it always did followed by the anger. Not anger at Wendy or myself but at whatever sent the shame or caused me to feel it.

"She's probably right."

"Then I hate war."

"It wasn't war. I was at the wrong place at the wrong time." I reached out and took her hand laying on the table but she pulled it away.

"Then I hate terrorists."

"Okay then." I drank some water. "Hate the terrorists. Now eat up."

9.

It was past seven o'clock when I finally woke and went to the kitchen to put on the coffee. Megan was still asleep on the couch. When the coffee was on I picked up the phone from the counter and unplugged the charger. I had three missed calls and two text messages. The first message was from Wendy reminding me to wake Megan by six.

Megan. It's time to get up. Megan! It's past seven. You've got to get ready for school."

She sat up, eyes half closed. "Why didn't you get me up earlier?"

"Be glad I'm not still asleep. Do you want breakfast?"

"Juice" was all she said as she walked sleepily to the bathroom trailing a sheet behind her.

The second text was from a private number. It was an address: shoreline, apt 4a, breakstone rd, m p. The coffee spit and sputtered as it finished brewing and the shower came on in the bathroom. I looked out the window at nothing as I thought about the address. I knew the apartments but didn't know anyone that lived there. I looked at the time it was received: 12:06 am. Wrong number. Then I remembered my trip to Columbia and leaving my number with Kasim. Maybe he decided to send me Khalil's address. I checked my incoming calls. One was from Wendy, one from Staci and the third was a number I didn't recognize. Wendy's message was the same as the text. Overkill. Staci's voice made my dick move in my pants. She wanted to know if I had made any progress on Khalil, reminding me Thursday was the deadline. Her message was all business, no mention of Sunday night and that irritated me. Then I was pissed at myself with being irritated. Get a grip, Peale. The last message drained any thought of sex from my being. It was Maggie. But what she had to say got my attention. She had information on Khalil.

As soon as I had dropped Meghan at school, I called Maggie as I followed the other cars in a slow line out of the school drop off lane.

"All right, Peale, what's the scoop? Why are you after Khalil?"

"Trying to track him down for a client."

"Who the hell are you working for, the CIA?"

"Why? What are you talking about?"

"Are you in your car?"

"Yeah."

"Find a place to pull over."

I pulled out of the line of cars and found an open space in parking lot.

"Okay. What is it?"

"I'm surprised I was able to get anything on this guy. He should be on a no-fly list."

Something like courage was sucked out of me leaving an empty place. "Why do you say that?"

"Because of the places he's been the past year: Lebanon, Libya, Turkey, Pakistan. Does this guy have a legit job like he's a journalist or something?"

"No, uhh, he's a banker."

"A banker. Right. Your banker has been doing business in a lot of hot spots with odd length of stays."

"Like what?"

"Last year, April, he leaves JFK for Turkey, doesn't come back to the US for two months. Another time, last January, he goes to Lebanon for only two days. In all, he's been to the Middle East seven times in the past year and a half, not to mention a couple of trips to Germany."

I sat in my car amid the normalcy of children being dropped off for school trying to make sense of what I was hearing.

"Peale. There's something else."

"What do you mean?"

"Like I said, this guy should be on a no-fly list. I shouldn't have been able to get this information as easily as I did."

"I'm not following you."

"A guy that is traveling this much, to these places, with his name, would usually be flagged, questioned, maybe put on a no-fly list if his answers weren't legit or he didn't respond."

"Maybe he was questioned." I didn't like where this was going, the implications it had for Staci.

"I checked. He hasn't been. The guy hasn't been touched."

"Well wouldn't that indicate he's clean."

"In today's world, it doesn't mean anything. If you ask me, he's being monitored. Watched."

I fought the impulse to agree with her. What she was saying made as much sense to me as anything. "So, is he in the US?"

"Yeah. As far as I can tell. He flew into Charleston from LaGuardia last Tuesday."

"Last week!"

"Yeah. Why the surprise?"

"Nothing. I just wasn't expecting that."

"Peale?"

"Yeah?"

"When do I get payment?"

My skin crawled and I noticed I was wincing.

"I'm working on it."

"Don't make me come looking for you. You still live over

on the Battery?"

How did she know that?

"You stay North of Broad, Maggie. You'll get what's coming to you. And Maggie?"

"Yeah?"

"Thanks."

"Fuck your thanks, Peale. Bring me payment. I wasn't doing this as a favor."

I drove straight to Mount Pleasant from the school. If Khalil was at the apartment in the text, I wanted to confront him, report it to Staci and get my money. What Maggie had told me bothered me on several levels. First, what did it say about Staci? I had been suspicious of her and her story since we first met, but did she know about the places he's been? Second, what was their relationship? I now knew what she had told me was bull shit, but what was the true story? Finally, if she has been lying to me all along, what did that say about the other night. I hadn't let myself think too much about it but when I did, I caught myself wondering if maybe something could be there. But that hope had been fading ever since it happened and this latest bit of news from Maggie told me I was being used from the moment I met Staci Turner. But why?

10.

The apartment building was almost completely hidden behind a strip mall of a grocery store, discount store, Chinese restaurant and a tanning salon. It was a two-story complex, probably built in the eighties when interest rates were high and builders couldn't afford to build anything more than what look like cheap boxes stacked on top of one another. Rivulets of orange brown rust stains striped the stucco that had been slathered on the exterior. Dry, stunted scrub palmettos planted next to the building were all that remained of the landscaping except for patches of weedy grass sprouting in the sand. I drove around once trying to see the apartment numbers, but the doors were out of sight inside the stairways that separated each block of apartments. So I parked and started the search on foot.

~ ~ ~

Mt. Pleasant is mostly an overgrown village, crowded with traffic and the noise of people driving to the beaches on Sullivan's or Isle of Palms or to the restaurants along Shem Creek. But this apartment building was an island of quiet amongst all of what goes on during the day. The silence emanating from the building made me feel uneasy. There were cars in the parking lot, but the place felt deserted. Whoever lived here laid low and didn't want to draw attention to themselves or whatever was happening behind those doors. There are places like this everywhere. A place where the chronically unemployed, the drug-addicted, the drug-dealing, the child pornographer, the single mom with multiple kids from multiple fathers, all gravitate to, drawn together by the low rent and low profile it offers. Over the years I had come in contact with the inhabitants of these places many times as a lawyer but it wasn't often that I had visited one. As a lawyer I had interviewed a reluctant witness at a place like this and even a couple of clients.. But if I could have avoided it, I would have stayed away.

Walking around I saw that each unit was a letter of the alphabet. I backtracked and found F, walked up a flight of stairs and entered a dark corridor, a hallway with doors on each side. The first door was 12F . Across the hall, the nearest apartment was 9F. I walked back down to check the floor below. At the bottom of the stairs was a padlocked metal door where the opening of the hallway should have been. It didn't make sense. Who padlocks the door to a hallway in an apartment building? I walked up the stairs to the third floor just to make sure the place wasn't numbered top to bottom. The first door on my right was 18F. Light shown through the far end of the hallway. 4F has to be on the far end on the first floor. I was more than halfway down the dark corridor when I heard a door behind me open then shut. I turned around and saw a little kid wearing nothing but blue shorts. We stared at each other for a second and I walked over to him. He just watched me.

"Do you live here?"

No response.

"Is your mama home?"

Nothing came from his mouth but his two brown eyes said he didn't trust me. There was no fear, just wariness.

"Does anyone live on the first floor?"

He shook his head quickly then ran off to the end of the hallway where I had entered and disappeared down the stairs. I turned and walked to the opposite end and down the stairs to the ground floor, all the while stupidly debating in my mind whether or not to believe the kid. I say stupidly because the answer was there in front of me. Another padlocked door. In frustration I walked up, grabbed the lock and yanked. The lock fell open in my hand as I released it. I looked around, removed the lock and pulled the door handle. It swung open smoothly and quietly, almost invitingly. Inside, the hallway was cool and damp with a faint odor of trash or something rotten. It was also completely dark except for the light from the door where I stood. I wanted to close the door but knew I couldn't see anything if I did. I opened it wider so it would look as much like the other hallways as possible. More light penetrated the darkness and I could now see apartment 4F on my left. I walked up to the door and knocked. The sound bounced down the hallway, disturbing the silence. What are you doing Peale? Nobody lives here. Try the doorknob. I looked down the hall into the darkness and then outside into the light. I saw no one. I reached for the knob and it turned in my hand. I hesitated, then pushed the door open but didn't enter. There was enough ambient light inside the apartment to see. A space opened around a corner to the left. Probably a kitchen. There was also a bare counter. I stepped forward beyond the corner, still half expecting someone to appear from another room. But it was obvious that no one lived here. Somewhere, deep within me I felt frustration, but that was overwhelmed by adrenaline. Something wasn't right, I could feel it and I walked further into the apartment. In front of me was an empty space, the den, faintly illuminated by light making its way through partially closed blinds that covered a rectangular window. Deja vu froze me and sent my mind racing after thoughts or feelings that stayed just out of reach. I shook it off and looked down a short hallway to the left. An open door at the' end of the hall appeared to be a bathroom in the half dark. Something in me suddenly grew impatient. Get this over with. Frustration replaced hesitation and I walked down the hallway and looked in a door on the left. With the flash light on my phone I could make out bare walls and floor and an empty closet with a few hangers. I turned to the door opposite the one I stood in, walked over and pushed it open for a quick glance before leaving. As the door swung open I jumped backwards into the door frame. That's how quickly your eyes can send an image to your brain and your body reacts. The body doesn't wait for another part of the brain to figure things out. Something deep inside, something primal says Run away. But I didn't. I remained motionless against the wall. All I could see was part of a mattress and two bare feet lying on top of it. My body was heavy and my heart was pounding. I had to push myself off the door jamb to walk into the room. With each small step more of the scene was revealed to me: the lower part of a man's body, naked, a mattress with a lime green blanket, then his upper body and a dark stain on the blanket over his body and then his face, black hair and beard, eyes and mouth open in a look of, what? Surprise? Fear? I moved closer to the body, shining the phone light around, being careful not to disturb what I now knew was a crime scene. With the tips of two fingers I pinched a piece of the blanket and flung it off of the body. There were six holes in his chest. I looked at the face again. It was Khalil. I had only seen pictures but I was sure. My gut erased any doubt my mind might have had, wanted to have. I walked around to the other side of the mattress. Clothes were laying on the floor but nothing else. There was another bathroom but it was empty as was the closet. I wiped down everything I could remember touching, including the padlock and left. Although I never saw anyone, I felt eyes all over me until my car was out of the parking lot and I was driving towards the bridge back to Charleston.

~ ~ ~

As I drove across the bridge I looked out at the green,

sun glinted water of the harbor and then at the blue sky behind and above the City. How normal it all was, like any other day. I could have gone home, ate lunch, watched TV, then picked up Megan at school. We would have gone out to eat and talked about her day, her life, then gone home and called her mom before watching a movie and going to bed. Nothing would have changed for anyone else because I found a murdered man. The sky wasn't darkening, a storm wasn't rising and thrashing the city. I was tempted by the thought that I could just ignore what I found, forget about it. And why not? What I found might change things for me and for some others, but not everyone else. For them it wouldn't create even a ripple in their lives. Why couldn't I just enter that world and leave the other behind? But I'd tried that before and knew that apparent normalcy would be a poor antidote to the reality of finding a murdered body.

There's the word. Apparent. Apparition. Nothing really there. For so long Khalil was just that and when he finally took form, he was lying dead on a blood-soaked mattress in a shit hole apartment.

11.

After my visit to the Shoreline I went to the Office. It was almost twelve but I wasn't hungry. I entered through the back door and went behind the bar and got a glass of water. After gulping down half of it, I leaned against the bar and confronted the question that had nagged me during the drive over from Mt. Pleasant: who sent the text with the address? Earlier, I thought it was Kasim., but doubt was creeping in. It was obviously someone who had my number and knew I was looking for Khalil. A short list and Kasim was on it. But there were two others. Maggie was one, but she would have told me when I talked to her. Plus, her number would have shown up on my phone when she sent the text, just like it did when she called. I wanted to throw out the final option immediately. Staci had my number and obviously knew I was looking for Khalil. So why leave a text? Why use a phone that wouldn't show a number? I didn't want to ask the more important question: why in the hell hire me when she knew where he was? I left that one unanswered and went back to my favorite choice. Kasim had my number and knew I was looking for Khalil. The more I thought about it, the more I was convinced he was my messenger. He wanted to maintain anonymity, so he didn't tell me at our meeting, he knew Khalil was trouble and wanted to help. I liked it. It was rational, made sense and it nudged Staci out of the top spot as the most likely choice. It should have troubled me that I was having to convince myself that it wasn't Staci, but it didn't. Despite just finding Khalil dead on a mattress and consciously ignoring the possibility that Staci sent me to find him, my mood improved. Proof of how thoroughly I had convinced myself that Kasim had sent me the message. I was about to raise my glass when Sam came out of the bathroom and saw me standing behind the bar.

"No calls. Hey, how is the case with K-K going?"

"Kay Kay?"

"Yeah. The Kardashian. Have you banged her yet? Even if you haven't, say you did and make up some really good shit and tell me all about it."

"Yeah. She asked me to meet her in this run-down apartment. The place was a real shit hole. Hookers, drug dealers, gang bangers. Bad place. So I'm thinking, >Why here?. What' going on with this woman.' But she told me she had something important to show me so I found the apartment ..."

"What was the number?"

"What?"

"What was the apartment number?"

"Why does that matter?"

"If you know the apartment number, the story could be true."

"I could make it up, like everything else."

"Not quickly."

"4F."

"Okay. Good." He was smiling as if he was satisfied it was all true. Not only could I put aside the fact I had just found Khalil's dead body, I could joke about it too. As far as I was concerned, what I was telling Sam was fiction. And the more fiction I told him, the more convinced I was that Kasim had sent me that address.

"I find the apartment and go in. There's no furniture. The place is empty. There's no power, no lights. But a window is open so there's enough light to see the curves of a naked woman in the room in front of me. I walk closer and can smell her. She smells like sun-warmed spices, carried on a tropical breeze."

"Wow. I need to write that down."

"Don't interrupt."

"Sorry."

"Then her voice in the half-light says >Come here. Closer. Let me show you something.' So I go up to her and we kiss and she's pulling my shirt off while I'm working on my pants."

"Shoes?"

"What?"

"Your shoes. Were they lace ups? That could cause a break in the action to get those off, right?"

"Flip -flops." He smiled again, satisfied.

"So, my clothes are on the floor and we're kissing and she starts walking backwards, pulling me with her, as we kiss, into a bedroom."

"Her tits. Were you grabbing her tits?"

"What? Yeah of course."

"What did they look like?"

"I don't know, tits. It was dark."

"But they were big?"

"You saw them. Yeah, they were big. Anyway, she turns me around and something that feels like a mattress is pressing against the back of my legs. So, we're kissing and groping when all of a sudden, she pushes me backwards through the darkness onto the mattress but I don't just land on a mattress, I also land on a naked body."

"There's another woman? A ménage?" His face lit up like a kid's in front of presents under a tree.

"No. A man."

His face fell and took on an odd look. "Oh."

"And get this. The dude was dead."

"What? You didn't..."

"Hell no."

"Did she?" The look on his face made me wonder if he hoped she did.

"Not while I was there. I came off that bed faster than I fell on it. Staci was gone. I grabbed my clothes and ran out of there naked."

"You tell a shitty story, Peale. I was dialed in for a while there. Hell, I thought it was actually true until the end."

"You got to work tonight. I can't leave you all stoked up around the female patrons."

"Why are you drinking water?"

"Oh." I looked at the glass. "I don't know. Just felt like it."

"You normally feel like a beer or three."

"Well today isn't a normal day."

Jess backed through the front door carrying a cardboard liquor box.

"Sam?"

"Yeah?"

"Go get all of that liquor out of the back of my truck and bring it in here. It's parked out front.

"Why don't we get liquor the normal way. The legal way?"

"Ask the boss. This is just left over from a party he threw last weekend. We're just storing it here."

"Right." Sam lumbered to the front door and propped it open with a brick. The sun light shining through the doorway made the black and white tiled floor look unfamiliar.

"This place would really look different if you opened up some of those windows."

"Are you drunk, Peale? Is that vodka?" I was in her way behind the bar so I moved around to the other side. "Thank you." It was said sarcastically. She took the bottles out of the box and put them out of sight under the bar. Sam appeared through the door, huffing and wheezing, carrying one box.

"Jesus Sam, hurry up. I can't leave a truck full of liquor out on the street all afternoon."

"I'll help." Manual labor might clear some of the trash out of my head.

"Thanks, Peale. By the way, did your buddy get in touch with you?"

"What buddy?"

"Some dude called. Said he was a friend of yours and was in town and wanted to hook up."

None of that sounded right. "Okay. Did he leave a name or number?"

"Nope. Said he'd try again or drop by your place later."

For some reason cold dread filled my gut. I don't have old friends that would drop by my place. Lately, only new acquaintances have been dropping by.

"Did he say anything else?"

"Not really. Just asked about when you might be here."

For every trip Sam made to the truck and back, I must have made three. I was a robot, going back and forth, bringing in box after box, lost in my thoughts, my good mood had been short lived, existing as it did on a delusion. What Jess said about someone looking for me toppled the barricade I had constructed with the argument that K.S. had sent me the Shoreline address, and the doubt poured back in. So Kasim sends me a text with the address at about the same time Khalil is being killed? And that's supposed to be a coincidence? My mind was scrambling, trying to fend off the simple, troubling conclusion my gut was telling me: Staci sent the text ... Staci sent the text ... Too much had to be ignored to conclude Kasim had sent the text. It wouldn't stand when I tried to reconcile it objectively with everything else that I knew: A gorgeous woman hires me to find her lost boyfriend who she later tells me isn't her boyfriend before she makes love to me. This is right on the heels of a visit from her step father who is the chief of police who makes a crazy offer to get my law license back if I keep him informed of my progress. Meanwhile every lead I got on boyfriend goes nowhere but I do find out he's been making a lot of trips to some rough places. There's the weird visit with Kasim at the Islamic center in Columbia. Then a mysterious text message sends me to an abandoned apartment where I find boyfriend dead. Now some guy claiming to be a friend but won't leave a name is in town and wants to hang out. So, knowing all of that, can I reasonably conclude that Kasim sent me that text? My mind gave me the answer by not answering at all. It had nothing to counter the conclusion my gut had already reached: You're being played.

~ ~ ~

I was standing on the sidewalk watching Sam stretch over the tailgate and reach for the last box in the back of the pickup when a sedan rolled to a stop behind the truck. The guy behind the wheel was dressed almost identically to Chief Carlton's escorts from the other night. A pair of aviator sunglasses stared at us from below a crew cut. He got out and stood in the open door of the sedan.

"Jackson Peale?"

Sam looked back at me but said nothing.

"That's me."

"Can you get in? We need to talk."

"I don't get in cars with strangers."

"That's not what I hear."

The little boldness I had acquired with my smart-ass remark abandoned me just as quick. "If you want to talk, come inside." I motioned to the door of the Post Office with my head. The crew cut paused then shut the door and walked over to where I stood on the sidewalk. "We need privacy."

"No problem. Come inside."

A row of booths lined the wall opposite the door where customers entered the bar. Of all the times I had set foot in the place, I don't think I had ever sat in one of them before. But I was now and sitting across from me was Agent Thursday of the FBI.

"Drink?"

"No thanks."

"Okay. What can I do for you?"

"Plenty."

"Such as?"

"Let's start with Staci Turner."

"What about her?"

"What do you know about her?"

"Beautiful. Smells like sex and looks like money. Or is it the other way around?"

"How do you think she'd look holding a Kalashnikov?"

I didn't respond.

"Hot? Sexy? Desirable?"

"I don't get your question Agent Thursday."

"What is your relationship with her?"

That should have been an easy question, but I hesitated answering.

"She's a client."

"What kind?"

"None of your business."

"If it wasn't my business, Mr. Peale, trust me, I wouldn't be sitting here."

He was right. I was dancing around it, holding it off because I didn't want to deal with it. But here it was and Agent Thursday was going to lay it on the table. I was going to make him.

"Why don't you just tell me then? Why is it your business?"

"Okay. If that's the way you want to do this. I was hoping we weren't going to dick around. But I don't have all day. This morning, after taking your daughter to school, you went to the Shoreline Apartments in Mount Pleasant. After looking around you found the apartment number you were looking for, the number that was sent to you in a text message earlier this morning."

My chest tightened and my throat was dry. The doom I had been vaguely aware of the past few days was now a dark, towering wall of water rising before me..

"You went inside the apartment – apartment 4F – which was empty except for a mattress and the dead man lying on it. He had been shot six times in the chest. The man was Mahmoud Khalil. You left the apartment and came here. You know all of this of course but you didn't know that I knew it. I can tell by the tight, pale look on your face."

He actually smiled, the prick.

"So let me tell you some things I bet you don't know. First Khalil was here in Charleston to commit a terrorist act."

At this point I started to feel nauseous. Why? I don't know. It was like I had been taking a leisurely walk in what I thought was a park only to be told I was standing in a mine field. Which way do I go?

"Specifically what, we aren't sure. But I'll get to that later. Second, he wasn't acting alone."

Here it comes.

"We know he had contacts here. What their roles are, we aren't sure, but Khalil was the guy that was trained to do the deed. Only something went wrong. We think he got cold feet. And that brings me to, third: Khalil's cohorts couldn't find him so they decided to hire someone to do it for them."

He stopped to let it sink in, not that it had to go far. My gut had already told me everything he was about to say. Almost everything.

"Staci Turner hired you to locate Khalil, or at least we are considering that possibility."

"What? Are you saying you don't know if Staci is involved or not?"

"Oh no, she's involved. We just aren't sure she hired you to find him."

"Wait a minute. I can assure you that is what she did."

Thursday leaned back in the booth and smiled. "She must be one hell of a lay to dull your senses that much. Can you imagine how a woman like that makes her way through life? What do you think the hard liners in Pakistan, Libya and Iran think of her? Maybe she hooks them the same way she hooked you, with money and sex. I bet that combination opens many doors for her, even over there."

Up until this point, I believed everything he was saying. But if Staci didn't hire me to find Khalil, what was the point? Agent Thursday smiled when he saw the >Oh Shit' expression come over my face. I was being framed for Khalil's murder.

"I'm impressed. You're quicker than I gave you credit for."

"But it doesn't make any sense. Why would I kill Khalil? There's no motive."

"Well let's see if we can make this work. Staci Turner will say she hired you to find a guy but your relationship quickly exceeds its professional boundaries. You become infatuated. Once you locate Khalil, he tells you to go fuck yourself, you pull a gun to show him you mean business. Khalil ends up dead."

I managed to get out a short laugh. "That's pathetic. It would never hold up."

Thursday nodded his head. "I agree except for one detail I left out."

By now my confidence was returning. Thursday didn't know everything. There were holes that had to be filled and he was trying to rattle me to see what fell to the floor. "Oh yeah? What's that?"

"Khalil was shot with your Sig 9 mm."

My mind went blank. No. That isn't accurate. It just stopped, like something important broke and it was no longer capable of functioning. For a few moments I just sat there, dumbly, letting seconds, maybe a minute, tick off my life, without a thought in my head. Then slowly, like someone knocked unconscious coming to, I came back to the there and then. It had started last Friday with Todd Burley, the hooker, the dope. I had been picked. But why me? Agent Thursday was looking around the bar.

"You know, I am kinda thirsty. Hey, miss."

He was waving his arm at Jess across the empty room, trying to get her attention at the bar. "Can we get something to drink over here?"

"We're closed ass wipe."

Thursday feigned a hurt expression. ABitch. Where's the southern charm I hear about?"

"To hell with that, where's my gun?"

"I would think the Mount Pleasant Police Department has it. If you didn't waste Khalil, the killer would have taken the gun with him – or her" He looked at me and smiled – "then returned after you left and placed the gun on the counter where it was found by the MPPD about an hour ago."

As Thursday was opining about the location of my gun, Billy Shores made his way across the bar on two crutches, one leg, no shirt, blood-caked dirt all over his body and a bloody, white bandage unfurling from his head. He stopped at the end of the table as Thursday finished. "Hey Sarge. Who's the nob?"

It wasn't long ago that I would just start talking to Billy. Didn't matter where I was, I'd start talking because it seemed so...normal. I learned that it wasn't but it's still hard not to respond to him and I have to stop myself before I do. It must look weird as shit to other people.

"Is there a problem, Peale?"

"What? No. No problem. Are we done here?"

"Not quite. You got to be somewhere? Look, this thing can go one of two ways: you either help me nail Turner and whoever else is involved or you go down for Khalil's murder.

"That's bullshit, Sarge. Tell this cupcake to go fuck himself."

I glared at Billy. To Thursday's eyes I was pissed off at him, looking away to control my anger.

"It's your call, Peale." He slid out of the booth and looked in Jess's direction. "Thanks for the tea."

12.

illie Carver sat at her desk in the Mt. Pleasant Police Department staring at the phone. She didn't want to make the call, didn't want to ask a favor. She didn't want to do much of anything, certainly not anything connected to work What she wanted to do was go home, pop a pill, crawl into bed, turn out the lights, and give in to the darkness that had been looming around her, wanting her. But she wasn't going to do that. Not right now anyway. There was still something in her that had always kept her from giving up. Something malleable but tough, seemingly indestructible. Had she been born with it, something nurtured and developed, or had it been installed by others? It didn't matter. It was there, still part of her. She leaned forward, picked up the phone and dialed the number.

She fell back into her chair. A strand of hair fell across her face as she held the phone to her ear. It annoyed her, like everything else that had happened that day annoyed her. She blew at the strand of hair as she waited on the call. It billowed then returned to the same place over her eye. Damn it! burst out between clenched teeth and she tucked the strand behind her ear.

Voicemail.

"You've reached Agent Brett Bone of the Federal Bureau of Investigation. Leave a message and I will return your call."

She stared at her computer screen, waiting on the beep.

"Brett. It's Billie Carver. From South Carolina. I need a

favor..."

She left her mobile number in case he no longer had it and hung up the phone. The home page of the Mount Pleasant Police Department glowed on the computer screen in front of her.

Mocking her.

Not a year had passed since she left the FBI Academy in Virginia and returned to a job as a deputy with the Charleston County Sheriff's Office. Those that knew her at the Academy saw her as the complete package, destined for quick advancement through the Bureau. Only a few of the male graduates were in better shape and no one in her class was smarter. She had a personality that exuded confidence, but a humble friendliness smoothed what could have been sharp and intimidating edges. It didn't hurt that she was physically attractive but there was very little jealousy of her because everyone around her could see she took nothing for granted. But there was also a quiet mystery about her, an emotional distance that all of her colleagues felt. There were no romantic relationships or sexual flings that anyone knew about. Brett Bone had thought he sensed signals from her one night at a local bar, but when he had moved in close to her she had turned her head away and muttered "no". He had never mentioned it and neither had she and the not-very-close friendship had remained until she left the Academy.

She never explained to anyone why she chose to return to Charleston as a sheriff's deputy, seemingly trashing a college degree, a master's and all that awaited her in a career with the FBI. No one knew her past and what motivated her.

At twelve years old she looked sixteen which was enough of an excuse for her mother's live in boyfriend to rape her one night when her mother was working late cleaning office buildings. "You tell anyone and I'll kill your mama." The same boyfriend would get drunk and high and beat her mother for the men he imagined she was fucking while she claimed to be at work. At times her mother would call law enforcement and the boyfriend would be arrested only to be released the next day. Billie's mother would grab her and take refuge at a relative's or friend's house but the boyfriend always coaxed her back home with tears and promises. And the charges would always be dropped. The cycle of beatings and rape, arrests and flights to safety continued until one day when she was fourteen her mother discovered the pregnancy Billie had been hiding for months. When Billie wouldn't tell her the father's name, her mother broke down in tears, screaming at her and calling her a whore. When the boyfriend came home drunk later that night, her mother laid into him, cussing him and calling him a child rapist. Billie would always remember the boyfriend turning to her and giving her a look that said "I told you what I'd do" before he picked up a baseball bat and beat her mother to death before her eyes.

The eyes. A one-way passage. The images go in and never leave. Trapped inside for other parts of her to deal with for – how long? For as long as it takes...

At some point, after the birth of the baby and giving it up for adoption, she had decided to protect women and girls from the bastards that treated them like trash. She would go into law enforcement and make the arrests and push for the prosecution of the crime, even against the will of the victim. Her mother's boyfriend had gone to prison for the murder and rape but Billie couldn't forget the number of times he wasn't punished. She also couldn't shake the thought that her mother would still be alive had he been prosecuted earlier. At first she thought she'd go to law school, but during an internship with the solicitor's office one summer she saw how the lawyers assigned to prosecute domestic violence cases would dismiss the case as soon as the victim went home. Once Billie asked a lawyer why a case was being dismissed and she was told that a case can't be prosecuted without a witness.

"What about using the arresting officer as a witness?"

"Maybe you could, if he was so inclined."

"Why wouldn't he?"

"You'll have to ask the officer."

So she did.

"I'm not wasting any more time on some chick that moves back in with a guy that just beat her ass."

"Isn't that your job?"

"Fuck you, dumbass. Do you really think a jury will convict a guy for beating on a woman when she's sitting next to him in court holding his hand? The judge would eat my ass if I pushed that case."

It was clear to Carver that she would be most effective serving as the prosecution's witness if the victim refused to testify. So she returned to college that fall with a plan to enter law enforcement after graduation. She also decided to double major in psychology and criminal justice. Her senior thesis was titled *The Psychological Impact of Domestic Violence on Victims*. It was 272 pages long. Her professor encouraged her to pursue a masters and doctorate. Although advanced degrees weren't part of the plan (she wanted to better understand the victims, not be paid to counsel them) she had also decided to attend the FBI Academy. Admission to the Academy required professional experience, however, and the graduate work would qualify. She agreed to the graduate studies with the understanding that she would also work full time with a woman's shelter while she worked on the master's degree. The combination of the two satisfied the admission requirements at the Academy and after earning the master's degree she left for Quantico as soon as she was accepted. At one point in college she had considered the Marines. But serving the four-year commitment didn't fit with her plans and there was no law enforcement training in the Marines. The FBI Academy offered state of the art training in law enforcement – witness interrogation, firearms, computers, tactical response – while demanding a certain level of physical and mental toughness that she wanted to prove she possessed. But postponing her career to earn the master's and attend the FBI academy hadn't been an easy decision. Although she was impatient to start working in local law enforcement on domestic violence cases, she knew that, as a deputy, she couldn't pick and choose her cases. It was her plan to present herself as a highly trained and educated law enforcement officer whose special skills and talents would be wasted on anything but domestic violence cases. She knew at the time her plan might not work, but she was determined to do whatever she could to make it happen. So, for five months she sharpened her skills as a future law enforcement officer at the FBI Academy before she was called before the review board and told that, although she had excelled in almost every aspect of her training, she had been deficient in her firearms course. While some members of the board wanted to make an exception and approve her for graduation, she declined, arguing that if she did not meet training requirements, she did not want to graduate. She didn't see any benefit in telling the board that she never had any intention of graduating from the Academy and serving as an FBI Agent. Intentionally failing the firearms course made her exit from the Academy easy on everyone.

Several months before she was hired as a deputy with the Charleston County Sheriff's Office the state legislature passed a law that directed and funded the establishment of a criminal domestic violence task force within each county's sheriff's office. If she had any religious sympathies at all she might have attributed the law's passage as part of God's plan for her. Instead she saw the legislature's action as an effort to combat a chronic problem in the state that just happened to parallel and compliment her own.

Her first arrest came the second night she was on patrol after being assigned to the task force. She and her partner, Tom (she couldn't remember the last name), responded to a call in an upscale neighborhood at a country club. It was close to midnight when they pulled into the driveway behind a Mercedes and a BMW SUV. The lights were on in the house but it was quiet when Billie and her partner walked up the steps to the front door. She knocked on the door and exchanged a glance with Tom whose eyes cut quickly away. Tom had been with the sheriff's office seven years and considered his assignment to the task force a demotion, although he received a bump in salary. He had made it clear several times that he saw the task force as a political stunt and waste of money, as did most of the more experienced employees in the sheriff's office.

The door opened slowly and a girl in her early teens stood before them with a look of fear in her eyes.

"Did you call 911?"

The girl looked over her shoulder at something or someone inside the house. She turned back to the officers and nodded slightly.

"Is there anyone else here?"

Another nod.

"Can we come in?"

The girl said nothing but opened the door wider. Once inside Billie could hear crying or what was closer to whimpering. She walked through the foyer down a short hallway into a kitchen where she found a woman in a chair at a dining table, her feet folded up underneath her. Her head was lowered to where Billie couldn't see her face. The girl who had followed Billie, now walked past her and went to the woman touching her on the shoulder. The woman startled and looked up.

"Mama, the police are here."

The woman's feet unfurled from under her and hit the floor.

"Oh, thank God! Please help me!"

Her hair was a mess, some of it sticking out in all directions and some of it stuck to her face with sweat, tears or makeup or some combination of the three. Then Billie saw the blood trickling down in front of her left ear.

"Ma'am are you hurt?"

"He hit me. He hit me with a glass. In the head."

This brought on more tears and sobbing. The girl stood beside her silent with her hand on the woman's shoulder, looking off in the direction of a patio door.

"Who hit you?'

The woman began sobbing. "My ... huh-uhz-bun."

"Where is he now? Has he left?"

She shook her head.

At that moment, there was the sound of something heavy crashing to the floor upstairs. The woman let out a screech and the girl jumped. Billie pulled out her weapon and looked at Tom who had been standing back at the entrance to the hallway. He was looking up at the ceiling.

Then there was a voice from upstairs. "Goddamnit! Who called the fucking cops!"

Billie turned back to the girl and woman. "Is that him?"

The girl stood frozen in place and wide-eyed, not saying a word.

The woman curled her legs back underneath her and hugged her knees with her arms. "Yes! Please help us!"

Tom drew his weapon and disappeared down the hall. Billie heard Tom's voice as she approached the hallway.

"Sir, put your hands where I can see them and come down the stairs."

"This is bullshit!"

"Sir, put your hands where I can see them!"

Plummet

Billie saw Tom with his weapon pointed to the top of the stairs. She called for backup and joined Tom at the foot of the staircase. At the top of the stairs she saw a man in dark pants and a white dress shirt glaring down at them. He gritted his teeth as if struggling to contain something inside.

"We need for you to come down stairs now!"

The man silently moved down the stairs with one hand on the rail and the other at his side. When he reached the bottom Billie turned him around, pulling his arms behind his back and cuffed him. Tom holstered his weapon and took him out to the car while Billie went back to the wife and daughter.

"We've arrested your husband. You're safe now. But I'm going to need to ask you some questions." Billie thought it odd that there was no thank you, just a small nod of the head before the woman stood out of the chair, wiping hair from her face.

~ ~ ~

Five days had passed since the arrest and the case still had not been assigned to a solicitor. Billie kept in touch with Lisa – the victim's advocate – and called the Solicitor's Office several times a day. Nothing was happening. The husband's name was Phillip Trask and he had posted bond the morning after the arrest. Lisa had assisted Judy Trask with requesting a hearing before a Family Court judge who issued an Order of Protection that granted her sole possession of the home and ordered Mr. Trask not to have any contact with her or their daughter. Lisa knew this was Billie's first Criminal Domestic Violence case and assured her everything was proceeding normally. But Billie wasn't sure. A voice inside of her was telling her something wasn't right. The voice was her intuition, her 'gut' but she thought of it as the 'the little old woman in her head' and although she struggled with accepting the possibility, she believed it somehow to be the voice of her mother, guiding her through life. And the voice was always right. There was never any specifics, just a general feeling that something was wrong. Billie hadn't heard from her in a while and tried to ignore it, telling herself she was just anxious about her first domestic violence case. But there was more to it than that. She had picked up on a vibe when she was interviewing Judy Trask following her husband's arrest, a vibe that had bothered her ever since. The voice in Billie's head wasn't sounding an alarm because Billie was inexperienced, she was warning her that something was wrong with the case. And the following day, a phone call from Lisa confirmed it.

"We've got a problem with Trask."

"Shit. What is it?"

"The girl, Abby, is changing her story."

"Changing it how?"

"Remember what I told you Trask's attorney said at the order of protection hearing, that the wife self-inflicted the wound to her head?"

"Yeah. The judge didn't buy it."

"Well, Abby says it's true."

"Dammit! He got to her somehow. He's not supposed to have any contact. Let's get her phone records and –"

"Billie!"

"What?"

"It's over."

"The hell it is! I can't believe you'd believe this shit. Look, the girl misses her dad, she's afraid he'll go to prison, she wants her family back again. Somebody from the dad's attorney's office reaches out to her, tells her what she wants to hear and she recants. We can't let the case fall apart that easily."

"Billie, listen to me. I confronted Judy with this."

"And?"

"She said 'Maybe I don't remember how it happened. He still needs to be taught a lesson.' I'm looking at the real possibility I helped a woman commit perjury in court. I can't have my reputation smeared like that. That's not fair to the real victims."

Billie's mind was racing. She had seen the anger in Phillip Trask's eyes that night and the fear in the eyes of his wife and daughter. That was real. But now the circle of violence was closing shut and it was up to her to straighten it out again. This is what she had set out to do, keep these cases on the court docket, make sure they were prosecuted with or without the victim's help.

She didn't remember hanging up on Lisa. The next thing she remembered was being on the phone with the receptionist at the solicitor's office, ranting about justice delayed and making threats to call the Attorney General's Office, until the receptionist was finally able to tell her that the case of State vs. Phillip Trask had been assigned. Billie apologized and in a calmer voice asked to speak to the lawyer who was going to prosecute the case.

"Christine McKinney."

"Ms. McKinney, this is Billie Carver with the Sheriff's Office."

"Hey Carver. Please, call me Chris."

"Okay, Chris, I'm with the Special Task Force on domestic violence and I understand you were assigned State v. Trask."

"I was. And you were the arresting officer."

"That's right."

"And you're calling because you heard the case is falling apart and you want to make sure the Solicitor's Office is going to go forward with the prosecution."

The words coming from the attorney sounded pre-recorded, a message played hundreds of times.

"Something like that, yeah."

"Right. I'll be honest with you, Carver. I see this getting booted."

"Booted?"

"Dismissed. Trashed. Earlier I spoke with the investigator for Phillip Trask's lawyer. The girl posted a video of herself on Facebook telling what really happened that night. Check it out. It should supplement your investigation which I noticed didn't include a statement from the daughter."

That was true and part of the reason the little woman in her head her was ringing alarm bells. The girl had refused to make a statement that night.

"I'm coming over there. We need to talk."

"Talking won't change the evidence."

"The evidence convinced a judge to issue an order of protection?"

"And by the end of the afternoon that same judge will be signing an order dismissing the PO after he sees the girl's Facebook post. This shit happens, Carver."

The voice was telling her the lawyer was right. There was something wrong with this case and she had known it from the night of the arrest. But she stubbornly ignored all of that, sticking to her principles.

"I'm coming over."

"I'll be in court."

"Then I'll talk to your boss." She hung up and left for the Charleston County Solicitor's Office.

The clock on the wall of the waiting area was ten minutes fast. Billie had looked at her phone at least fifteen times as if the world would catch up with the clock or the clock would decide to wait. It was irritating her. Why do that? So your employees would get to work early? They'll just leave ten minutes before they should in the afternoon...During the forty-five minutes she had been waiting to see the Solicitor, she had seen people walking through waiting area, either entering or leaving the office, but none of them was Daniel C. Baker, Solicitor of the Third

Judicial Circuit. The receptionist she had spoken to when she arrived, had been answering the ringing phone almost non-stop since then and seemingly forgotten Billie was there. Billie wanted to say something but reminded herself of her status. I'm a drop-in wanting to see the Solicitor. There will be a wait if I'm lucky to see him at all. And she had decided on the drive over that she needed to see him. She needed to tell him that with the passage of the Domestic Violence Prevention Act and the state's funding of the task force, there had to be changes in how these cases were prosecuted. She didn't need to talk with an assistant solicitor. She wanted to know if the man elected to prosecute the laws of the State in Charleston County was going to do that.

"Deputy Carver?"

The voice brought Billie back to the future world of the waiting room.

"Yes." An attractive woman stood in a doorway smiling.

"Come with me. Solicitor Baker will see you now."

Billie told herself that the Solicitor would be on the phone when they walked into his office and he was, standing behind his desk and motioning with his free hand for her to come in and have a seat while he finished his conversation. Important men are always on the phone.

"I hear you, Henry, but it's not going to happen. Not in this case. You file whatever motions you need to cover your ass on the record. It's just another day at the office for me." He hung up without another word and smiled at Billie.

"Mr. Baker, this is Deputy Carver."

He looked quizzically at the woman until he heard the name.

"Right. Of course." He broke into a wide smile and extended his hand to Billie. "You're with the Domestic Violence Task Force, right?"

She relaxed as they shook hands and she smiled. This

was starting better than she had hoped.

"Yes. It's a pleasure to meet you. I didn't think you would know that."

"Give me some credit deputy. I mean, the legislature may pass the laws but it's our job to actually do something with them, right?"

"I'm sorry that's not what I meant. I just didn't expect you to know me."

"Well, I've been meaning to put something together on this, you know, like a joint meeting between the Sheriff's Office, my office, the Victim's Advocates ..."

"Family Court?"

"Yeah, right. Them too." He paused a second. She had interrupted him and he let it register before finishing. "You know, to get on the same page with this."

Other than the slight irritation he showed at being interrupted, it sounded promising. Everything he was saying could have come from her own mouth. Billie began to feel she had an ally. A powerful ally. Until his next statement.

"We can't be going in different directions. You'd agree with that wouldn't you?"

She felt things turning. Returning was more accurate and her mood darkened. The world seem to want to exist at an equilibrium she couldn't accept.

"Yes. That's why I wanted to see you."

"Good. At least two of us are on the same page." He smiled and seemed to want to bring the meeting to an inconclusive end.

"I don't think we are."

He leaned back in his chair with an expression she hadn't yet seen on him. It unsettled her.

"How's that?"

"I made a domestic violence arrest the other night – Philip Trask is the suspect – and I was told earlier today by an assistant solicitor that the case would most likely be dismissed."

"And you disagree with that?"

A dry sound came from her that would have been understood by anyone that heard it as meaning 'no shit.' It wasn't professional and she immediately regretted it. "I definitely disagree with that."

Daniel C. Baker stood up and walked towards the three large, arched windows that filled one wall of his office. From the second floor of the building, the windows provided an elevated view of the intersection of Meeting and Broad Streets, an area known as the "Four Corners of Law" in downtown Charleston. Buildings representing the municipal, county and federal governments surround the intersection along with St. Michael's Episcopal Church, representing God's Law and the fourth Acorner." While he stood before the windows with his back to Billie, hands in his pockets, Daniel C. Baker may have been pondering the absence below him of a building representing the State's law. Whatever occupied his thoughts, the silence lasted only a moment.

"We have the tough part, Carver." He was still facing the windows, not her.

He's still playing the politician she thought. She rather have it out, for them both to tell the other where they stood. That wasn't how he was handling it.

"The legislature in Columbia holds press conferences, announces the passage of laws and the dedication of tax dollars to fund the prosecution of those laws but it's a sham. They know we're drowning in cases. The money they give us doesn't come close to what we would need to do the job. What they don't say in those press conferences is that the money they give us won't pay for the additional courtrooms, prosecutors, judges, court reporters and public defenders we would need to adequately address the problem of domestic violence in this state. Not to mention more prisons to put them in." The speech had been made with his back to her, as if from a balcony overlooking the streets to a crowd of people below.

Billie felt her face flushing. This was the same bull shit she had heard as a child when her mother was being beaten and she was being raped.

"Mr. Baker, it's true we do not live in a wealthy state and our judicial system is not adequately funded. That means decisions have to be made right? Decisions about how to allocate limited resources. And those decisions necessarily involve priorities. Well the legislature – the source of money for this office – has made domestic violence a priority. They have told you to make it a priority." There. She had said what she had come to say. She had challenged him and it was either going to go for or against her, but at least it was done. He turned from the window. A small, quick smile acknowledged the boldness of her lecture.

"Deputy, you are right. Decisions have to be made. And ultimately, the guy – or gal – at the top has to make them." He sat at his desk again and leaned forward in his chair. "I'm one of those guys." He stared at her for a moment. "You're not one of those gals."

She didn't respond.

"If you do this job long enough Carver, you'll see that the prosecution of criminals is an assembly line. Ideally, the end product of that assembly line is the conviction. There are many different people that work on the line and everybody has a job to do to make sure the line keeps moving. You have a job on that line Carver. So do I. But our jobs aren't the same. They don't overlap. One of my jobs as a lawyer is deciding which cases should be prosecuted and which cases shouldn't be prosecuted. It's a vital part of the process, because if it's not done properly, the whole line bogs down."

"The legislature ..."

"Fuck the legislature!" The words blew out of him like something suddenly broke and he sat back in his chair, running a hand through his graying, brown hair.

Billie stood up. "I think we understand each other. I won't waste any more of your time." He said nothing and remained seated behind his desk. "But I'm not done. I'm going to the Attorney General if I have to." The threat sounded weak and she wish she hadn't said it, or, rather, wished she had said it with more confidence. He slowly stood from his chair. They stared at each other for a moment as he considered her bold and reckless statements while she tried to look confident, in control.

"Well, deputy, if you talk to the AG, will you give him a message for me?"

"What's that?"

"Tell him he cheats at golf."

She couldn't tell if the solicitor grew larger or if she suddenly shrank but a realization came over her that made her feel small, as small as she felt as a child when her mother would take her back into the home of her abuser, when she was helpless to stop his attacks. No matter how long she lived, how hard she fought, she kept returning to the same place, that place the world wanted to be, where she was small and insignificant and the lives of others crowded out her own.

The phone call that ended her career as a sheriff's deputy must have been made during her drive back to the office. When she arrived, she was told to report to the captain who told her to turn in her badge. She was stunned and later she would realize that being stunned proved how naive she really was. She removed her badge – was she actually supposed to do that? – as the captain continued talking about something she didn't hear. She placed the badge on his desk, looked him in the eyes but said nothing, knowing she either had too much to say or nothing at all. As she walked down the hallway to her locker it occurred to her that it might all be over. Maybe not a career in law enforcement, but she would never get the opportunity to work on a domestic violence task force again. This would follow her wherever she went. Her dreams and plans were finished before she had been on the job a month. Hurt and angry, she wanted to scream, but held it in. But the tears couldn't be stopped. By the time she reached the parking lot she was sobbing, unable to face the question that repeated in her brain: What now?

~ ~ ~

The five weeks she had been with the Mount Pleasant Police Department was a blank space in her life. She had done little real police work since arriving, probably due to the Chief intentionally not giving her much to do. And she hadn't complained. She spent most of her time mentally wandering through the wreckage of her career, consciously avoiding the question that still haunted her: What now? She was eating fast food every day, not exercising and going straight to bed when she got to her apartment in the evening, sleeping through the night with the help of medication until her alarm blasted her awake in the morning. There were times, when she was alone, that she allowed herself to cry. She was depressed. And now she had to find the energy somewhere and somehow to work her first case. The day before, while on patrol, she had responded to a call from dispatch. An anonymous caller had reported gunshots at the Shoreline Apartments. Not an unusual occurrence apparently. But the place had looked deserted when she arrived. It had taken her twenty-seven minutes to find the body. She had also found the presumed murder weapon on the counter in the kitchen. Nothing about what she had found at the scene or learned afterward made sense to her. But instead of stoking her curiosity, the questions annoyed her. She was at a dead end in her life and wanted no part of an investigation that required passion, diligence or creative thought. She wanted routine. A routine that required her to do little more than go through the motions. That's all she could offer her profession right now.

So she was more bothered than surprised when Chief Baskin came to her that morning and told her that the case of the murdered man in the apartment was hers.

"I'm not an investigator."

"You are now. Congratulations."

None of it had made sense to her.

"It doesn't make any sense. Give it to Joey."

"Look. You're not a traffic cop. It's time for you to get off your ass and do what you were trained to do."

She hadn't agreed so much as she didn't refuse. When she hadn't responded to the Chief's locker room speech he just ended the conversation with 'Good' and walked back to his office, leaving her to wonder if she had the motivation to meet the professional demands of what had just been dropped on her. Plus, the voice inside her was pushing back against this, refusing to accept the reasons the Chief had given for handing the case off to her. But in spite of how she felt, she couldn't avoid that part of her that had pushed her to survive the abuse and her mother's death, that same something that had driven her to be a top student in college and at the academy. It was still there. Beaten down and buried beneath a pile of emotional garbage perhaps, but still there. Billie told herself the investigation would be routine and that the Chief had assigned her the case because he knew that and wanted to bring her along slowly. Convincing herself that expectations were low, she had decided not to quit and give it a try. What else am I going to do? Quitting would be giving in to the depression and there was nothing but the darkness waiting for her if she made that choice.

There was nothing to do but put blinders on and forge ahead. Each day, she told herself, it will get better. So her investigation began that morning, by asking questions around the office about the Shoreline Apartments. That's when she learned that shootings were a regular occurrence at the Shoreline and were always the consequence of either drugs or domestic violence. Ignoring any evidence that would suggest otherwise, the morning ended with Billie feeling a small surge of optimism that her victim would fall under one of the two categories.

What the Chief hadn't told her was who had decided Billie Carver should investigate the murder at the Shoreline. The night before, Tom Baskin had received a call from Charles Davis Carlton, the City of Charleston Police Chief, requesting a favor. An off the record favor.

"Tom, the FBI has been following a guy named Mahmoud Khalil. He's the guy your people found at the Shoreline today. They're worried his death may blow up their investigation before they can find out why he was here or who sent him."

"So why don't they call and tell me this."

"They may – at some point – but right now they want to stay in the background and let things play out."

"What's your interest in this Charles?" The ambitions of Charles Davis Carlton were presumed by most everyone that knew him to exceed far beyond law enforcement in the Holy City.

"Whatever Kahlil was working on, Charleston seems to have been the target. At least the FBI thinks so. They aren't telling me much, Tom. Honestly, I don't know how much they actually know."

Tom Baskin smiled when Chief Carlton used the word "honestly." He didn't think for a moment Charles Davis Carlton was telling him everything he knew.

"So let me get this straight. A possible terrorist that the

FBI has been shadowing ends up dead in an apartment in Mount Pleasant and instead of dealing with me directly, they have you call. Is that it so far?"

Both men knew what was being said. Baskin didn't believe what he was being told and if Carlton wanted Baskin to play along, it was going to cost him.

"Tom, I realize this isn't protocol, but I need for you to slow play the investigation, let things play out awhile."

Baskin noticed it was now Carlton that needed a favor, not the FBI. Maybe he mis-spoke. Maybe he didn't.

"And why would I not diligently try to solve a murder in my city?"

"I can think of five thousand reasons."

"I can think of ten."

"You know your jurisdiction better than me. If there are ten, there are ten."

Only then did Tom Baskin realize he had misjudged the situation. This was more important to Carlton than he had thought. He could have gotten more. Carlton was ready to pay whatever it cost. I'll get more later, once I find out what's going on.

"Don't you have someone new, a girl that came over from County?"

"Billie Carver."

"Yeah. Carver. I'm thinking she'd be good for this."

"You've done your homework. This case may grow moss on Carver's desk."

"Well, it's your investigation, Chief. I'm sure you know the best way to handle it."

Right.

"Oh, give my best to Carol."

"I will do that, Charles." Chief Baskin silently marveled at how smoothly Charles Davis Carlton could operate the machinations of corruption. He couldn't think of Carlton's wife's name. He remembered it was foreign-sounding. "And when can I expect a visit from you to discuss those reasons?"

"How does tomorrow afternoon sound?"

"I'll be waiting."

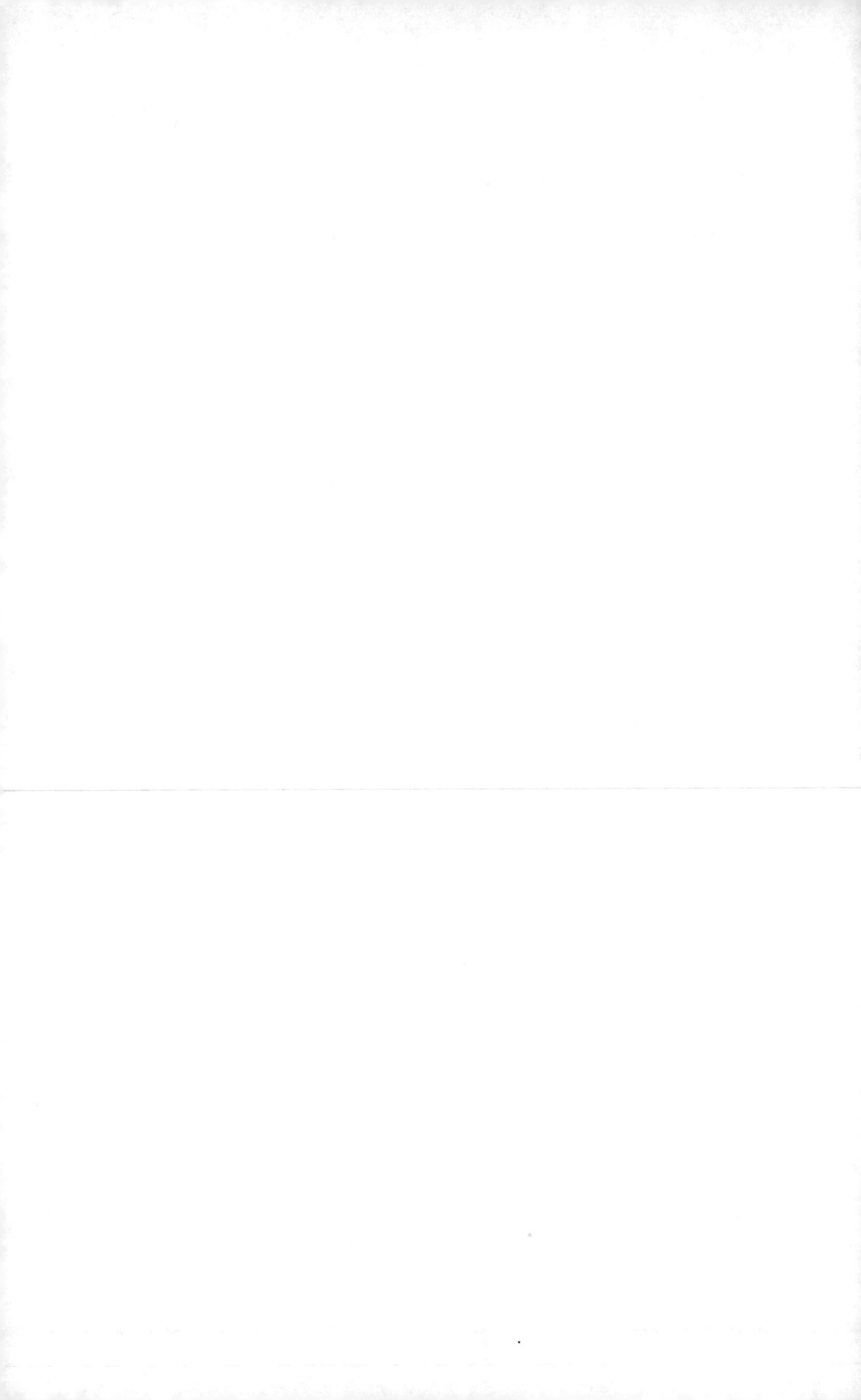

13.

Her desk sat in an open area with four others more or less like it. It wasn't her desk but it was the one she always used. There were twelve officers and two investigators who shared the five desks. From where she sat she could see the Chief's Office and the work station of every other employee. There were three interview rooms if more privacy was needed. The department had outgrown the building years ago but that wasn't her concern. Deep down she knew she wouldn't be there long.

Her phone rang.

"Carver."

"ATF on line two." ATF was the Bureau of Alcohol Tobacco and Firearms. Although there was no federal computerized database of firearm sales or ownership in the U.S., if the gun had been used in another crime or reported stolen, it might have been registered in the database along with the name of its owner. The ATF kept a record of such things. She had also put in a routine request with the FBI's National Crime Information Center which also maintained a database of stolen firearms. Both were routine requests and she expected nothing from either. Even if the gun found at the Shoreline had been used in a prior crime or reported stolen, the probability that any information the feds had would lead her to the person who shot the Shoreline victim was very slim if not nonexistent. She punched the flashing light. "Carver."

"Yeah, we've got a match on a serial number for a

127

firearm. Are you Officer Billie Carver?" She stopped herself from saying anything more than "I am."

"Well, we got a match."

Billie sat up in her seat. The information may prove useless but it was more than she had expected.

"Okay. Give it to me."

She grabbed a pad of blue sticky notes and wrote down the name and address of the owner of the Sig 9 mm that was found at the apartment and hung up. She got up from the desk and walked over to the Chief's office. He was looking at his computer.

"Watcha got, hot shot?"

He'd been calling her that since the week after she arrived and she hated it. From what she could tell, he had a nickname for all of the officers.

"Chief, I wish you wouldn't call me that."

"Right. Watcha got?"

"The gun found at the Shoreline Apartments? I got an owner's name. It was reported stolen.

The Chief looked up from his computer with an expression she hadn't expected. He looked confused. His reaction flipped a switch inside her that put her on self-protect mode.

"No shit? Where did you find that?"

"NCIC."

"The feds had a file on this gun?"

"Not that unusual is it? Gun used in a crime is most likely stolen. Here it is."

The chief stood up and walked over to her and took the sticky note from Billie's hand. With one phone call his inexperienced, lethargic officer had made more progress in the investigation than he thought she would have made in three months. Normally, it would take weeks to get information on a gun's owner from the feds, if you got it at all. Not that the feds didn't want to help. They were prohibited by law from maintaining a federal data base of gun owners. Carver was right. Since she had found the owner's name at NCIC, the gun had most likely been reported stolen. Still, Carver was further along with the case than he had expected her to be and the chief began to worry a little about his deal with Carlton.

Billie watched the pinched look on the chief's face relax into a smile as he read the name. He laughed and handed the note back to Billie.

"Peale! That fuck up."

"Who is he, some blue blood?"

"Shit no! Peale? Tainted blood's more like it." The Chief's laugh faded.

"Jackson Peale is a former lawyer. Before your time. Ran into some trouble a few years ago. Booze. Drugs. Fucked up his practice, lost his license. Works as a private detective now, I think."

"Whitsett is South of Broad, isn't it?"

"Don't know. Is it? Look, if it's Peale's gun, invite him in. No house calls."

"Will he show?"

"From what I know of him, yeah."

"I'm going to call the City and County. Find out who reported it stolen. "

"Right."

She turned to leave and the concerned look returned to the Chief's face. He knew there was no way the FBI wouldn't have Peale's name too. Nothing about this felt right to Baskin and it certainly didn't sync with Charles Carlton's wild story about the FBI and terrorists in Charleston. The introduction of Jack Peale into the scene only made matters more confusing. Ah hell. It's just Carlton trying to throw Carver – or anyone else – off the trail. That's what he told himself so he could go back to his game of online poker Carver had interrupted. Still, he couldn't shake the concern he had for Carver if someone was going through the trouble of manipulating federal databases to confuse what had happened at the Shoreline.

"Carver?"

She stopped in the door and looked back. "Yeah, Chief?"

"Are you good with this?"

She nodded. "I am."

"I think you are too. Otherwise, I'd have given it to someone else."

She nodded again and started back to her desk.

"Carver?"

"Yes, Chief?"

He almost said be careful but stopped himself. "If you need anything ..."

The look on his face and his words confused her. It all seemed out of place and a little disconcerting.

"Right."

She walked back to her desk wondering if she was Carver now or still Hot Shot. When she sat down, the phone buzzed and she picked up the receiver.

"There's a reporter on 3. Said she talked to you earlier at the apartments where the body was found. Said she's left several messages."

Billie's shoulders slumped. She had run into the reporter in the parking lot of the Shoreline when she was leaving after forensics had wrapped up their investigation. She had blown the reporter off at the time, promising her an interview later. Billie watched the blinking light and tried to decide what she could and shouldn't say.

"Carver."

"Hi. This is Jennifer Lott with *The Sun*. I spoke to you at the Shoreline Apartments yesterday."

"Yes. I remember."

"Do you have time for a few questions?"

"Sure."

"Do you have an ID on the victim?"

"No. Still John Doe."

"Suspects?"

"No."

"Anyone called about the victim? Family? Friends?"

"No."

Billie was starting to feel confident in how this was going. Some reporters could ask questions in a way that any answer you gave made you sound like you weren't telling the truth. She could answer yes / no questions all day.

"There was a gun found at the scene, right?"

The question made Billie hesitate. "Yes."

"Have you traced the serial number?"

"It's been requested."

"Any idea on who the owner may be?"

"If I did, I wouldn't give it out. Yet."

"Any reason?"

"I would need to speak with the owner first. It wouldn't be fair to her if she discovered her gun may have been used in a murder by reading *The Sun*."

"So, it was murder?"

Billie cursed herself for the slip up. "That's what we're thinking. Six holes in the chest rules out suicide."

"Do you have a ballistics report?"

"Not yet."

"So you've got a John Doe at the Shoreline knocked off with a stolen gun."

"That's not what I said."

"What part is wrong?"

"Well, the 'stolen gun' part."

"The owner could be involved?"

"We don't know that yet."

"But it looks like a drug deal gone bad."

"Except there were no drugs found. Three hundred and some change in the victim's pants pocket. No motive at this point."

"So he had money but no ID?"

Billie had wondered about that also. If his ID was taken, why not the money?

"That's right."

"Why was he naked?"

Now Billie found herself shifting in her chair. The reporter was focusing on questions that Billie had been avoiding. Questions that complicated things. She had hoped it was just another drug deal gone bad. Maybe a page three story read over morning coffee then forgotten. But she knew it wasn't. If a murder story wasn't printed on page three it belonged on the front, above the fold. And that meant it was news. News that lasted for days, weeks, even a year. And she would be part of the story. As soon as this reporter came to the same conclusion, her investigation would go into hyper drive. She had to keep thinking it was drug related.

"I can't comment on that."

"Never heard of a drug deal where the buyer or seller was naked, unless it took place at his home. The victim wasn't living at the Shoreline was he?"

"We don't think so. Looks like a meet."

"Okay. You were the first to arrive at the scene?"

"Yes."

"Why were you there?"

"Someone reported gunshots, I was on patrol, dispatch sent me."

The reporter made a sound that said she questioned what Carver had just said.

"Is there a problem with that?" Carver immediately cursed herself for the question. Don't drag this out. Keep your mouth shut except for giving the shortest answer possible. Dammit.

"Well, it's just that I questioned everyone in that

building, well, the ones that would come to the door, and not one said they heard gunshots. So who called it in?"

Carver was at first intrigued by what Lott was asking but that quickly turned to irritation.

"That's all I can give you right now. I've got to go."

"But ... wait —"

"What?"

"Are you available to go out sometime?"

The question stunned Carver. Not only was it completely unrelated to what they had been discussing, it was inappropriate."

"What paper did you say you were from?"

"*The Sun*. It's a smaller, local paper. Mostly an on-line alternative to print."

She had heard of it but never read it.

"What would your editor say if he knew you were asking out the investigating officer of a case you were covering? Ever heard of a conflict of interest?"

"I don't think he would care as long as it didn't interfere with the reporting."

"How could it not? That's my point."

"So, you would go out if not for me covering your investigation?"

"No! What made you think I would?"

"I don't know. I just picked up on a vibe when we spoke at the scene."

"Well, your sensor for that sort of thing is way off."

"Okay. No problem. Won't happen again. So if I call again, it's about the case, okay? I don't want you avoiding my calls with the excuse that I'm asking you out. Deal?"

Billie paused. She wanted to tell her not to bother calling again, that she'd crossed a line. Instead she found herself saying "No problem."

And she knew why. She hadn't been hit on like that in a while and never by a woman. She had to admit, it felt good, no matter who it came from. She wasn't feeling very attractive these days so the reporter's invite -although inappropriate – gave her ego a boost. But then she wondered about what Lott had said about her giving off a vibe? What vibe? Sure, she had been around women that she thought were attractive but not in that way. But she had rarely felt that way about a man either. A darkness crept over her thoughts as she was sucked down a tunnel, back in time to the rapes and the pregnancy, her mother's death. I built a wall, shut it all out. How many hours had she sat through lectures in psychology, studied the texts and research, analyzed others but never once looked into her own murky, messed up self? She shuddered and looked around the normalcy of the office, bringing her back to the present day and the current version of herself and felt a tear sliding down her cheek. She rose from the desk and left the office. She needed to have a talk with Jackson Peale.

14.

greeing to keep Meghan was starting to look like a mistake. How was I to know the guy I was asked to find would end up murdered? With my gun? And the FBI would put me at the front of the line of suspects? Then there was Billy Shores dropping in unannounced. He wasn't going away like I had hoped. The shit was piling up in my head so when I picked Megan up from school I wasn't the most attentive father I could have been. She was talkative and upbeat and I tried listening at first, but my mind slid back to dead terrorists, dead soldiers, prison. Sexy Staci. It didn't take her long to pick up on the fact I wasn't listening to whatever it was she was saying and she was quiet by the time we reached Broad Street. I wasn't proud of my ability to ruin my daughter's mood but at the moment I couldn't work on that particular problem in our relationship. Besides, a new situation was about to detract us both.

When I pulled into my driveway, there was a black Mercedes convertible parked in front of my apartment.

"Whose car is that?" If anything could drag Megan out of the funk I had put her in, it was a shiny, expensive sports car.

"A client's. Why don't you stay in the car for a second, ok?"

"Where is he? Why can't I get out?"

I shut the door on her questions and looked around as I walked to the wrought iron stairway leading up to my apartment. Megan's second question was a good one.

135

Plummet

Where was she? I didn't want to alarm Megan so I casually walked up the steps like nothing was wrong. But there was something wrong. I hadn't really let myself think about it until then. There was a strong probability that Staci had killed Khalil. Somehow, during the few feet from the car to where I stood on the steps, I had suddenly become smarter. I found myself wishing I had a gun. Who the hell else would have killed Kahlil? And she framed me for it! And now she's at my apartment?

I glanced down at my car. Meghan was looking up at me from behind the windshield, her face asking the question "What's wrong?" I patted my pockets as if trying to locate my keys then held them up in my hand and dangled them so she could see as I pulled open the screen door. It was lame but all I could think of.

The door wasn't locked and the realization that she was inside flashed in my brain just before I saw her standing near the kitchen with her back to me. I froze in the door way and the screen door shut behind me. As she turned around I was expecting to see a gun pointed at me. I was wrong. Again.

She was crying and walked quickly to me, wrapping her arms around me and buried her face in my neck.

"Thank you." It wasn't a whisper, just a weak voice cracking with feigned vulnerability. She started kissing my neck then my face and made her way to my lips, between each kiss a "Thank you."

In just seconds I had gone from expecting Staci to shoot me to wanting to take her into the bedroom. My mind was mush. I grabbed her arms and pushed her gently away but didn't let go.

"Wait a minute. What the hell is going on? Why are you here?"

She looked up at me, mascara smudged around her eyes, black tears on her cheeks.

"You killed him." A strange smile creased her face. " You killed that bastard. I had to thank you."

She turned out of my grip and walked away from me, sliding one hand down my arm until her hand closed around mine. She pulled me in the direction of the bedroom.

"Hold on, Staci." She stopped, looking confused, then smiled and tossed her long hair. Never-mind my kid was in the car downstairs, I had questions that needed to be answered before I could think of getting a hard on. Then I remembered Thursday's request that I get closer to her. I also remembered what he had said about her getting her way with her body and her money.

She walked back to me. Her smile was replaced with a small, playful frown.

"What's wrong, baby?"

"You've got to get out of here."

"Not just yet ..."

"Look, my daughter's downstairs in the car."

Her expression changed with a quickness that bothered me.

"Oh."

"And Staci?"

"Yes?"

"He was killed with my gun." I was looking into her eyes for something, probably the truth.

"I know. Do you know how rare you are, a man that knows what has to be done and does it?" Her fingers moved through my hair and her eyes were moving over my face, taking as much of me in as they could. How did she know it was my gun? Did Carlton tell her?

"I feel so lucky, so grateful." She pressed her tits into me and we kissed, her hand sliding down my back and squeezing gently when it reached my butt. My mind was falling away from everything but her when a knock at the door broke the spell. I turned and saw Megan standing in the door with her book bag in one hand. She was looking away from us, giving us time to untangle and put on a false front. For Staci, that wasn't a problem. She walked straight up to Megan.

"Hi, I'm Staci."

Megan glanced at her, then me then to her book bag. "Hi."

"Please don't be mad at your dad, he didn't know I was coming by. Oh, I love those jeans. I used to have a pair that looked like that ..." And the small talk began about clothes and hair and other things I couldn't say three relevant words about. Staci was transforming herself in my daughter's eyes from the stranger groping her father to a very attractive and friendly woman interested in everything about Megan. I stood there watching and wondering how many times a day she could pull it off, being whoever she needed to be at that moment, to get what it was she wanted. As they continued talking, a darkness came over me, brought on by the question, what does she want? The image of her standing in front of the door, chatting and laughing with my daughter just moments after trying to seduce me didn't sit right. The darkness wasn't just a warning that something was wrong, but a realization that just about everything I wanted to believe about Staci was a lie.

"Alright, ladies, I'll be the bad guy and break this up. Megan, you've got homework to do, I'm sure. And Staci ..." She was smiling at me and reached out and lightly grabbed the fingers of my hand in a way that made it look like she didn't want Megan to see but made it impossible to miss. Her touch made me unsure of myself and I could only manage a sound above a whisper. "We'll talk later."

Staci squeezed my fingers, said bye to Megan and left,

Batista never said hello when he answered the phone, just launched into the conversation as if he already knew what I wanted. And why wouldn't he? When I called Batiste, it was only for information and if he had it, he would know what I wanted. I could see him trying to spin that as some kind of extra-sensory perception. For once though, I wanted him to be wrong.

"The bottom open up beneath ya feet, mon?"

"Something like that." Talking to Batiste was like talking to a character from a late night TV skit.

"Yeah. Not literally. Not yet literally."

His tone, what I could detect through the bull shit accent, bothered me. A mendacity creeped around in it. "What do you mean?"

"I told you bad people were asking 'bout you. Now bad things have happened. Were you lissenin? Were you careful? No. No."

"Who was it?"

"What does that matter?"

"Quit fuckin' with me, Batista." My voice was louder than I had wanted and I looked up to the bedroom door as if I could see whether Megan could hear me or not in the den. I could hear the TV and went back to Batista who had been taking offense to my attitude.

"... should be tankin' me you ungrateful, gun-less, murderin', swingin' dick."

"You know I didn't kill that guy?"

"How I know that?"

The questioned bothered me. Why? Had I come to regard Batista as some well of truth in which I lowered a bucket of questions and pulled up the answers?

"Look. The whole stripper thing the other night was planned, a scheme to get my gun to frame me for killing Kahlil."

"Bullshit, mon. People buy hot guns to kill people every day."

"Isn't it a coincidence that it was my gun that killed the

guy I was hired to find? And that someone sent me a text to go find him after he was dead?"

"What do the FBI say?"

Batista knew more than I was assuming he did. "That Kahlil was a terrorist and Staci Turner is connected somehow. They want me to get close, let it play out."

"And you?"

"Right now I've got to play along."

There was a pause before he spoke. "Go back to the beginning. If it was rigged, where did it start?" I didn't know if he was giving me advice or information.

"You mean the stripper?"

"You are a dense, fuckin' white man. Take you five years to figure dis out."

"Then quit acting like black Yoda and tell me."

"Who the fuck you with that night?"

Todd Burley. I hung up the phone without another word. My ears were ringing with what? Truth? Anger? It was anger because all I could think about at the moment was doing Todd Burley harm. But I couldn't. I had Megan with me. I needed to think this through anyway. I opened the door and went into the den.

"Who were you yelling at?"

"Nobody. It's business."

"I thought it was mom but I heard another voice. It was weird."

Was the phone on speaker? I couldn't remember. Damn that's careless. I went to the kitchen for a beer. Megan was curled up on the couch watching TV. Her eyes never left the screen as she fired question after question at me. That was fine, it was taking my mind of Burley.

"Are you still doing private detective work?"

"Yeah."

There was a pause. "Is that what you are doing for Staci."

I thought I could see a smile bending the corners of her mouth. Maybe not.

"Yeah. She, uh, hired me to find someone." I drank some of the beer and pretended to look for something in the cabinets.

Another pause.

"Is she paying you?"

I turned around and looked at her. She hadn't moved, just kept looking at the TV as if she had never said a word. Do women learn this shit or is it packaged in that extra x chromosome?

Then she looked right at me. Her expression said she had a right to know. I always thought she looked like me but at that moment she was her mother. It was that same sweet, feminine power that could punch me in the gut and fold me over. And it was coming from my daughter.

"Well?"

"Quite well, actually." It was the truth and had the added bonus of suggesting sex. Maybe that wasn't appropriate but she brought sex into it, not me. I was reminded again that I didn't know my daughter at all.

"Why was she crying?"

"Those were happy tears. Look, tomorrow after school we're going to see Martha."

"Dad, I have a test Thursday in biology."

"You can study there."

She groaned and went back to the TV. "What's for supper?"

"Don't know. In or out?"

"Do you have enough money for something on Shem Creek?"

Shem Creek was across the bridge in Mount Pleasant. The thought made me lose my appetite and the question about money reminded me of something I had somehow forgot. It was Tuesday and I had found Kahlil. Staci owed me ten grand if I found Kahlil before Thursday. And, in a way, I did. But she hadn't brought any money with her. How could I let ten grand slip my mind? I needed some quite time alone. I looked at Megan. She shouldn't be here. When I agreed to keep her, Kahlil was a routine missing person case. Now it's murder and someone has gone through a lot of trouble to make it look like I'm the killer. Bad things could happen in the next few days and Megan didn't need to be with me. Her mother's trip to the mountains needed to end. But in the meantime, I had to make everything look routine and normal.

"No. Let's stay in and order delivery. Get started on your homework."

15.

The GPS had taken Lott to Whitsett Street but it couldn't find her a place to park. After driving through the tight, one-way street twice she decided to just park in what she guessed was Peale's driveway, unable to explain to herself why she did not want her car to be seen. She knocked on the door of the house several times but no one answered. After a few minutes she walked around the porch until she had a view of the back yard. To her right was a smaller, two story building. Green jasmine covered most of the corner of the building nearest her, climbing up to and stopping just below a window on the upper floor. A light was on.

As she reached the top of the stairs leading to a door, she could hear what was probably a television playing inside. A girl answered the door when she knocked.

"Is Jack Peale here?"

"Who wants to know?" The girl stood behind the screen door.

"Jennifer Lott. I'm a reporter for *The Sun*. Is he here?"

The door closed without any response from the girl. Lott decided to wait. The TV was still on but there were no voices. After a minute, the door opened and the girl appeared again.

"He isn't available."

"But he's here?"

The girl's head turned slightly as if she were about to look at something or someone out of Lott's view, then stopped. "He's not available." The door closed.

As Lott descended the iron staircase, she was smiling. There was more to the Shoreline murder than she had thought and it now had her full attention.

16.

A message from the Mt. Pleasant Police department was waiting for me at the Office. Officer Billie Carver wanted to talk with me. I called and told her I could meet her around 12:00. I had almost suggested a restaurant but guessed I probably wouldn't feel like eating after talking with her. So we agreed to meet at the station.

On the drive over to Mt. Pleasant I reminded myself that my gun had been stolen and that I could tell her exactly what happened – well, maybe leave out a few details – and the facts wouldn't implicate me any further. Still, I was bothered by something. As I pulled in to the police station parking lot I realized what it was. A few years ago, when I was a lawyer, I represented a man charged with murdering his wife and her boyfriend. All they had connecting my client to the crime was motive and the generally accepted fact that most murders are committed by someone close to the victim. Not enough to convict my guy but they had the murder weapon.

Ballistics and the coroner's report left no doubt that a gun found in a dumpster outside the hotel where the bodies were found was the gun used to kill the victims. But the solicitor had to connect my guy with the gun, which seemed simple enough because there was a serial number on the gun. But there was no readily accessible database of gun owners in this country. The most likely reason a gun's serial number would be found in a federal database is if the gun had been reported stolen. In the case of the murdered wife and boyfriend, the solicitor's office was told by the feds that the gun used in the crime had been previously reported stolen. However, it had taken them weeks to get that information. The Mt. Pleasant Police department had somehow been able to track me down in a day. And although my gun had been stolen, I had never reported it. When I had agreed to the meeting with Carver I was confident that I would be seen as the victim of a crime and there was nothing that would implicate me in Khalil's murder. But how was my gun in the federal database? I didn't know the answer but one of the possible answers was ominous: it wasn't in the federal database. I know I didn't kill Khalil but someone was going through a lot of effort to make it look like I did. The possibility that the same people could manipulate the search of a federal database drained most of the confidence I had left my apartment with. By the time I was walking into the station I had decided that agreeing to the meeting was a mistake.

The sight of Billie Carver was a pleasant surprise. She was attractive. Even a police uniform couldn't hide that fact. I had to remind myself that she probably thinks I killed Kahlil. And luckily, she showed none of the beguiling charms of Staci Turner.

"Mr. Peale, I'll get straight to why you're here. A man was found dead in the Shoreline Apartments yesterday and a gun registered to you was found at the scene."

"That's terrible."

"Terrible that a man was found dead or that your gun was at the scene?"

"That the man was killed."

"I didn't say he had been 'killed', Mr. Peale. How did you know that?"

My confidence was returning. This was amateur hour. Did she really think I would just confess to the murder right here?

"Why else would law enforcement be involved?" The question embarrassed her and she lost some of her momentum.

"Can you explain why your Sig 9 mm was at the scene?"

"It was stolen sometime between Friday night and Saturday morning."

"Where was it stolen?"

"From a hotel room."

"Which hotel?"

"The Midway Motel in North Charleston."

"And why were you at a motel in North Charleston.'

I was hoping she would ask that. "I was entertaining a woman. Or two."

She had been scribbling on a pad until I said this. She looked up and stared at me for a moment. "Mr. Peale, this is serious."

"Believe me – I know."

She paused again and I got the impression she doubted herself. A fatal flaw in a law enforcement officer.

"Names?"

"Excuse me?"

"The names of the women you were with."

"Oh. I don't know."

"You don't know?"

"And there may have be only one woman. I'm not sure."

She was getting mad now. "Mr. Peale, I know you use to be a lawyer so you are aware that providing false information is a crime?"

"Yes. But you have no probable cause to believe any of what I've told you isn't accurate."

At this point I asked myself why I was fucking with her. Maybe she could help. It certainly didn't help me by pissing her off. But it was too late for that. She was pissed.

"As a former lawyer I'm sure you are aware of what little information I need to obtain a warrant for your arrest, and how long you will sit in jail before you get a bond hearing. Is that the way you want this to play out?"

She was mad. She was inexperienced and I was being an asshole. "Officer, let's start over okay. You are telling me my gun was found at what I'm guessing was a murder scene and assuming that ballistics will connect my gun to the wounds on the victim, you are certainly justified in bringing me in for the obvious questions that raises. I apologize for seeming frivolous."

She leaned back in her chair and closed her eyes for a moment. When she opened her eyes and sat back up in her chair I decided to fill her in on what happened in the hope it would get me out of the place sometime soon.

"Friday night I went to a pub in Charleston, the Post Office. From there I went to the Paradise in North Charleston. It's a strip club. From there I left with a woman working as an independent contractor at the Paradise and we went to the Midway. The next morning, the woman insisted I owed her money in an amount I did not have at the moment so she took all of my possessions she could find – including my gun – and told me she would return them when I paid the money. When I met her manager later to do just that, they returned my clothes but not the gun."

"And when was that?"

"Saturday morning."

"Five days ago?

"Yes."

"And do you have witnesses to any of this?"

Up to that point I was feeling in control. She was the novice, she was going off on tangents that would lead nowhere and she was asking the wrong questions. But how quickly it all changed. Her question, an obvious one, drained all of my confidence onto the floor in a puddle at my feet. I realized I had a problem. "Well yeah. The, uh, the night manager, he'll remember."

"The night manager saw her take your gun?"

"Well, no."

"Mr. Peale. You say your gun was stolen by this woman you met at the Paradise. Where's your proof?"

There had to be proof. I mean, it happened, didn't it? I scanned what little memory I had of that morning. The only name I had was Cody's and there was no one else around.

"Why did you have your gun in the motel room anyway?"

Isn't she going to wait for my answer to the first question? I need time to think. I know there is something there, something that proves she took my gun ...

"Show her the text message Sarge."

I look to the chair next to me and there's Billy Shores, propping his crutches against Carver's desk and settling in like he was late for the appointment.

"The what?"

"That girl sent you a text message about getting your gun. You didn't delete it did you?"

I reached in the front pocket of my pants and pulled out the phone.

"Uh, Mr. Peale, did you say something?"

"What? Oh, yeah, I mean, no. I just remembered I have a text message from the woman I was with. It references the gun."

"Well, that would be something."

I scrolled through the messages and found the text. Carver took a picture of it with her phone as well as the other one I received telling me where to meet.

"What is this address?"

"That's where we met."

"You paid them money?"

"No. Not exactly."

"Did they have your gun?"

"No."

"So what happened when you met?"

I didn't want to go this far but there was already one question I hadn't answered. Anymore and I could find myself charged with murder.

"There was an altercation."

"A fight?"

"Yeah. It was a shake down. They wanted more money. I didn't have it so there was a fight."

"Who fought?"

"Me, the woman and her manager."

"What happened?"

Damn I didn't expect to get into this. What the hell am I to do, admit to kicking their ass and stealing their car? Admit to violence and crime? Isn't that exactly what I'm suspected of?

"Tell her Sarge. You kicked their ass and took their fucking car. Tell her."

I stared at Billy wondering whose side my hallucination was on. Carver must have seen me staring at an empty chair and took it for what it probably was: an admission that I didn't have a good answer.

"Mr. Peale? Are you going to tell me what happened?"

"Yeah. We, uh, got into to it. You know, shouting and stuff and then I left."

"How did you get there?"

"I drove. My car." Shit I lied. Why in the hell did you lie?

"Oh shit Sarge. That's not what happened. You better tell the truth. Oh shit ..."

"I can't tell her the fucking truth!"

Yes. I said that. Right in front of a cop who suspected me of murdering Khalil. And what's worse, I said it to a torn up, shredded Marine that's been dead for thirty years. Why am I allowed to walk the streets?

"Excuse me? Would you care to repeat that, Mr. Peale?"

"Repeat what?"

"You just said 'I can't tell her the fucking truth.'"

"No. No. I said 'I'm trying to tell the fucking truth.'"

"Mr. Peale, I'm going to be straight with you even if you aren't with me. I am considering the very real probability that you are responsible for the death of the person found at the Shoreline." She stopped and stared a moment, for effect I guess. It worked. "The only reason I'm not placing you under arrest are these text messages and lack of motive. I was hoping you would give me more when I asked you to come here today, but frankly, you've done nothing but implicate yourself."

"Fuck her, Sarge. You're gonna solve this case way before she ever will. Let's get the hell out of here." Billy started grappling with his crutches and trying to stand from the chair.

Should I just come clean? Tell her everything I know, everything about Staci, Khalil, the FBI, Carlton? She doesn't know a damn thing but is just one skipped meal away from throwing me in jail. My mind was racing, I couldn't think straight but somewhere a voice pierced the shit storm in my head and it was telling me to keep my mouth shut. Just get out of there.

"I'm sorry, officer. Check with the motel. They can confirm I was there. And ... well you've got those text messages."

"Mr. Peale, you know that doesn't mean shit. If you wanted to create an alibi, you go get a hooker, by a burner phone, send yourself these text messages, then come up with a bullshit story about your gun being stolen, a gun that you still haven't explained why was in the motel room that night."

I sat there and listened as she gave her speech and slowly my lawyer brain returned asking a very simple question: Why isn't she arresting me? She didn't need a motive, she just made her case. There's no other suspect. She doesn't believe I did it. But why? I sure as hell would. Confidence restored, I stood from the chair.

"I guess the girl just liked playin' with my gun."

Billy was gone and Officer Carver remained seated, staring at me with what I guessed were unkind thoughts.

"Will you take a polygraph?"

I might have laughed. I know I smiled. Not at the question but at the law enforcement agent's unwavering belief in the utility of the polygraph. They couldn't use the results in court but God how they believed in it. Pass and they'll cut you lose from an investigation. Fail and they'll bear down on you with all the conviction of a religious zealot. I considered the polygraph more like a metal detector. You see those guys on the beach, scanning the sand for treasure but when the metal detector goes off, more likely than not they found a beer can, not gold. I let her question hang in the air.

"If that's all ..."

She said nothing, just stared at me. I could see that something was running through her mind and I wondered what it might be as I turned and left.

17.

Brett Bone's voice was friendly and familiar on the message he left but also more formal than she had hoped. She needed his help, help that a friend would possibly provide. But the tone of his voice wasn't encouraging. It sounded like they were nothing more than acquaintances.

"Hey Billie, it's Brett Bone at the Bureau ..."

He had left his mobile number and she returned the call as soon as the message had played. His reaction to her call dispelled her concerns.

"Billie, it's great to hear your voice ..." and after the initial chit chat that comes when two friends that haven't spoken in years finally do talk, Billie explained why she was working at the Mount Pleasant City Police Department. At first Brett didn't say anything so she prodded him.

"Go ahead and say it."

"Say what?"

"I told you so."

"You should be with the Bureau. You know that even if you won't admit it."

"Well, that's not why I called."

"Oh yeah? You just called to check up on me, see how I'm doing, if I'm married ..."

She cut him off. "No, this is about a case I'm working ..."

"... because I'm not."

"Not what?"

"Married."

So Brett Bone is still the flirt, she thought. Maybe that will help.

"That doesn't do me any good."

"Billie, I'd be there by dinner time if you told me to."

She suddenly felt hemmed in and awkward. She wasn't good at flirting but there was something else. She could handle getting hit on, but this time she was uneasy, not flattered. Brett Bone hadn't seen her since the academy and she was no longer the fit and vibrant woman he had tried to kiss that night in the bar. Instead of giving her ego a boost, the flirting made her feel self -conscious. The last couple of years had broken her down. She felt unattractive. Would Brett be disappointed if he saw her? The thought angered her and she clumsily changed the tone of the conversation.

"I've got a John Doe murder vic that I was hoping you could help me identify."

Brett Bone wasn't offended when Billie responded to his invite by changing the conversation. He was glad to be talking with her.

"I'll do what I can. Your people can't help you with this?"

Yeah, Billie. Can you explain why you aren't asking SLED to check this out instead of the FBI? Brett's going to assume this is all just a pretense to touch base with him. Well, let him. It might help. He may try to impress me. But why are you asking the FBI for this? She had instinctively called Brett without thinking about it. But now, during the brief silence that followed Brett's question, the answer came welling up from deep within her. Because something isn't right about this case. I'm being lied to.

"I have my reasons." She hoped the cryptic response would put him off.

"Okay, what do you need?"

"Run what I've got on John Doe through your biometric

database and see if there's a hit."

"Do you have any photographs?"

"Just of the corpse."

"That may be a challenge. Our facial recognition technology isn't what you would expect. But if he's in the system, his palm and finger prints will ID him. Your office doesn't have facial recognition software?"

"I work for a city, Brett, not the federal government."

"I don't think it costs that much."

"But it costs something. City Council isn't going to raise taxes for facial recognition software."

"So you need my help due to local fiscal restraints and other undisclosed reasons?"

This time she was better prepared for what he was implying. Probably because he was assuming what she had hoped he would assume. She smiled but didn't respond.

"You know, you'll owe me after this."

"Not if you don't get me anything."

"Then let me get started. Send me what you have."

She emailed the prints and photographs and reminded herself that she needed to go for a run later that night.

18.

arver's law enforcement training told her Peale was the guy and if he wasn't the guy, he knew more than he was telling. So arrest him, put him in a cell and let him consider telling more. If he was the guy after all, she would have him locked up and he wouldn't go anywhere. If he wasn't but knew something, maybe sitting in a cell would convince him to talk. But she couldn't arrest him. Three hours earlier, after she had told her chief that she suspected Peale for the murder and was bringing him in for questioning and possible arrest, he had let her know different.

"Question him. But no arrest."

When she asked why he told her that there wasn't enough evidence. She should keep looking and report to him if she finds more.

Billie had left the meeting with the Chief confused and frustrated. She agreed there wasn't much other than the gun, there was no motive and the death could be something mundane that turned bad at the end of a stolen gun. The victim associates with the wrong people, makes someone unhappy, he's led to the Shoreline where he's executed with a stolen gun. She told herself that was the most likely scenario, but she didn't believe it. Why was I given this case? The question was laying unanswered underneath all the evidence she had gathered. And why, after I tell the Chief I'm bringing in Peale for questioning, am I told not to arrest him?

Plummet

While her cop brain was telling her Peale was the guy, her gut was, ironically, telling her exactly what the chief had suggested: keep looking. And it was the irony of it that bothered her the most. Why is it ironic, Carver? Why? Maybe the Chief has the same suspicions. Maybe, but her gut was telling her he didn't. He had other motives. Unknown motives and motives that were separate from what a cop's motive should be: solve the crime. She could feel it and more than that, she believed it. The voice inside her was telling her something wasn't right. She might have believed it to be the voice of her mother, a spiritual guide that knew more than what the visible world had revealed so far. A guide that would not reveal the Truth to her but could prod her further by raising these doubts within her. It was a comforting story but one she no longer believed. If she'd been taught one lesson in life it was to be a realist. Her mother wasn't talking to her.

She knew enough about the enteric nervous system to believe that her gut was a source of knowledge. It could tell her when something was wrong even when her brain told her different. And her gut had been telling her just that since she was given the case.

It was time she heard from Brett Bone.

19.

Every Saturday, four maids arrived in a van to clean and wash what needed cleaning and washing at Charles and Rasha Carlton's home. They worked for four hours, from 9:00 am until 1 p.m. and this was in addition to the housekeeper who worked Monday through Friday. Although the house was a home, it could never look lived in, except for those rooms that were off limits to guests. Rasha stood in the doorway of one of those rooms, watching a young woman from Mexico or some other Latin American country dust around pictures that were displayed on a table next to a window with a view of the harbor. The pictures were of Staci and Laura and herself. None of her husband. When the maid turned and saw Rasha she was startled then smiled in embarrassment.

"Sheets? Change sheets?"

Rasha looked at the bed thoughtfully and fingered the necklace below her throat. When had the linens been changed last? When was the last time Staci had slept here? What she really wondered was where Staci slept, where she lived. She knew of the spacious apartment overlooking King Street that was over an empty commercial space, but she had the feeling Staci didn't sleep there much. The family trust had bought the building at Staci's request. When her husband had suggested that the first floor be upgraded and leased to a business, Staci had dismissed the idea with "maybe." It had remained vacant ever since. Rasha had visited the apartment several times but only when Staci invited her. It had been furnished with a stylish mix of antique and contemporary furniture that had to have come from the eye of someone other than her daughter. But when Rasha had complimented the look and asked who had been the designer Staci had only replied "a friend" and Rasha knew not to ask more. Her daughter was an iceberg, her beauty visible to anyone, but there was also an emotional detachment felt by those who knew her. Some even glimpsed the danger that smoldered beneath the surface, a danger to anyone who dared come close. In her teenage years she had rebelled, not with drugs, sex and music, but with religion.

Obsessed with Laura's death in Palestine, Staci began visiting a mosque in London that was known for its support of Palestinian political organizations that had been labeled terrorist groups by the British government. There she made friends that Rasha never met and that her former husband did not approve of, but nothing Rasha said or did deterred Staci from what over time seemed to be her fate. Only a permanent move to the United States when Staci was sixteen removed her from the influence of the mosque and Rasha did her best to immerse her daughter in the secular culture of the U.S. At first Rasha had planned for her daughter to attend school in New York but when William Turner told his wife he had bought a second home in Charleston, South Carolina, she reconsidered. New York was a multi-cultural city and it wouldn't take her daughter long to find and associate with the same type of people that had caused their flight from London. She had never been to the southeastern United States and she saw Charleston as she did the rest of the region: a mono-culture of white, Christian backwardness that would provide a potent antidote to the radical ideas coursing through her daughter's mind. If she, herself, could survive living there.

For a while it seemed to work. Rasha marveled at how

quickly Staci made the transition from London to Charleston. She was enrolled in an all-girl's private school where her British accent and foreign beauty made her instant friends with enough of the other girls for Rasha to believe that there would be little or no >shock' from the change in culture. There were high school dances, trips to the mall and Friday nights watching the all boy's high school football team play. There were times when she spent the night with a friend or had one spend the night at their home. At least three boys called on a weekly basis asking if they could take Staci out on a date. She always refused. Remarkably, it had seemed as if she was fitting into the new culture that was so different from what they knew. She had begun to worry that perhaps she was even losing touch with her daughter as she watched her become a southern American teenage girl while she, herself, still struggled with the change.

Those worries had ended one weekend when her husband was away and Staci had come to her with a plan. A plan that she said would avenge her sister's death and punish the one that was truly responsible. The worry that her daughter was becoming Americanized had been displaced that weekend by another, greater worry for her daughter. A worry that had never gone away.

~ ~ ~

Downstairs, Staci was listening to her step-father lecture her on a topic she did not need to hear anything about. Not from Carlton anyway.

"The only way out of this is for Peale to take the fall."

The garnet painted walls, fireplace and the pictures of eighteenth century hunting scenes hanging in gold lacquered frames around the room made Staci feel as if she were sitting in a scene for a Christmas card. The room was nothing more than an elegant set that bore no relationship to her step-father, her mother or herself. She would never feel at home here or in any other room in the house. The only comfort she derived from it was the wealth it exuded which was all she ever asked of a home, wherever she lived. What her step father was suggesting had been the plan all along and his insertion of himself into the, situation, at the final hour would have amused her except for the pedantic way he was talking to her. She didn't respond, choosing instead to calmly stare at a painting of men on horseback, wearing long coats and top hats, chasing after a pack of dogs and one red fox. The painting depicted the fox leaping over a log and looking back on his pursuers with what looked like, to Staci, a grin on his face.

"Hello? Are you listening? We either come to an understanding about how this thing goes down or it doesn't happen. Do you understand?"

She closed her eyes on the painting and when they opened again she was looking at Carlton, standing far enough away and holding a glass containing a brown liquid with no ice. He stared at her for a moment then took a drink to insert an interlude in her silence. She wasn't going to argue and didn't want to respond at all but knew she had to say something.

"This won't touch you."

"That's not what I —"

"Because it won't touch me. It won't touch mother." He stopped trying to talk and looked like he was considering the sufficiency of her response. "It won't touch us. I won't let it."

20.

Phone call from Bone to Carver. Info on Peale and that FBI was tracking someone on a watchlist in Charleston – no name?

21.

Staci said nothing when she walked through the door. She smiled and took my hand and led me to the bedroom. If I was a stupid man, I would think this gorgeous woman sat around her home somewhere waiting for me to text her for sex. I wasn't stupid, but the hooks were sinking deeper into me.

Afterwards, we were lying in bed, Staci's cheek was on my chest and my arm was holding her lightly against me. It was nice, no matter the reason she was here, but I was going to jail if I didn't find out what she was up to. And I reminded myself that she would let me go to jail, watching with fake tears glistening those eyes from another place.

"How did you know about Khalil, that he had been killed?" The question had been hanging around, wanting to be asked. I knew what she would say, but I wanted her to know that the question was there.

Her head lifted from my chest and she pulled her hair behind her neck. "From Charles. Where else?"

I nodded a little, more to indicate that I had expected that answer.

"And the money?"

"What are you talking about?"

"Our deal was, you would pay me $10,000 if I found Khalil by Thursday. I found him."

She sat up in the bed. "But you killed him."

I almost said, "So what?" but realized playing along with her lie served no purpose. Looking at her I reminded myself again I was being used. But with her sitting there, naked, with a questioning look on her beautiful face I wondered if I had this wrong. I wanted to be wrong, but was I? Living in a fantasy world would land me in a real prison. I reached out and with my fingers moved her hair out of her face. She pressed her cheek into my hand and closed her eyes. She can't be this good, can she? There was little doubt she was somehow mixed up with Khalil and his plans, but she may not be the one that killed him, or even know who did. I could feel my convictions shifting, giving way.

"You didn't say I had to find him alive."

She looked at me with something like anger in her eyes. I'd never seen it from her so I wasn't sure. But when she spoke her voice was louder, no longer a bedroom whisper. "I thought things were different with us now. I mean look at us. Why am I here? I thought you killed him because he was a threat to me." She stopped and searched my eyes for... what? The truth? That was impossible.. "Maybe I was wrong." She got out of bed, picked up her clothes and went to the bathroom.

Peale, you are screwed. What the fuck is going on? If she was acting, it was brilliant but everything I knew about people told me she wasn't. She really thinks I killed Khalil. But why not pay me the money? Okay, we're sleeping together, so what? I never agreed to swap it out. Maybe I'm wrong. Maybe she thinks we are in a relationship and paying me the money would say something about her that she doesn't want said. Hell, I don't know what's going on. She could be in there smiling at herself in the mirror, congratulating herself on her acting job.

The bathroom door opened and she came out dressed and in a hurry. She dropped her purse on the bed beside me while she pulled her hair up in a pony tail.

"I'm going to get you your money but this ends." She jerked her chin slightly to indicate the bed and, I'm guessing, the sex. With her hair pulled back she picked up her purse and made for the door. I jumped out of bed.

"Wait. Staci."

She stopped but didn't turn around.

"Let's talk."

"Where do you want to meet to get your money? I'm not coming back here."

"Staci, I don't care about the money. I don't want the money." I turned her around and looked into her eyes. "I want you."

And it was true. I wanted her and if there was any chance of having her I was going to take it, no matter the cost. Without smiling, her eyes searched mine in a way that made me wonder. And worry.

"I'll have to think about it." She kissed my cheek and left me standing in my bedroom, naked and alone. Within a few seconds of hearing the door close as she left the apartment, it was as if she had never been there. If told I had just woke from a dream I couldn't argue against it except for the smell of her fading in the air. The idea of Staci and me together was so improbable that anytime spent with her became detached from the rest of my world, becoming another one. But I was never completely in Staci's world either. I was straddling the two. And as I hung there, suspended, parts of me in one and the rest in the other, I couldn't shake the feeling that this was exactly where Staci wanted me.

22.

The sky was blue over the harbor with a few white clouds drifting lazily in from the Atlantic. Sea gulls dove and dipped over the dark green water and here and there people walked as couples or alone along the edge of the Battery. It was probably a more public place than Carlton would have wanted for a meeting but, if he showed up without his caravan, no one would even notice us. I stood next to one of the cannons that sat in the park, its barrel pointing towards Fort Sumter in the distance, a reminder that people can always justify killing other people. I had chosen this spot for our meeting and told Carlton to come alone. It wasn't long before he was standing next to me, also gazing across the harbor. I looked behind us and saw two of his crew cuts standing outside the lone SUV, surveying the slow action on the Battery through their aviators. For a man that wanted to have a private conversation, he sure knew how to draw attention to himself.

"This isn't an ideal location for a private talk."

"You knew the location. You didn't have to bring an entourage."

He squinted and looked out over the harbor as if taking in the view. "She's using you."

No toothy smile, no chit chat. Maybe it was the location but Carlton was all business.

"Okay. For what?"

He looked at me. "You aren't recording this?"

Now I looked out at the harbor. "Recordings are too

rigid. I prefer memory. It's more malleable."

I could feel him staring at me and I guessed he was wondering if this meeting was a mistake. Whatever he was thinking, he decided to go forward with it.

"If I know my stepdaughter, she's going to ask you to do something for her that will sound crazy. But when she does, I want you to say yes."

"That's too vague."

"I don't have details. Look, Jack, we can help each other. I know you've got, well let's call it a 'gun problem'."

I looked at him and he smiled in a different way when he saw the look on my face. There must have been a flash of confusion in my eyes when he mentioned the gun. And why shouldn't there be? Every one of these characters I was mixed up with seemed to know more than I thought they would and always, it seemed, more than me. Did Thursday tip him off? Maybe, although it didn't make sense. Carver may have called the Charleston PD after discovering the gun was registered to me. But if that has happened, does Carlton also know about the connection between Khalil and Staci? And me? His comment implied as much. Then I remembered the conversation Carlton and I had had in my driveway a few days ago. Again, I had the feeling I was about two or three days behind everyone else.

"You're still not giving me enough detail to give you an answer." If he did know more than me, I needed to catch up. I wasn't going to play along with Carlton's subtle suggestions and innuendo. If he wanted my help and I take the fall for something, he won't be able to claim "plausible deniability" when I point the finger at him.

"She's got something planned. Don't have the details but it is probably violent and will involve people getting hurt. Innocent people."

The expression on my face gave me away.

"You already know. His head dropped and shook slowly

as he smiled to himself. "Sonuvabitch."

"Excuse me?"

"Not you, Jack. My life is full of them but I wasn't talking about you. How much do you know?"

Now I shook my head. "It's not happening that way. You tell me what you know." He looked away and I thought I saw a wince but it could have been caused by the glare of the sun on the water. He turned to look at me but said nothing at first, as if he was deciding how much to tell. No, that wasn't it. He knew he had to tell me and was coming to terms with that but it was ripping him up inside. Something in me enjoyed watching him do this balancing act as he inched his way out on the limb where I was perched.

"I have a feeling I'm telling you what you already know, but maybe it will fill in some blanks. Anyway, none of what I'm telling you came from me, agreed?"

I knew what he meant but it still sounded stupid and confirmed how desperate he was.

"Sure." I was trying to give the impression that this was a waste of my time and the look on his face told me it irritated the hell out of him. But what he said changed my demeanor.

"From what I've been able to uncover, Staci and my wife have agreed to facilitate an act of terrorism here in Charleston."

What he had uncovered? Does that mean this didn't come from Thursday?

"What are you talking about?"

"So this is news to you." He smiled vaguely and continued. "They are both tied up with some bad people from the middle east. I don't know how or why but for some reason they have agreed to do this."

"What do you mean? They've agreed to do what?" If he wasn't getting this from Thursday, it was confirming what Thursday had told me.

"Facilitate. Pick the target. Provide logistical help. Money."

He seemed too calm about all of this. The man had ambitions and if what he and Thursday were saying was true, those ambitions would be destroyed along with the target.

"You're telling me that Staci and your wife are going to help a terrorist attack Charleston?"

He paused and looked me in the eye. "Yes. That is what I'm telling you."

"I don't believe it. You're information is wrong. That doesn't make sense."

Now he was agitated. "Goddammit! Why would I make this shit up?" I got the feeling he wanted to tell me more. But, as if remembering he was in a public place, he quickly relaxed his posture and smiled. He wanted me to believe him but he was holding out on me.

"Tell me what you know."

"Mahmood Khalil was supposed to do the job."

"Bullshit." I knew this much but decided to play ignorant.

"Bullshit? My friend, Staci paid you to find Khalil because he had refused to go forward with the plan. Whoever is behind this had trained him, put too much time, effort and money in him – not to mention the risk – to have him walk away. They put the heat on Rasha and Staci to get him back on board or take care of it. For some reason, Staci chose you to find him."

Finding the truth in what Carlton was saying was like trying to catch a butterfly. I stopped trying and just watched to see where it was going.

"Khalil was a trained terrorist?" I laughed a little when I said this.

"Yeah." Carlton looked away, as if taking in the beauty of the harbor again. AAnd now he's dead."

He continued looking at the harbor, the boats, the birds, whatever, giving me time to put all this together, to see where it went. And anyone looking at this would see it led back to me. I was paid by Staci to kill Khalil. But Thursday had already told me as much. What I couldn't decide is how many teams were playing here. Was Carlton just telling me what he learned from the FBI, trying to help them out, or was he working solo, for his own reasons? The FBI could care less how this turned out for Carlton. He knew that, and if true, his political career was ruined if it became public knowledge that his family was supporting a terrorist plot in Charleston. Or anywhere else for that matter. But how does he think he can keep this quiet? His last comment gave me a hint. He could have me arrested or Staci's jihadist friends may want their own revenge.

"Big picture. How does any of this turn out well for you?"

He looked at me again, smiled and looked off behind me as if checking out the row of historical homes along the park opposite the harbor. The park was part of the neighborhood where we both lived and where neither of us belonged.

"Shouldn't you be asking the same thing Jack? There's a way out, for both of us. Neither one of us wants this to ruin our life. We have that much in common, so why shouldn't we work together?"

I couldn't argue with what he was saying, but I didn't like it.

"Okay. So Staci comes to me and asks me to help and I say yes. Then what?"

"Find out what you can, as much detail as possible and let me know."

It was the same thing Thursday wanted me to do for him.

"Any way out of this for Staci?" I felt like a fool asking

the question but he knew her better than me and she seemed to be trapped in all of this. Or at least that was my hope, that she was some sort of victim. His face lost the smile, replaced with something more serious.

"Don't trust a word she says." He was looking straight into my eyes. "I don't think she knows what the truth is."

"What does that mean?"

"She's fucked up, psychotic." He shook his head as if warding off thoughts of things he couldn't understand. "Clinically I think she is a sociopath but I don't have time to get into all of that. Just know that you can't trust her. Anything she says or does is a lie. Do you understand?"

I nodded. But that was my own lie. Who I was lying to was a question I didn't care to answer.

23.

It was time for Wendy's vacation in the mountains to end. Whatever was going to happen in the next few days, Megan didn't need to be around for it.

When I called Wendy and told her I had important business that had suddenly come up and I needed for her to come back for Megan, she didn't believe me.

"That's bullshit."

"Believe me. It's not."

"Can't you be a parent for once?"

"I'm trying to do the right thing."

"Jack, when life happens, you can't ignore the fact that you are a parent, that you have responsibilities. You handle it. What if you were a single parent? What would you do?"

It was a good point, and luckily one I didn't have to deal with. "Wendy, if there was anyone else, I wouldn't call. But this is important."

"Does it have anything to do with your girlfriend?"

"What girlfriend?"

"The one that you were groping in front of our twelve-year-old daughter. Are you fucking her while Megan is there? Please tell me you aren't."

I wanted to cuss her out but I stayed calm because I needed her cooperation. "This is out of my control. Are you coming back or not?"

"Goodbye, Jack. You'll be a better father for this."

Plan A had failed, so after picking up Megan from school I put Plan B into action. Plan A had been a long shot but I had decided to give it a try because exposing Megan to Plan B might be considered child abuse by those with an expansive definition of such things. Like Wendy. But at this point, I had no choice. If I was going to be dealing with people that would blow up a bomb in downtown Charleston, Megan didn't need to be anywhere near me.

Sitting in the passenger seat, Megan's phone had her full attention. She hadn't noticed I wasn't driving to my apartment.

"Honey, I've got to go somewhere on business. It will take about an hour."

"Whatever." She didn't look up and continued messing with her phone the entire drive to the apartment building where Todd Burley lived. When I stopped the car, her head looked up.

"Where are we?" She surveyed the detritus around her. "This place is a dump."

It was a dump. The Fox Run was nothing more than a run-down motel that had been converted to apartments. The parking lot was full of pot holes, trash and broken up asphalt. One of the windows was shattered. Rotting furniture sat outside the door to one of the rooms. Anyone that lived here didn't have options.

"Daddy, I don't like this place."

"Megan, look at me. This will all be over quickly. You are not in danger but do not get out of the car. Do you understand?"

She nodded and her lip trembled. I felt like shit for doing this but it was the only way I could get Wendy to come get her. As soon as I shut the door Megan would be texting her mother giving her an only slightly exaggerated description of what was happening.

I backed the Taurus up to Burley's apartment, got out and opened the trunk. From the inside of the trunk I retrieved a Taser and walked up to Burley's door. I banged on it with the bottom of my fist. Part of the closed blinds separated quickly then I heard the door being unlocked. I considered the possibility that Burley might not open the door for me if he, in fact, drugged me and sent me off with that hooker. But Burley wasn't smart and he was probably drunk.

The door cracked but was stopped from opening fully by a chain lock. Burley's face appeared in the opening.

"Jack, buddy, how'd you find me?"

"Just asked around. Can I come in?"

Burley's eyes surveyed what they could of the parking lot. They fell on the open trunk of the Taurus and laid there a moment.

"Hey, you aren't pissed at me for the other night are you? I mean, your friend said you'd be okay with it and she wanted to do it as a joke."

"What friend?"

"Good looking girl, black hair, great body. She gave me the pill. Said she was a client and she wanted you to have a good time but not to tell you, but I'm telling you now cause I heard you had a tough time. I'm sorry about that."

"Did she say anything else?"

"Just that she had a party planned for you at the Paradise and she would meet up with us there. She also gave me five hundred bucks and told me to start the party without her if she wasn't there. She never showed."

Todd Burley was a low life and it gave me the creeps being at his door but I felt bad about what I was going to do. But then I remembered the woman he raped and whatever compassion I had was gone. I kicked in his door and it hit him across the forehead. By the time I was inside he was trying to get off the floor. I shoved the Taser in his gut and Tased him until he stopped struggling, then pulled him by the arms to the door. That's when I noticed a large naked woman lying on the bed. She raised her head and looked at me with tired eyes.

"I'm his probation officer. He hasn't been reporting."

She closed her eyes and let her head drop back to the pillow. I dragged Burley to the trunk and worked his limp body inside where I duct taped his ankles and wrists. I put a strip over his mouth also, closed the trunk and got back into the Taurus and drove away, looking around as I left the parking lot for any witnesses.

"Daddy! Was that a man you put in the trunk?"

"Yes. And you did a great job honey. You did exactly what you were supposed to do."

She was ignoring everything I said, rapidly texting someone instead on her phone.

During the thirty-minute drive to Maggie Felton's home Wendy must have called my phone thirty times. Megan quit asking if I was going to answer after the sixth or seventh time when I tossed the phone in the back seat.

Megan was a nervous wreck saying things like "I want to go home and "I want my Mom" and "Where are we going now." I really felt bad, but I blamed Wendy for this. She's the one that told me that you can't stop being a parent when life happens. So here I was driving down the highway with my daughter next to me crying and a duct taped Todd Burley in my trunk heading for a world of hurt. My life. Happening.

After dropping Burley off at Maggie Felton's house I drove straight back to my apartment. Megan began packing her things as soon as she was inside.

"Mom's coming to get me."

"I know. Megan, I'm sorry you had to see that but I have to work and sometimes I can't control when I have to work. That was a bad man I picked up and if I hadn't gone when I did, I might not have ever caught him."

"Who was that person you took him to?"

"Oh. She's, uh, a federal agent."

She seemed distrustful of my answer and continued to look around the apartment for anything she may have missed. I went to the fridge to get a beer. Wendy would be on her way back to Charleston, still a few hours away. We had nothing to do but hang out till then. Megan sure as hell wasn't going to leave with me again. She was sitting on the sofa with her bag next to her, texting away. There was no way I would come out of this looking good, although I did it to protect Megan I had the feeling that our few days together would end up driving Megan and me further apart. Turned out to be a lot further than I had feared.

24.

illie unbuckled the belt and threw her weapon and holster onto the bed and undressed. She walked over to her dresser drawers and took out a T-shirt and running shorts. Before changing her clothes, she stood in front of the mirror and looked at herself, wearing only panties and a bra. The muscle tone in her arms and thighs were fading and she thought she could see her mid-section slouching around her waist. Yesterday, the sight of her softening and growing body would have added another shade of darkness to her mood. But today she felt irritated. I'll go for a run in the morning. She changed her clothes, the too-snug running shorts increasing her determination to lose weight. Billie Carver had never equated physical fitness with physical attractiveness or sex. During college and the FBI academy, she had considered the training of her body to reach higher and higher levels of performance on an equal level of importance with training her mind to do the same. She had decided that how her body looked and what it could withstand sent a message to others that she was serious and determined about her job and her life.

For her, being physically fit sent the message that she was disciplined and serious. She still felt that way, but now knew that others – especially men – didn't infer such positive traits from her sculpted body. When she left the Academy, she was 5'8" and weighed one hundred twenty-eight pounds. She would run five miles a day in thirty-five minutes and consider it a leisurely jog. During those daily runs, she would wear the same type of running shorts and tank top that she had just put on and thought the sight of her toned arms and legs would stir admiration in anyone that saw her. But real-world experience, as it had repeatedly in her life, mocked her abstract ideas. The men who would stare, whistle or even shout at her, did not see determination and muscle, they saw mocha colored tits and thighs bouncing and flexing down the street for their entertainment. Had she any interest in sex, she might have changed her route or covered her body more. But she had the ability to marginalize the unpleasant and the offensive. Since she had never explored her own sexual feelings about men or women, what she experienced during those runs was no different than coming upon roadkill. Gross and unexpected, it was soon passed and forgotten.

During her run the next morning at 5:00 am, Carver's mind was occupied with the same thoughts and questions that had kept her awake most of the night: Why was Mahmoud Kahlil murdered at the Shoreline? He was middle eastern. Why would he be involved in a drug deal at the Shoreline? It could have been a sex hook up, but why meet at a dump like that? The vic was well groomed and had nice clothes. Maybe he was meeting a prostitute? There were no answers yet, but they would come. The important thing to Carver was that the questions were no longer a burden. She felt energized, even after little sleep and the morning run. Later that morning, as she walked across the parking lot of the Mount Pleasant Police Department she admitted to herself that for the first time she was looking forward to her job.

"Officer Carver?"

The voice came from behind her as she approached the entrance to the police headquarters. Billie turned knowing who she would see.

"Ms. Lott. Using ambush tactics?"

The reporter smiled a confession. "Not what I prefer but when phone calls aren't returned…" She shrugged.

"Come in then. You caught me in a good mood."

Billie decided to talk with the reporter at her desk instead of an interview room which had been her first inclination. She pulled up a chair for Lott and they both sat down.

"You get five minutes."

"Great. Uh. Any news on the who the vic was?"

"No."

"Okay. What about the gun? Have you talked to the owner?"

Carver hesitated because she didn't won't to give out a name. "Yes."

"Name?"

"Not yet."

"Is he a suspect?"

"No comment."

An exasperated look came over the reporter. "Come on. I'm going to get the name sooner or later. You're just making me more and more curious."

"Later. Not sooner."

"Work with me, Billie."

"We may need to interview him again. I don't want you to screw that up."

"So the owner is male?"

Carver realized that no good would come from talking with the reporter. Just by stringing the conversation out a little further, Lott made her give up more about Peale than she had intended.

"I used the pronoun as a conversational convenience. You should read nothing into it. Now, I've got work to do. So, if you don't mind?"

"What about the gun?"

"What about it?"

"Was there one of those things that people use to muffle the sound, a silencer?"

"It's called a suppressor. No, there wasn't one."

"Then why didn't anyone hear the shots?"

"Someone did. They called it in."

"Couldn't that have been the shooter?"

"Why would the shooter use a suppressor – so no one would hear the shots – then call it in?"

"I don't know. But it's a good question, don't you think?"

It was a good question that irritated Carver. She didn't want more questions, especially interesting ones that had no answers. She wanted this to be simple. She stood but Lott wasn't ready to let her go. She hadn't got much and didn't want the opportunity to slip away. A voice called Carver's name from another room. While Carver' was distracted, Lott's eyes fell on a blue sticky note stuck to Carver's computer screen. It had a line of numbers and letters with a name and address written beneath. She had time to make out part of it before Carver's attention returned to her.

"So, Ms. Lott, can you see yourself out?"

"Yeah. Thanks for the time. I'll give you a call later? Are you talking with the owner again soon?"

"When and if we need to. And she agrees."

"She?"

"Good day, Ms. Lott."

25.

The phone call came as I was getting out of the shower. Normally I'd let it go to the machine but I hadn't heard from Staci since she left. In spite of everything that was going on, Staci was on my mind most of the time. Randomly, thoughts of Thursday, Khalil, Carlton, Megan and even jail would interrupt throughout the day, each time intruding on the hope that Staci wasn't a deranged terrorist, that she really cared for me, and that there was a way out of this for both of us. It was an unlikely dream, but it kept me from taking a boat out to the Gulf Stream and beyond.

I picked up the phone dripping with water. "Hello?"

"Hi."

"I'm glad you called."

"I said I would."

"I know. But when you left, the way you left, I wasn't sure."

"That was my fault. I let things get out of hand. I have that problem, going with my instincts, seeing what I want and grabbing it. Or him."

She was saying everything I wanted to hear and so much worry and stress left me at once I wanted to fall to the floor and sob or scream in triumph. My voice was unsteady when I talked again and I was thankful she couldn't see what a mess I was.

"Forget what I said about the money."

"No. That isn't fair to you. I've got the money and I want you to have it. But we need to talk about everything else.

About us."

"Staci. We need to talk about more than just us." My own words overwhelmed me. I was finally admitting to her and myself that I had been living two lives, the real one and the fantasy I had created around Staci. Until now, in my mind, I'd kept them apart, keeping the dream world with Staci walled off from reality. But I had just told her that I wanted her to go with me across that wall. And in doing that, I took a risk. I was also telling her I knew what was going on, that she hadn't completely fooled me, but also that I didn't care.

"Yes. Of course. Let's talk about everything."

"When can you come over?"

"I can't right now. I'll call you when I get free."

That didn't sound reassuring, but what choice did I have?

"Okay. Call soon."

"I will."

When she called again I was on the phone with a reporter who had called asking questions about the Shoreline. Staci gave me an excuse to end the conversation without answering any of questions. But to say the call unnerved me was an understatement.

Staci wanted to meet. I thought of the Post Office but something in me rejected the idea.

"What about Colonial Park?"

"Twenty minutes?"

"Okay. And Staci -"

"Yes."

"A reporter just called asking me about the Shoreline."

There was only silence for a few seconds. "See you in twenty."

I was there in ten, sitting on a bench pretending to watch the ducks on the water as I considered what it meant if a reporter was calling me about Moody's death. I was so deep in thought that I jumped when Staci sat down beside me.

"I'm sorry. Am I that frightening?"

I turned to her and put an arm across the bench behind her but didn't get too close. Anyone watching would think we were friends, nothing more. But when she looked at me I didn't care what anyone else thought. How quickly she could make me careless.

"Staci, if a reporter called me it can only mean one thing."

"They traced the gun."

"Right."

"So tell them it was stolen." She was calm and logical today, not the sultry girlfriend who saw me as lover and protector. The woman next to me didn't need protecting. She opened her purse, took out a small mirror and examined her look.

"You don't just make a call and get the name of a gun owner. It doesn't work that way. This was way too fast."

Staci returned the mirror to the purse and snapped it shut. She turned to me and took my hand.

"Jack, I haven't been completely honest with you."

I felt like the bench disappeared beneath me and I was falling down through time. Her voice brought me back. She paused for effect and then dumped.

"When I was younger and we were living in England, I had an older sister. Laura. One summer she went to Lebanon to stay with my uncle and his family. She said she wanted to learn more about my mother's side of the family and Lebanese culture and that was probably true. But I knew she had become obsessed with the conflict between the Israelis and Palestinians also. My mother was worried but my father was unconcerned about the dangers and said she could go. On July 16, 1990 we received the news that she had been killed by Israeli soldiers ..."

Plummet

She kept talking but I was hearing only parts. My mind was grappling, searching for something to grab on to as the past and present collided, crushing me in the ruin.

"... Since Laura was a British citizen there was an official inquiry by the British and Israeli governments. My mother paid for a private investigation. The government reports cleared the soldiers of any wrongdoing. The private investigation uncovered enough evidence to support bringing war crime charges against the Israeli officer and soldiers involved. But when my father was presented with the report, he did nothing."

She opened her purse again and pulled out a handkerchief that she used dab at the corner of her eyes. Looking at her calmed me and I took a deep breath but I couldn't think of anything to say.

"Mother and I begged him to use his contacts to do something, to make sure those soldiers were held responsible. But all he said was >she was at the wrong place at the wrong time'. Can you believe that? Can you believe a father would dismiss his child's death like that?"

The tears were flowing now and she held the handkerchief to both eyes for a moment. When she lowered her hand, mascara was smudged around her eyes. After a sniff she composed herself enough to throw the bombshell.

"Years later, while exploring for oil and gas reserves in Indonesia, my father's plane went down in the ocean." She looked me in the eyes. AHis death was not an accident."

I stood up and walked to the edge of the artificial lake for no reason other than to put physical distance between me and the truth. But that wouldn't help. Staci appeared at my side.

"Jack, look at me."

She turned me to face her, to look upon her, be taken in by her. She would pour the truth in my ear then hold me close and whisper lies to me.

"We are being blackmailed."

I managed to finally speak. "Who?"

"Me, my mother. But the real target is Carlton."

I thought about our conversation the day before, what he had said about Staci. Were the blackmailers the terrorists Carlton talked about? I didn't want to hear her say anything about terrorists, but I had to find out if what Carlton told me was true.

"What do they want, money?"

"No."

"Then what?"

"I need your help. I lied to you about Moody. He didn't owe me money. He was trying to help."

I fought off the obvious conclusion that everything she might have told me since we met was a lie. She read my mind.

"Not everything I told you was a lie. Moody was a friend from college – a former boyfriend. But I hadn't seen him since college. Over the years he somehow got involved with the same people that are extorting us now. He was the one that approached me first."

"How do you know he was connected to the blackmailers?"

"Because after he contacted me my mother and I received a visit from someone we know from Lebanon."

"Who?"

Staci looked out over the lake and pulled her hair back behind her ear.

"Who?"

"I can't tell you anymore. Please trust me."

How could I trust someone whose story changed every day? I told myself that I didn't have any idea who Staci really was or what her role in any of this might be. But another voice was telling me that Staci was the obvious suspect for framing me for Khalil's murder. Proving again she was telepathic, Staci put her arms around my waist and held me tight, her face pressed against mine. I ignored that other voice.

"I need you, Jackson. No one else can help me."

"What is it exactly you need from me?"

She told me about the visitor from Lebanon and I didn't believe her. She also told me she wanted to come to my place later that night, which she did. Her visit had me considering all kinds of far-fetched scenarios where she was an innocent player in all of this and she really cared for me. It reminded me of when I use to snort cocaine before going to work in the mornings, convinced it made me a better lawyer for my clients, a better partner to the firm, a better provider for my family. It wasn't hard to believe at the time. In fact, it was harder to believe the reality when it all came to an end. Lying in bed that night after Staci had left, I ran it all back through my mind several times. Each time I came to the same conclusion: I was being used. I didn't have all the pieces and not everything made sense to me yet, but I knew I had to stay close to Staci and play along, just like Thursday and Carlton had suggested. But I wasn't doing it for them. I had to clear my name and the only way I could do that was to find Khalil's killer.

26.

Jennifer Lott parked her red Toyota RAV 4 in the parking lot of an office building that housed the law firm of Trotter, Davis & Stone, PA and waited. The law firm was Jackson Peale's former employer. Three times she had been turned away by the firm's receptionist when she had tried to meet with one of the partners – even after setting an appointment the first time – so she had decided an ambush interview in the parking lot was the next step. She had positioned her Toyota in a space directly across from the Mercedes sedan owned by Robert Stone. She guessed it was Robert Stone's Mercedes because there was a sign in front of the space that said "Reserved for Robert T. Stone, Esq." According to an archived article she had found in a local business magazine, Jackson Peale had been enjoying a prominent rise in the legal community before he crashed to earth. A picture from the article showed Peale and Robert Stone talking with reporters outside of the Federal Courthouse after they had successfully defended some businessman on racketeering charges. With a copy of the article in hand, Lott was prepared to shove it in Stone's face if he tried to deny knowing Peale.

At 6:23 p.m. a man in a dark suit emerged from the office building and walked to the Mercedes and opened the door. Lott hesitated. Was it him? It looked like an older version of the guy in the picture with Peale but these guys tended to look alike to Lott. He's getting in

Stone's car, who else could it be? How do you know that's Stone's car? Someone could have borrowed the space ... As the doubts froze Lott to her seat, the man closed the door and started the engine. When the reverse lights lit on the Mercedes, Lott cranked her Toyota and pulled directly behind Stone's car. If he wanted to escape, he'd have to jump the curb and squeeze his expensive car through a small lawn that buffered the building from the parking lot. Lott kept her car running, turned on her phone's recorder and got out and walked to the driver side window. She froze when she saw the panicked look on the man's face and the gun in his hand. Instinctively she raised both hands and stood there frozen, wide-eyed and heart pounding. Oh shit! What have you done? The window cracked a few inches.

"Get the fuck away from the car!"

She started to run but didn't move. Tell him who you are and that you have a recorder.

"I'm Jennifer Lott, from *The Sun*. I just want to ask you a few questions about Jackson Peale." The man's eyes narrowed when she said Peale's name. "I'm recording this."

The man looked around, cursed and told her to get in. She turned her car off, walked to the passenger side of the Mercedes and sat down in the front passenger seat.

"Make it quick. You're clogging up the parking lot."

"Are you Robert Stone?"

"Yeah."

"Jackson Peale use to work here?"

"Yeah."

"When did he leave?"

Stone's face twisted into a sneer. "The firm or reality?"

"What do you mean?"

Stone turned and looked at her. "What do you want with Jack?"

"I'm doing a piece on lawyer's in Charleston and his name came up and ..."

"Bullshit." He continued staring, searching her face for the answer. "Turn off the recorder."

When the recorder was off she placed the phone in her lap. Stone picked it up and placed on the hood of the Mercedes and rolled up the window.

"Hey, I turned it off."

Stone ignored her. "I don't know why you're digging around on Peale but it's been long enough. I'll talk but it has to be off the record and no mention of the firm. If you don't agree with that, get the fuck out and move your car."

"Deal."

"One more thing. You've got five minutes."

"Start talking."

"Okay. I may be revealing protected information here but this conversation never happened so here it goes. Peale was good. Damn good. Better than me and anybody else in the firm. But there were signs something wasn't right. I'd walk in his office and he'd be talking to himself and I'm not talking about rehearsing a closing argument. I mean he'd be having a conversation like there was somebody in the room. When I'd ask him about it, he'd get flustered and embarrassed. At first I blew it off as him being eccentric, but then it was obvious he was drinking and getting high at work. We quietly sent him to a clinic in New York for the drugs and drinking. It was supposed to be a two-week program but he stayed three months. When he returned he seemed great and was ready to go back to work and he did. But a few days later, a local psychiatrist called looking for him. He said that jack had missed an appointment and he wanted to know if he was okay. The guy didn't want to say much more than that, but he eventually let us know that Jack was sick. Really sick. And he had been told to stop working and concentrate on getting things under control. So, were thinking >okay, he's an alcoholic, addiction issues, we get it' I mean that's not unheard of in this profession, right?"

"Who was the shrink?"

"Uh, I don't remember. Never talked to him again."

"Okay, so what happened?"

"Everything seemed normal, Jack was doing okay until about three months later. He and I were in court arguing a motion to suppress or something. It was his first time back in court since being hospitalized. Well, we're sitting at counsel's table waiting for the judge to get ready and Jack leans over an says to me >Do you mind if Billy sits at the table with us?' I say >who the fuck is Billy?' Jack says >My buddy Billy Shores, from the Marines. He's sitting behind us. He wants to know if he can sit up here.' My first thought is >Hell no he can't' because I'm focused on the argument we are about to make before the judge and I'm pissed because he knows only lawyers and the clients sit at the table. Then it hits me. I get this sick feeling and look behind us. Nobody is there. Before I can say anything to Jack, he's standing up asking the fucking judge if his invisible friend can sit with us. The judge is totally confused, thinks he's talking about a lawyer. Jack walks over to the railing that separates the gallery from the bench and opens the swinging gate as if he's letting someone walk through but there's no one there. Jack tells the judge that his good buddy from the Marines is here and wants to sit at counsel's table and although he isn't a lawyer he is a war hero and so on. The judge is pissed thinking it's a joke. By now, the attorneys from the solicitor's office are watching this and they are confused and amused. I ask the lead prosecutor to join me at the bench where I tell the judge what I think is happening which is evident to everyone because Jack is standing by the rail having a conversation all by himself. The judge grants a continuance and I get Jack the hell out of there. We had him committed to the Thompson Center later that day."

"What is that?"

"The Thompson Mental Health Center, over off 17 North."

"Why are you telling me this?"

The lawyer let out a sigh and closed his eyes then opened them again. "Jack's been through enough. Very few people know his history and blow him off as a coke head and a drunk and that's wrong. He has serious problems that have nothing to do with drugs and alcohol. The last thing I want to see is some reporter printing a bunch of bull shit without knowing the truth. Or at least part of it. I guess I'm hoping you won't write anything about him."

Lott could almost believe what the guy was saying except for the obvious fact that anything printed about Jackson Peale would almost certainly include the name of his past employer, smearing Thomas, Davis and Stone, PA with whatever shit Peale had gotten himself into.

"What interest do you have with Jack anyway?"

"A gun registered to him was found at the scene of a murder in Mount Pleasant."

Plummet

"Jesus!" The lawyer looked as if he might become ill. "You have to go." He was rolling down the window." Look, you call me before you print anything and goddammit don't put the firm's name in your story!" He was becoming angry now and Lott decided it was time to leave. She had more questions but they would have to wait. She got out, walked around and retrieved her phone from the roof of the Mercedes and got back in the Toyota. As soon as she had her car out of the way she expected Robert Stone's Mercedes to back out of its spot. But as she watched in her rear-view mirror, the car remained parked and then she saw the tail lights go out. Before she had left the lot, Robert Stone was running back inside the offices of Thompson, Davis and Stone, PA.

28.

Carlton looked at the name and number of the incoming phone call and wondered if Congressman Davis was calling to tell him something he wanted to hear or to drop another load of bullshit for him to deal with. He used to look forward to talking with the congressman. It made him feel special, important when Clarence Davis called. But since his last phone call, when he had told Carlton that Staci was being watched by some unknown group, the congressman was just another potential source of bad news for Carlton.

"Congressman."

"Don't be formal with me. It's 1:30 am and I'm drunk."

"Okay, Clarence. Where are you?"

"Well, physically, I'm at my condo in Georgetown. Metaphysically, I'm between the Scylla and Charybdis with the sword of Demosthenes hanging over my head..."

"Then let's stick to Georgetown. I know where that is."

"You know the other too."

He paused, irritated. "I wouldn't know."

"Oh yes you would. Chief, we both know you want another title. Everyone knows you want another title. You, my friend, are in a boat, intent on your destination, storm tossed and side tracked, god-hindered. But determined."

"Okay."

"I'm forecasting fairer seas."

"Clarence, it's late. Don't speak in riddles."

"You will be running for Congress in a couple of

months."

The seat was held by a white man. A millionaire with family money. A conservative Republican who had the freedom to say whatever needed to be said to garner the most votes in a congressional district that hadn't elected a Democrat in over twenty years.

"Why would I waste the time and money?" He thought he heard the sound of a powerful man taking a drink of liquor and savoring its taste.

"He got caught."

"Who?"

"Richard. He got busted getting a blow job from a male prostitute. Probably underage, but that hasn't been determined ..."

"Hold on. Richard Haynes got caught with a male prostitute?"

There was deep laughter on the other end of the line. "Yes he did."

Richard Haynes, other than being a United States Congressman, was a White Man's White Man. Successful businessman, beautiful wife, two handsome sons, Deacon in his church and sportsman to boot. Getting his knob polished by a boy toy turned the public image inside out.

"Will it be public? I mean, it's not going away?"

"Shit no. We can guess why, but there's no protection for the asshole."

After the Emanuel A.M.E. Church shooting, instead of condemning the murders and supporting the removal of the Confederate Flag from the State House in Columbia, Congressman Haynes chose to take the very public opportunity to remind South Carolinians and the Nation of the Confederate Flag's importance in honoring those who fought and died defending the rights of states against an oppressive federal government. Although seen as an anachronistic buffoon by most people, Chief Carlton knew that Richard Haynes didn't injure himself politically with those statements.

"I don't see how that helps me."

"Your right. To a point. But look. Times are changing. Run for the seat. Make your Republican opponent take a stand, one way or another. If he's against Haynes' position on the flag, the Haynes vote will go to a third-party candidate. If he supports it, we go after the Republicans that don't want to cast their votes for a racist. I think it will work."

Carlton did too. He would never admit it to Congressman Davis but he could feel the political landscape shifting along the coast of South Carolina. It would be close, but if his opponent was foolish enough to take the wrong positions on a couple of issues...

"Of course, everything has to be right on your end."

The musing over imaginary campaign stratagems came to a stop and an awkward silence ensued.

"Things are right, aren't they, Charles? On your end?"

"Yes. Of course. This is what I've been preparing for." Then, the tag line, "you know that."

The seasoned politician could sense insincerity in the slightest inflection or hesitation. "Well, Charles, as you are aware, you have a lot of people that are making sacrifices for you, and it is my expectation that you will come to me if you ever believe there is anything that might become an embarrassment or liability for any of those supporters."

The weight of the congressman's words made Carlton want to sit down. The heavy expectations that came with the support of powerful people made Carlton consider telling the congressman >no'. But this is what he wanted, or a step in the direction of what he wanted. The opportunity couldn't be squandered. He had to do it. So what should he tell Davis? There is something that could become very embarrassing for not only his soon to be supporters but also the congressman himself? He wouldn't tell him. Not now anyway. Only if there was no other way.

"When will you be in Charleston?"

"Next week."

"Let's plan on talking then. Over dinner. My treat."

"In that case, I know just the place. We'll spend some of your wife's money and plan your campaign."

Again, the reminder that without Rasha's fortune, they wouldn't be having this conversation. Carlton forced a laugh before hanging up the phone.

28.

Peale had just left the Office when his phone rang. "Peale."

"Why haven't you called?"

"Ain't Thursday. I had no reason to."

"You are supposed to keep me updated on Miss Turner."

"There's nothing to report."

"You met with her."

So that's the way it's going to be. Followed around town by the FBI every minute of the day.

"That was personal. Nothing you'd be interested in."

"I'm interested in everything. Tell me."

"She hasn't said anything about ... you know."

"What? Murdering people? Damn, Peale. You are hopeless. Right now, you're girlfriend and some other equally nasty people are planning something. You need to find out what it is so we can stop it before it happens. And Peale?"

"Yeah."

"If for some reason I've got this wrong and she isn't responsible for Khalil's death, that means you are the only suspect."

"Thursday, do you sample the shit you talk or do you just expect others to eat it?"

Thursday made a sound that came across as a sarcastic laugh. "Peale, what did Staci say about Khalil's death?"

Peale had hoped this question wouldn't come up,

Plummet

"What do you mean?"

"Well, she hired you to find him, then he turns up dead. I'm sure the topic has come up."

He had hoped it wouldn't come up because he didn't like the answer. What it said about Staci and, more importantly, what it said about himself.

"She thinks I did it."

Thursday was laughing again, this time with what sounded like legitimate humor.

"Oh that's great. And what did she say when you denied it?"

Peale didn't say anything. What could he say that wouldn't come back and bite him later?

"You didn't deny it! You horny old fuck! Playing the hero so you could lay that young thing. Oh shit! ..."

He was still laughing when Peale hung up.

29.

Chief Carlton liked to be visible in public, not just in the City of Charleston, but wherever he went. He wanted people to see him, tell others they saw him, tell those who didn't know him who he was. And to be visible you had to stand out. So he traveled in a caravan of black SUVs, oblivious to the possibility that most people would see him and his entourage as a nuisance or at least ridiculous. When Chief Baskin called and told him they needed to meet, Carlton suggested a restaurant on Shem Creek.

"That's very public."

"So?"

"You aren't concerned?"

"Why can't the chiefs of police of neighboring cities get together for a bite to eat?"

Baskin had reluctantly agreed and was waiting outside the entrance to the restaurant when the caravan arrived. He cringed. Although it was 11:30 on a Friday morning, the not-big-enough parking lot was almost full. Baskin wondered where the five vehicles in Carlton's caravan would park as he watched them circle the lot once then come to a stop where he stood, idling in a line. Carlton got out of the second vehicle along with one of his crew cut companions.

"Vance, just keep them right here. The Chief and I will go in alone."

A surge of optimism rose in Baskin when he heard this, thinking the meeting would be brief. But when they sat down at a table overlooking the water and Carlton ordered appetizers and asked for a menu, the optimism drained.

"I'm starving. You're not eating?" Carlton was more ebullient than normal and normally – in public – he was very ebullient. He would exude a charming confidence that made those who didn't know him come away with a positive impression when they met. Baskin knew him well enough to know something was up to elevate Carlton's personality to the obnoxious.

"No. It's early for me."

"Got to eat when I can these days. That's why I suggested this place. Well one of the reasons."

Baskin didn't want to ask but did anyway. "What other reason?"

Carlton smiled his big, toothy, silent smile and looked around the restaurant before fixing his eyes on Baskin.

"Did you see the paper this morning?"

For a moment Baskin imagined that Jennifer Lott had already written her piece on the Shoreline shooting and that Carlton had obviously lost his mind now that his career was plummeting back to earth. Baskin felt sick knowing what it meant for him when the story got out. His career would be over too, not to mention being prosecuted for public corruption.

The waitress brought out hushpuppies with honey butter in little white paper cups. "Your shrimp cocktail will be out in just a sec, hon."

"Wonderful." When the waitress had walked away, Carlton held the hushpuppies out to Baskin. "Come on, eat." Then he saw the expression on Baskin's face. "Tom, you don't look too good. Do you need something?"

"No. I'm good. Just not hungry."

Carlton sat the basket down away from Baskin. "So? What do you think?"

Baskin's expression confused Carlton. "What do I

think?" He wanted to scream "I think you and I are going to jail!"

"Yeah. About our congressman?"

Now the look on Baskin's face explained the problem. Carlton laughed. "Come on man, you're an elected official. Don't tell me you don't read your own paper." Baskin read the paper every day and was awake and waiting on it when it was thrown in his driveway at 4:45 am that morning. He had poured over the entire edition twice and saw no mention of the Shoreline or of Jackson Peale and had thrown the paper on the kitchen table and left for the office. He hadn't paid any attention to the other articles.

"Apparently the story broke late last night on the internet. I saw it on cable news around 12:00 am. Not much detail. Only that he'd been arrested and no statement had been given. Got to hand it to *The Sun*, in the dying days of print journalism they showed that they can get in front of a story if the timing is right." Carlton laughed to himself and bit into a hushpuppy while Baskin stared at him bewildered.

"Arrested? Who was arrested?"

Carlton was enjoying this and laughed. "Richard Haynes."

Baskin still looked confused.

"Congressman Richard Haynes. You've heard of him?" Carlton shook his head in bewilderment and smiled his silent smile as he spread honey butter on the end of a hushpuppy with a knife.

"What are you talking about?"

Carlton lowered his voice but was smiling. "Goddammit, Tom, our congressman was caught having sex with a male prostitute and arrested in DC last night. Or maybe night before. Not all the details are out. *The Sun* had the story online this morning. Hell, you might be the last to know."

"So, this has nothing to do with the Shoreline or

Jackson Peale?"

"What? Peale? Hell no." He smiled again and drank some water. "Where is my shrimp cocktail?"

Relieved that Lott hadn't printed what she knew, Baskin was once again irritated by Carlton's exuberance, although he could guess the reason for it. If what he said about Richard Haynes was true, Haynes would resign and there would be a special election to fill his seat in Congress. Carlton was already campaigning.

"Here she comes." The waitress walked up to their table smiling, carrying the shrimp cocktail on a platter and placed it in front of Carlton. "Will you be ordering lunch?"

"I think I will. Tom?"

"No thanks."

"Just me then. But give us a few minutes darlin' "

"Sure thing."

When the waitress was out of sight Carlton's expression changed. "I wasn't expecting any news on the other thing." He tossed a napkin in his lap then dunked a shrimp into the small bowl of cocktail sauce. "There haven't been any developments have there?"

"Yeah. There have. And something needs to be done about it or *The Sun* will have a decision to make on which story should get the headline."

A plump pink shrimp crowned with cocktail sauce stopped in front of Carlton's open mouth.. Carlton lowered the shrimp then dropped it in the icy bowl with the others and began wiping his hands with a white napkin. He was no longer smiling.

"Tell me."

"Yesterday Billie Carver, the officer I've got on the Shoreline case..."

"Yeah, right. Carver. Go on."

"... well she tells me that a reporter for *The Sun* is investigating the death at the Shoreline and Carver is convinced it's not drug related."

"Okay. What does she know? What could she know? It's been four days for Christ's sake."

"She knows it was Peale's gun."

"So?"

"She thinks Peale's involved. She thinks there's more to it than drugs."

Carlton sat back and threw the napkin on the table. "She knows nothing. Peale's a coke head. It fits."

"She's looking. That's the point. This was supposed to go away. Unsolved drug killing." He lowered his voice and leaned closer to Carlton. "What if she finds out who this guy was, that the feds are involved?"

Carlton wanted to continue telling himself that she wouldn't find out so he could focus on putting together a campaign for a congressional seat. His mood soured and his appetite for food was gone.

"Anything else?"

"I don't think we had an accurate read on Carver."

"Why's that?"

"She talked to the FBI."

"Goddammit." Baskin could see Carlton's jaw muscles working, grinding out emotions between his teeth. "And?"

"They ID'd the corpse."

"Goddammit." Carlton was seething, trying to remain calm but about to explode behind the table in the booth. "Motherfucker."

"The waitress appeared out of nowhere. "Are you ready to order?"

Carlton threw on a smile. "Sorry. Change of plans." He pulled a wad of bills from his pocket and handed her a hundred. "Will that take care of the bill and you?"

"Sure. Thanks! Can I get you anything else? More water?"

"No, sweetie. We're good. You've been great."

The more he talked to the waitress, the calmer he became. When she left them alone he was more controlled.

"What else does she know?"

"I'm not sure. She's not telling."

Carlton looked Baskin straight in the eyes. "What do you mean?"

Baskin returned the stare. "What are you not telling me, Charles?"

There was a pause, then an unconvincing "I've told you everything I know."

"Okay. It's just that Carver asked me a strange question."

Carlton leaned back in the booth and looked out the window in the direction of a boat slowly motoring down the creek. "What did she ask?" The day had started out beautifully and he had been in such a good mood. He knew it wouldn't last but he thought it would have lasted longer than it had.

"She asked me about you."

The boat passed, leaving nothing but a wake that moved through the green marsh grass, the small waves of water unseen but for the swaying grass. Did they tell her about Khalil? Does Baskin know? Is that what this is about? Blackmail? Carlton's attention swung back to Baskin. "Why me?"

"I don't know. She wouldn't tell me."

Carlton was silent for a moment, allowing the silence to convey its own message, that Baskin was approaching a line that shouldn't be crossed.

"What did she say, specifically?"

Baskin held his gaze on the man across the table, impressing on Carlton that he too, should be careful in how he chose to proceed.

"She asked me How well do you know Charles Carlton?
"

Electric pains shot through Carlton's gut, contorting his face for a second, long enough for Baskin to notice.

"Anything else?

"I asked her why and she said something like it's probably nothing and that was it."

Carlton slid out to the end of the booth as if he were leaving. He didn't know if he believed Baskin was telling everything he knew or not but it didn't matter. The FBI had said something to Carver that compelled her to ask the question. Something about Khalil or Staci or Rasha. Or the fact that the FBI wasn't following Khalil at all. He had to assume the worst.

"Tom, it's time we identified Mahmoud Kahlil's murderer."

"And who would that be?"

"Jack Peale, of course. The body and gun were found in a drug den. Peale's a druggie. Like I said, it fits."

"Peale may have something to say."

Carlton looked into Baskin's eyes. "Not if he can't talk."

Baskin didn't respond other than to slowly shake his head, not to say he wouldn't be part of what was suggested but to deny the reality of what he had involved himself in.

"Carver won't go for it."

"Why not?"

"She was convinced it was Peale at first – I had to practically order her not to arrest him – but now, she's looking at other possibilities."

Carlton leaned over the table. "Why?"

"She wouldn't say, but her attitude has changed towards Peale. If I tell her to arrest him, she'll be suspicious. More suspicious."

"I can live with that. And if you heard me correctly, I'm not saying he needs to be arrested, or that Carver needs to be involved."

Again, Baskin was silenced for a moment when

confronted with where things now were in Carlton's mind. "And the reporter?"

He had forgotten the reporter but his reaction to her as well as to Carver and Peale and whoever else may pose a threat to him was different now than it had been just a few minutes ago, before Baskin had told him any of this and ruined what had started as a fine day. It was no longer a cloudless day in Charleston where he could look as far into his future as he dared. There was darkness on the horizon of his mind. He would do what had to be done to weather the storm to come.

"Never mind her. Let her write her story on Peale. Hell, encourage it. This is what we'll do ..."

Their meeting had lasted just a few minutes more, during which time Carlton had quietly laid out what would be done. He would have kept talking had the growing lunch crowd not filled the tables around them. But there was no need for him to. Baskin understood what was being said. He felt himself sinking deeper into the mess but had the strange notion that Carlton was standing by, safe, watching him go down. It may have been Carlton's willingness to pay him another $100,000 for his silence and his role in what was going to happen. But there was something more. A man who openly tells you his plan to kill someone is also telling you that he will kill you too, if necessary. It wasn't just the bribes that entangled him in all of this but fear also. And he felt it. A coldness that dried his mouth and created a dull pain that started at the back of his skull and spread over his head to his eyes. His arms and legs felt heavier and he numbly made his way through the restaurant. Outside, as he watched Carlton's entourage leave the parking lot, he felt sick. Baskin steadied himself on the railing and closed his eyes as people passed him on their way inside. When he had recovered enough, he walked slowly to his car, fighting the urge to vomit.

When he returned to the station he phoned Carver.

"Where are you?"

She was waiting on Jennifer Lott outside a restaurant in downtown Charleston. Based on his reaction when she had told him about talking to the FBI and Jennifer Lott pursuing the story on the Shoreline, she was hesitant to tell him where she was and what she was doing, "Meeting a friend for lunch."

"I need for you to talk with Peale again."

"Peale? Why?"

"Confront him with the what the FBI told you. Get his reaction, see what he has to say."

Carver didn't see the value in what the Chief was asking her to do. Not at this point anyway. "I don't see how that will get us anywhere. If he's not involved he won't know anything, if he is, he'll warn Staci Turner. We should turn this over to the FBI."

"The FBI hasn't contacted me about any of this and I've got a murder to solve in my city. I'm not waiting around for them. Go to his place and question him again."

"To his home?"

"That's what I said."

"Chief, he lives South of Broad remember? That's not Mt. Pleasant. We should bring in the County on this."

"Carver, quit worrying about jurisdiction and go question Peale. At his home. Try to rattle him. He won't be expecting you."

"And he probably won't talk to me either."

"Just try it, Carver. Tonight."

"Tonight?"

"Yeah. And I expect to hear how it went tomorrow morning."

~ ~ ~

When the reporter arrived at the restaurant, Billie told her that she wasn't hungry but needed to tell her something.

Plummet

They walked over to East Bay Street and stood on a sidewalk that overlooked the harbor. A large cruise ship preparing to take on passengers dominated the view. Down the street buses were parked along the side of the road where a few people mingled but there was no one else around.

"So what have you found out? It wasn't a drug killing was it –"

"Listen to me." Billie looked around then started talking like she didn't want to be overheard. The reporter thought the cop's behavior was strange and her instincts told her she was about to hear something useful. She knew when to ease up on the questions.

"Okay. Go ahead."

"I don't know why I'm telling you this other than I'm having really bad vibes."

"I'm listening." Lott was choking on a barrage of questions she wanted to unleash and didn't know how long she could keep it up. A little longer. See what she'll tell you.

"Ok. I've got a friend at the FBI. I asked him to check on the vic ..."

A name! She's got a name ...

"I can't tell you everything right now ..."

"Oh come on Carver. I know Peale's involved. I know his background, the drugs, the psychosis. I'm not stopping-"

"Stop talking. There's much more to this but nothing can be proven at this point and honestly, it could go in different directions." Carver pulled out a key from her pocket and held it up to Lott. "This is a key to my apartment. If anything happens to me I want you to go there. Pull up the floor vent in the bathroom. There is a package inside that will tell you everything I know so far."

"Really? We're doing this?"

"What do you mean?"

"I'm writing a story here. I need information. Give me

something I can write. Not a key to a secret stash of documents that I'm to look for after something 'happens to you.' Are you hearing yourself? I'm supposed to wait until you're dead? Really? Give me something I can use now."

"I can't. I can't trust you with it yet."

Lott took the key. She couldn't argue the trust issue. If Lott got something printable, she'd go with the story.

"And what if nothing happens to you?"

"You'll get what I know and whatever else I find out."

Lott wanted to ask When? but knew the answer to that already. "And what stops me from going to your apartment now?"

Carver looked out in the direction of the cruise ship for a moment. "Because if I don't get your word that you'll do what I ask, it won't be there when you look."

Lott looked at the ground. She didn't like this, being strung along, but what choice did she have. She didn't know Carver but she seemed honest, although the key and the package and the cryptic if anything happens to me made her sound overly dramatic. This woman is really naive or has no other person to turn to. Or she's nuts. No, she's probably in over her head. Whatever she's found out just freaked her out a little. I'll call her tomorrow and see if she's ready to talk.

"Okay. Deal."

30.

It was strange being in Staci's apartment for the first time. Having been through all that we had been through together, I didn't expect it to surprise me. But there was the real world and there was the fantasy world where my relationship with Staci existed and this apartment was part of the real world.

At the back, where we had entered the second floor of the building, there was a kitchen with a refrigerator and a small table and chairs. Nothing there looked like it belonged to Staci. It wasn't stylish. The appliances were dated as were the cabinets and flooring. The same dated decor continued as we walked down the hallway to the front of the building to a living room area. There was a couch and chairs a table and a TV on the wall. There was a fireplace with a mantle. On the mantle was a clock that did not have the correct time. Unlike the kitchen, everything in the room looked expensive and newer. But there was nothing personal about it. Nothing that said anything about Staci. Nothing I wanted to know anyway.

"Have a seat."

I fell into the couch and stretched out, I wanted to go to sleep.

"Jackson, sit up. I have to talk to you about something very important.

If I keep my eyes closed it will go away and when I open them again it will all be gone. It's true. The child in us never leaves. I can see him sometimes, standing alone, holding a something precious …

"Jackson."

I open my eyes and see a stranger sitting in a chair, leaning forward, legs crossed, looking at her phone. She's wearing a casual dress the color of sand with brown, knee high leather boots. Her sunglasses are parked on top of her head. She put the phone on a table and came over to where I was lying on the couch and sat next to me. She put her hand gently against my face and stroked my hair, her eyes looking into me, seeing me.

"Do you love me?"

I nodded. I couldn't say the word because I would have heard my voice and if I heard my voice …

"Can I trust you? With my safety? With my life?"

Another nod. She hesitated with a look that seem to question my response.

"I believe you." She leaned down and lightly kissed my lips. When she parted from me she stared into my eyes again, then stood up, running her hand heavily across my chest. She walked over to a closet and took out a blue gym bag with an apparel company logo on the side. She carefully placed the bag on the table next to her phone. I sat up and listened as she told me, then showed me, what was in the bag, then told me what it was she needed me to do.

31.

Back in my apartment, I was still in two parts, unable to bring myself together. I needed to talk to someone, so I picked up the phone and dialed Batista's number.

"You in deep mon."

"Looks like it."

"And you called Batista wanting advice on what to do?"

"I don't want to lose her. I – I want to believe her. I..."

"Okay, okay, mon. try to pull it together. Now, let me guess. Your mind tells you to do one thing, your heart another. I'm right?"

"Yeah."

"Of course I'm right. Batista is always right, mon."

"I've got to tell the feds. They told me this was happening but I didn't want to believe it ..."

"Hold on, hold on you ball-less bastard. Who do you have on dis earth that gives a shit about you?"

I had to think for a moment for someone other than my daughter but couldn't come up with anyone else except Staci. "Well, Megan ..."

"After that shit you pulled. You'll be lucky you get to see her in a park for two hours on a Saturday surrounded by police. If she would agree to see you. Anyone else?"

"Staci, maybe."

"Right, she tells you she loves you, she needs you and will take you away with her. It sounds like you have one person who gives a shit about you and you are gonna throw her to the FBI. Dumb, ball-less, friendless white mon."

"So you think I should do it?"

"Ask yourself, where do you want to be in a year, here in Charleston doin your shitty PI work while everyone looks down on you or off somewhere far away with Staci Turner?"

He was right. What was holding me here? My relationship with my daughter was over probably. My ex would see to that. And there was nothing in front of me but a repetition of the same crappy work. And when Martha dies, I'll be homeless. Batista's voice interrupted my thoughts.

"There's someone here with me that wants to talk to you."

It jolted me. Who could be there that wanted to talk to me? I'd never known anyone to be with Batista when we talked. I had always considered our conversations private, almost as if I was talking to myself.

"Sarge?"

At the sound of his voice the floor beneath me opened and I fell. A familiar feeling. Not familiar in a comforting way but always anticipated. After the bombing it had stayed with me, the expectation, the knowledge that the ground beneath my feet would one day open up again and swallow me, only I wouldn't crawl out the next time. I often wondered what it was like not to have that inside of me. I couldn't remember. During my life after the Marines I came to consider it normal, this feeling of doom, as if it's concealed within all of us, only the knowledge of it had been revealed to me, as it had been to others. A foreboding. A foreboding that only I and the other chosen ones felt. These were my thoughts as I fell and entered the darkness that had shadowed me. As I fell, the voice of Billy Shores talked to me.

"Sarge, it's time to come down. What Staci wants you to do is right. It was the Jews that killed her sister. And why were you and I in Lebanon when that truck blew us to hell?

The Jews. Killed me and did everything but kill you. Left you walking around, seein' and talkin' to dead people, people that ain't real. But it's a gift. You just see more than other people. Staci understands. She's been changed and sees things different too. You belong together ..."

It went on like that for, I don't know how long, the falling accompanied by the voice of Billy Shores. It felt like hours had gone by when a knocking on the door woke me up. I was lying on the floor. I sat up, my mind trying to make sense of what had happened. Then I saw my phone on the floor. One of the last things I remember Billy saying was "they'll be comin' for you. They can't let you live ..."

Knocking again. Louder this time and I could feel my heart pounding in my chest as I sat on the floor staring at the door. Then a voice.

"Mr. Peale. It's Billie Carver, from the Mt. Pleasant Police. Can we talk?"

Carver? Why would she want to kill me? She wouldn't, or would she?

"Uh yeah. Hold on a second." She was talking again but I couldn't understand what she said because I was in the bedroom, pulling a box off the top shelf of my closet. I put the box on the bed, took the top off and pulled out a Smith & Wesson .38. I checked the chamber for bullets and stuck it in the waist of my pants against my back. I put the box back on the shelf in the closet and went to the door and opened it.

"May I come in?"

I didn't say anything but opened the door. Is it her? Should I kill her now? No. Wait. It may not be her. She walked in talking but I wasn't listening. I was looking for Billy Shores but he wasn't here. Cold fear began swirling in my chest, tightening my lungs and I reached back and felt for the gun.

"... apologize for barging in like this unannounced and

I won't take but a few minutes. We just had some follow up questions we'd like to get answered before tomorrow."

She was looking at me like I was supposed to say something. "Okay."

"Great." She was looking at the couch. "Okay. Well, I talked to the FBI yesterday and..."

Two strange, muffled sounds cut her off mid-sentence and she fell towards me with a confused look on her face. I pulled the gun out of my pants and aimed at a dark figure in the doorway as she crashed into me. Falling backwards, I heard more muffled shots as I squeezed the trigger of the .38. The sound of two shots from the .38 exploded in the apartment and the dark figure disappeared. We both hit the floor, me in one direction, still trying to point the gun at the door and Carver to my left with the sound of dead weight. I scrambled to my feet, heart leaping in my chest, my eyes and gun pointed at the screen door and waited a moment, listening. I walked slowly to the door and kicked it shut then looked over at Carver. She wasn't moving and looked dead. I've got to get out of here. The cops will be here soon and they'll take care of Carver. But what about the shooter? He could be outside, waiting. I don't have a choice! I had to get to Staci's place on King Street. It was the only place I knew where I could go and the cops wouldn't look for me.

Although one end of King Street was a block from Whitsett, Staci's place was on the northern end. I went the opposite direction, towards the harbor where I dumped the .38, then headed back towards Staci's apartment, staying on the smaller, residential streets that were close to and paralleled East Bay. It was going to be a hike. I tried to look as ordinary as the other people walking the streets of Charleston at that time of night, but I kept looking around in different directions and when I heard the sirens, my heart started pounding again and I had to fight the urge to run. I stuck my hands in my pockets to force a more leisurely pace.

Near the port I started angling towards King Street and eventually came to Calhoun Street where the traffic was almost bumper to bumper and the street wider and more open. Sirens continued to wail, moving off towards the Battery. I stood at the pedestrian crossing, feeling like everyone passing by was looking at me and waited for the crosswalk sign to turn green. Only the thought of getting run over kept me from running across the street through traffic. After crossing Calhoun and making my way through smaller, neighborhood streets I turned left and crossed Meeting. Eventually I came upon a music hall. A crowd of people mingled in front on the sidewalk and even blocked part of the street. Being part of a crowd gave me a chance to breathe and I thought about going inside to hide during the show. But I had to find Staci. So I crossed King Street then walked through parking lots and alley ways until I could see the back of Staci's building. The light was on upstairs. There was no one in the back near the stairs and I walked over and quietly climbed the steps. At the top I quickly knocked on the door.

"Who is it?"

Staci's voice.

"Jack. Let me in."

The sound of locks unlocking and when the door began to open I squeezed my way in.

"What's wrong?"

"You got to get me out of here, now!"

"Wait —"

"Listen! Someone just tried to kill me! There's a dead cop in my apartment! I've got to get the hell out of here! You said you had a plan. Let's do it."

She stood there considering something. "Okay. We will. But not yet. Jackson, I've got to do this or running won't matter." She paused, just looking at me. "I'll do it tomorrow, then we'll go, like I said."

Plummet

Shit. I'm not getting out of here tonight. We, aren't getting out of here tonight. I felt the walls closing in on me. What did I expect? That she'd ditch her crazy ass plan and take off with me? Probably. I could leave alone but where would I go? She's got connections, a way to disappear. I've got nowhere to go and no one to go to.

"And Jackson, tomorrow, after it's done, if I don't make it on time, leave without me. I've given instructions to the others to take you."

Defeated, I walked past her down the hall to the kitchen and sat down at a table.

"I'll do it." The words were garbled and quiet.

"What did you say?"

I looked at her and made sure I got it out of my mouth. "I'll do it. The bomb." Is this what she intended? Is she that good after all?

She walked over to me and ran her hand through my hair. "No. This isn't your fight. I was wrong to ask you earlier."

"I'm not going anywhere without you. If something happens, I want it to happen to me. I've got to know you are okay."

Her voice changed. Its tone was disconcerting. Colder. "Are you sure you can do it? I mean, it has to be done. If it doesn't happen, they'll kill me ... if I'm lucky."

Somehow I believed her. That part anyway. "I've got my reasons for wanting it done, apart from you."

Yeah. Sure I did. And what was it going to be, this bomb? One last kick in the crouch of the country that sent me half way around the world to get blown up, that patched me back together and dumped me on the street? A middle finger wave goodbye to the city whose streets I was dumped on, that gave me a job, a family a career, dreams, then took them away and told me my place was in the alleys, off the sidewalks, out of sight. Hell, by tomorrow I'll probably want to blow myself up. No more child support, no more imaginary people, no more questions about dead guys in motels killed with my gun or cops gunned down in my home, no more pretending that lies are truth just so I can tell myself there's something worth living for ...

"Thank you. Jack, I don't know what I'd do without you."

I stood out of the chair. She slid her arms around my waist and pulled me close to her, holding me with her cheek against my chest. But I was numb. If it had been another night, I would be taking her clothes off and throwing her onto the kitchen table. Instead, I just wanted to lie down some place and drift. I gently pulled her arms away, kissed her forehead, then looked for a place where I could try to sleep.

32.

Twitter was supposed to keep her up to date on breaking news but nothing beat a police scanner for knowing what was happening with law enforcement as it was happening. Jennifer Lott kept one at her home and it was there, while she was in her kitchen scooping ice cream into a bowl that she heard about the shooting on Whitsett. Standing there staring at the scanner she listened to the voices of the officers and dispatch and thought Isn't that Jackson Peale's address?

The ice cream was left on the counter as she ran downstairs to her car.

"What the fuck happened?"

"One down one to go."

"Don't give me that shit! This is a colossal fuck up! Who the hell got away?"

"Maybe we should meet and not talk on the phone..."

"Fuck that! I thought this guy was a pro! How the fuck did one get away?"

There was a pause to let the other know he needed to calm himself. "Peale had a gun. Got off some shots. The guy had to go or risk getting caught."

"Peale's on the loose?" He considered it and decided that was the best option if he had to choose. "So Carver ..."

"She's dead."

Hearing the words made him nauseous. Yeah, he had agreed to it, but talking about it was different than knowing it had happened, that she was gone. She didn't deserve this. How did it get to this ...?

"I know where Peale is. We'll have him by tomorrow."

33.

From one end to the other, Whitsett Street was clogged with vehicles flashing red or blue lights. From her previous visit to Peale's apartment she knew to look for a parking spot two streets over and found a place where she could park her car off the road. It wasn't a legal, but there was no time to find anything else. She locked the doors and ran towards Whitsett. Instead of walking down the sidewalk where she was sure to be stopped by law enforcement, she went through a neighbor's yard that backed up to Peale's apartment. She climbed over a stone wall and fell into some bushes that poked and scraped her as she forced her way into the backyard. It was dark where she stood but not thirty yards away was the main house and the driveway, lit up with portable klieg lights. Police were combing the ground for evidence. How can I get inside? She looked up at the apartment and could see the flash from a camera through the window. Is there a body in there? Peale? Her mind wanted to question why shots would have been fired at Jackson Peale's apartment. Suicide? That would make sense but she was sure the call on the scanner said multiple shots. That would probably rule out suicide. Only one way to find out. Get a look inside. Entering the apartment could contaminate the scene and she considered waiting but decided to try going up the steps to the door.

As she walked around to the driveway, she saw an officer at the foot of the steps, she retreated backwards into the darkness before he could see her, then, keeping in the dark, ran around to the side of the house and climbed onto the porch. The street in front of the house was lit up with flashing lights. Every few seconds someone would hurry by on the sidewalk or in the road intent on whatever had to be done. Neighbors were standing on their porches watching the spectacle. In all the commotion, Jennifer Lott walked across the porch to the front door, found it open and walked inside. She closed the door slowly, then walked up the stairs and looked for a window that would give her a view of the apartment. Light from a back bedroom flooded through an open door onto the hallway floor in front of her. She walked into the bedroom to a window and looked out over the driveway. She also had a view of the stairway to the apartment, not twenty feet away. There was no one on it but the officer at the bottom of the steps.

After ten minutes of waiting and watching, Lott was at the point of leaving the window and take a chance with the police when the door to the apartment opened and someone backed out guiding one end of a gurney. He said something to the officer at the foot of the steps who climbed up and helped hold one side of the gurney as it slowly emerged from the apartment. As it was moved through the door she could see the top and back of the head but not the face. It wasn't Peale though. It looked to be a woman. The daughter? No. As the gurney was carefully guided down the steps, Lott was surprised to see a police officer's uniform come into view. Her mind was trying to make sense of what she was seeing when the face came into view. Cold fear poured through her body. She leaned against the wall for support and turned from the window. Is it really her? You've got to be sure. She looked out the window again but the gurney was already being carried across the driveway and she couldn't make out the face. Forcing herself across the room she made her way down the steps and to the front door. She saw an ambulance to her left and ran out into the street towards the back of it and stopped. She watched as EMS escorted the gurney to the back of the ambulance. No one stopped her as she moved closer until she could have reached out and touched the body.

"Hey. Who are you? Travis, get her out of here."

A hand grabbed her arm and started dragging her away from the ambulance but not before the reporter had seen the face. It was Carver and she was dead.

34.

She hadn't noticed how scared she was until she tried to open the door of Carver's apartment. The key in her shaky hand danced around the door handle as if intentionally avoiding the key hole. She stopped, closed her eyes and dropped her hands to her side. Calm down. After a few deep breaths she opened the door. Inside she turned on the light and immediately felt exposed, making her want to turn the light out again. Then she noticed the room. It was empty and for a moment she wondered if she had somehow entered the wrong apartment. Where there should have been a couch, coffee table and TV there was nothing, as if the apartment was vacant. It wasn't until she looked into the kitchen and saw a coffee maker on the counter that she thought differently and the fear she had felt was replaced with sadness. What else could she feel when only a coffee maker told her that a person had lived in a place. She looked for the bedroom half expecting to find box springs and a mattress on the floor but found an unmade bed elevated from the floor by an unseen bedframe. There was a mirror above a chest of drawers against a wall and a clock radio sat on a small table next to the bed. There were no pictures, nothing that would make the place a home. Carver had been existing here, not living.

She went to the bathroom, turned on the light and scanned the small space finding an air vent on the floor. She knelt down and pried it up with her fingernails. Inside was the envelope Carver had told her would be there and her heart beat faster as she reached in and pulled it from the duct. Sitting on the floor she began opening the envelope when a thought stopped her. Carver was dead. Someone killed her. They may be coming here. She replaced the vent cover and hurried out of the bathroom into the den but was stopped by another thought before opening the door. They could be here already, watching. She considered this for a moment. I can't do shit about that now and she put the envelope inside her blouse and left the apartment as calmly as she could manage.

She didn't return home, going to a late-night bar instead, just in case she was being followed. The place was busy but not packed and she was able to find a table that gave her a view of the front door. After ordering a beer she opened the envelope. Inside were handwritten notes on white legal paper. The script wasn't clear and looked to have been written in a hurry. She looked over each sheet for no other reason than to see how much was there when her eyes stopped on words that were underlined:

`info classified — FBI infmnt .`

She flipped back to the first page as the waitress brought the beer.

"Anything else?"

"No. I'm good."

As the waitress left she started to read what she could make out on the first page:

```
5/30/17 p/c w/ Brett bone FBI.
Vic name mahmood Kahlil egyptian national
connections w terror group
staci Turner — charles Carlton rasha Carlton
```

The police chief's name made her stop. Why is Chief Carlton showing up in these notes? And Rasha is his wife. The name Staci Turner was familiar but she wasn't making the connection. Who is Staci Turner?

She began reading the second page:

```
M K
info classified — FBI infmnt
```

What did that mean? She looked at the words again. MK is Kahlil so Kahlil was an FBI informant? With connections to a terror group? Remembering she couldn't call Carver for clarification, she thought of something else: Carver knew she was in danger, she said as much. That was after she had a phone call with ... she picked up the first sheet and looked at the name ... Brett Bone at the FBI and found out the vic was an informant with connections to a terror group. So who was she afraid of and why? She took a drink from the beer bottle and stared across the bar into her thoughts, her mind snatching at bits of information, trying to find something that fit with what she had just learned. Then something occurred to her without any fact to fully support it but she knew it was true despite everything. Peale didn't kill Kahlil. It was a set up and Carver knew it. Whoever set him up knew that she knew and killed her. If she maintained her journalistic principles she wouldn't eliminate Peale as a suspect and she told her self that she hadn't. It's only a theory. But in her heart she knew she was right because Carver believed it too. She continued to read:

```
S Turner has ties w/ terror group. R Carlton?
K infiltrated
If MK dead he was discovered
```

The last part made sense to her. Khalil was killed for being an informer. That doesn't explain what he was doing at the Shoreline and why he was naked but Lott decided to put that to the side for now. Who is S Turner? And is this saying that the wife of the Chief of Police is connected with a terror group? It was so preposterous that she began to question everything she had read until she thought about

Carver. Why would she be dead if it weren't true? Maybe the note about Rasha Carlton doesn't mean she's connected. She was frustrated by questions with no clear answers and her instinct told her to find the person with answers to the questions. She looked at the name of Brett Bone on the top of the first sheet. I'll call Mr. Bone. At first it seemed like a reasonable idea. But Carver was alive until she talked to Bone. Maybe I won't talk to Mr. Bone right away. In fact, I've got to be careful about who I talk to period. She looked at the last two notes:

```
No active op in ctown
Mk off grid
```

Again, she needed more information, or clarification from someone. But she read it again. Khalil was "off grid," meaning he wasn't in contact with FBI? "No active op" in Charleston meant the FBI had nothing going on with Khalil. Whatever he was doing he was doing on his own. She drained the rest of the beer. She was fairly confident no one was following her and she was ready to go home. But she sat for a moment, thinking. I can investigate Carver's death. That will give me some cover. If Peale isn't dead he's going to be the prime suspect. But if Peale didn't kill Carver, who did? And was she the target? If Carver was the target someone knew she would be at Peale's or followed her there. Was Peale there too? They carried her body out of the apartment so she had to have been killed inside, meaning someone let her in. So Peale lets her in, she's shot by someone other than Peale, Peale isn't shot but can't be found. Was he abducted? The questions were taking her in circles, each leading back to Peale as the best choice for Carver's murder. But you're ignoring Carver's notes. She wanted you to have them and knew her life was in danger.

But why? Because of the notes?

She told herself that tagging Peale as Carver's killer was

lazy and it ignored everything else she had learned since talking to Carver the day before. She had to find someone who could answer her questions, someone other than Jack Peale. Not because she didn't want to question him. She did. It just didn't seem likely she would be able to find him. Go back to Carver's notes. Find the people in the notes and question them. She looked through them again. There was Chief Carlton, his wife Rasha, and Staci Turner. Brett Bone, an FBI agent, was also mentioned. Would he help? Again, it occurred to her that one of the people in the notes was possibly responsible for her murder. And if Jack Peale didn't murder Carver, it was more than possible that one of the people in the notes was responsible for it.

She left the bar as the journalist in her struggled with her instinct to survive.

35.

Rasha listened to what was being said, said nothing herself and hung up the phone. It was an older phone, its color and style out of place among the expensive interior furnishings of her home. But if they had to contact her by phone, they insisted on a land line. It had always been that way, even before her first husband's death. The preferred communication was face to face, the words dissipating as they were spoken (if not recorded), existing only in the mind of the hearer and speaker. Next came the written note, but it had to be destroyed after the communication was delivered. If it was, the communication would be as covert as the spoken word, without the risk of recording. Last was the land line phone. It could be tapped but not surveilled as easily as mobile phones. They would always call from public places. They would never use a mobile phone to contact her and she would never use one to contact them.

These were the rules of communication insisted upon by the people that had contacts in Indonesia, that had someone working as a mechanic at the airport where Rasha Turner's husband boarded a plane to fly over a newly leased oil field. The rules were delivered in person at a table of a café in Sienna that overlooked the Piazza del Campo. The man who delivered the rules was a young Saudi. He was attractive, neatly groomed and wore an expensive light grey suit and white shirt with no tie. When he had finished talking business he looked across the piazza and his outstretched arm casually swept from one end of the space to the other, drawing Rasha's attention to his new subject of contemplation.

"Do you know what is significant about Sienna's piazza, Mrs. Turner?"

The question seemed so random and unrelated to what they had just been discussing that she wasn't sure she had heard him correctly. She hadn't said anything, only looked at him with confusion. He smiled.

"It's size. Compared to the piazzas of Montepulciano, Pienza, any of the other hill towns in Tuscany, it is much larger. Able to hold more people. Do you see?"

She had seen it was large but not his point. Again, he had smiled.

"Those that built this, the ones in power at the time, wanted to create a space where hundreds, even thousands of people from the city and the countryside could come together, in public and discuss whatever needed to be discussed. The rulers of the other hill towns feared large public gatherings and kept public spaces small because the people were poor and often hungry. If the people were allowed to congregate in the city in such numbers, revolution would be inevitable. But the rulers of Sienna wanted to make a statement. Do you see?"

She looked out over the expansive bricked floor that sloped down from where they sat in the shade into the sunlight at the lower end of the piazza. The entire space was surrounded by buildings of different sizes and shapes, rising up and forming a wall that encircled the piazza. Narrow streets leading into and out of the piazza created breaks in the wall of buildings, preventing, what had seemed to Rasha, to have otherwise been a large, beautiful enclosure.

"People will tell you it was an experiment in democracy. But it wasn't. It was something far more clever. And useful."

Late that night on a flight from Florence to London, she had been kept awake by what the Saudi had said. But it was what he had said about the piazza that her mind couldn't let go of, not what would be required of her and Staci for the killing of her husband.

"Who owns the wealth in the world? The masses of people that populate it? No. One percent. One percent owns ninety percent of the world's wealth. You and I, Mrs. Carlton. Your husband. That is the way it has always been and always will be. It doesn't matter what governments are in power, wherever you go in this world, the few have power over the masses. It is the natural order of things. It cannot change. Communism tried changing it by force but failed. And democracy? The United States is no different. Corporations, institutions, bureaucracies, these hold the power there. The people simply elect the managers, the caretakers. That brings us back to the piazza. Sienna's piazza is nothing more than a symbol of an illusion, the illusion that power had been given to the people. When the masses revolt, who takes power when the revolution is over? The few. And when the masses are hungry, scared, angry, who do they turn to? The few. And when the masses demand power, who gives it to them? The few. But what they give them is nothing but an illusion. The masses never have power. It is always held by the few."

He had gone on to tell her that the people in the United States only needed to experience fear and they would give up their freedom without admitting that they had done so. The 9/11 terrorists attack had shown this. What was needed was more attacks. Smaller perhaps, but in places people felt safe. She had not asked why, she didn't want to know and didn't care. Her thoughts had been occupied with what she was asking the Saudi to do, not why he was doing it.

He had included her in his "one-percent" but at the moment she did not feel powerful. Staci was with them now and since the bombing was considered a failure, a price would have to be paid. Until the phone call, she had not known the price. Now that she did, she felt helpless. Money and influence could not get Staci out of this. Only the currency of fear had purchasing power in the world she found herself in. And in that world, she was a pauper. She wanted to scream but couldn't. It was if her body knew the futility of it. She was overwhelmed with the fear that Staci was going to die and there was nothing anyone could do about it. She looked out the window across Charleston Harbor. In the distance an American flag fluttered in the offshore breeze above Fort Sumter.

What have we done?

36.

It took Jackson Peale thirty minutes to make his way on foot back to Whitsett Street. He had stopped several times, leaning against a tree, a car, a fence, whatever he could find for support. At each stop, he looked around, breathed deeply and told himself to keep moving.

Sirens continued screaming and Peale recognized not only the sound of law enforcement but also those of the fire department and EMS. Only then did Peale wonder if the explosion had hurt or killed anyone. The thought made him stop and his chest tightened and he nearly collapsed again. But this time it was guilt that froze his lungs, not fear, and it demanded that he die. Part of him agreed. Death was the only escape from this shit. But another part told him to keep moving. It was an old, familiar voice. The same one that told him to have another drink when he thought he shouldn't, the same one that told him to go along with Staci Turner's games as long as it meant more sex. A voice to be wary of, normally, but one to listen to at a time like this. He stood straighter, looked around and took a deep breath and didn't stop walking again until he was in sight of Whitsett Street.

The driveway of 107 Whitsett Street was sealed off with yellow police tape. There was one officer standing at the foot of the steps leading to his apartment. There was no police car, however, parked on the road or in the drive. Peale thought that his only concern at the moment was not being seen by one of his neighbors, any of which would be eager to turn him in. Thursday watched Peale as he walked onto the porch of Martha's house, unlocked the door and went inside.

Thursday waited a few minutes then climbed the steps of the house and stood listening at the front door. He could hear nothing and turned the door knob and pushed slightly. It gave way to the push and he opened it some more, surveyed the street a last time, then went inside, quietly closing the door behind him.

The suitcase was where he had left it on a shelf in an upstairs closet. Peale took it down and put it on the bed and hesitated before opening it. If the money is gone, I'm stuck here. He opened it and breathed a deep sigh when he saw the money in the zip lock bag next to a towel he had wrapped the taser in. A release of emotion shuddered through him and tears welled up in his eyes. The adrenaline from the explosion had masked a deep loneliness and sadness that had been with him ever since he had realized Staci meant for him to die in the explosion. He had been ready to give up everything for her, a concession that now seemed so foolish, that shame racked him into quiet sobs. All he wanted at the moment was his daughter. The pieces of his broken relationship with her now seemed to him the most valuable possession he could wish to have. He fell to his knees and cried into the musty comforter on the bed.

Downstairs, Thursday wasn't sure at first what he was hearing. It sounded like the moaning of a wounded animal, but as it grew louder, it was clearly the sound of a man crying.

Pathetic. I can't wait to kill him. What's the saying? Pity someone long enough and the pity turns to hate? Something like that. But I already hated him. No. That's not true. I despised him. But that's not hate.

Jackson Peale. A pathetic piece of shit defined by his addiction to pleasure. Despicable. I can't wait to kill him.

He waited at the bottom of the staircase, listening to the sobbing and growing more impatient. He considered a slow ascent of the stairs but decided against it. The house was old, the stairs made of wood. Stairs creak. Thursday wasn't inclined to announce his presence. If the target knows it's a target, the kill becomes more difficult, if not impossible. The night before proved the point. Thursday dismissed the idea that Peale recognized him as the shooter, but his cover as an FBI agent wouldn't help bring him downstairs since Peale would think he was being pursued for the explosion. No. Peale couldn't know that Thursday was here. He would have to wait. He took out the gun and attached the sound compressor to the barrel.

The police officer who had been standing guard at Peale's apartment needed to use the bathroom. He had been told not to enter the apartment. Going in the bushes of the backyard crossed his mind but the thought of being caught by a neighbor made him think of something else. The bathroom in the house was the only option and he was sure he could get in and out without being caught. He walked down the driveway and around the house to the front door.

Both Peale and Thursday heard the footsteps on the porch. Peale stood up, took out the taser and closed the suitcase. Thursday stood flat against a wall that gave him a view of the stairs and the front door. He calmly watched as the officer opened the door and walked in and looked around. He first saw Thursday and then the gun pointing at him. He could only say 'Wait!' before Thursday put a bullet in his forehead.

Plummet

Peale heard the muffled shot and thudding sound from downstairs. Cold adrenaline froze his body. Then came the pounding of footsteps on the stairs. The door to the room was partially open and he flattened himself against the wall next to it as the footsteps slowed then stopped at the top of the stairs. He's listening. Peale's heart pounded in his chest and ears and he thought he might have another anxiety attack. Get it together! You're going to die if you don't get your shit together! He blocked everything out except for what he could hear, focusing on the sound of soft, approaching footsteps on the old, wooden floorboards. He crouched with the taser, knowing the man would come in fast, ready to fire at the first sight of him. His only chance was to avoid the end of the gun while hitting the man wherever he could with the taser. It was the same taser that had taken down Todd Burley, who was bigger than average. As long as this one wasn't much bigger, it should do the same. That's what Peale was telling himself as the silence outside the door told him the man had stopped. Peale's thighs were burning and he wanted to stand but couldn't. He could come in any second now. Be ready! He kept his eyes fixed on the opening of the door, ready to explode at the first site of anything crossing the threshold.

For a moment the gun was pointing downward, directly at his head and Peale thought he was dead. But as he lunged forward, one hand reaching for the wrist holding the gun and the other stabbing the taser at the man's rib cage, the gun lifted and pointed towards the bed, giving him an open shot at the man. Thursday saw the movement below and to his left and swung the gun back in that direction but it was too late. The electric charge stopped all movement in Thursday's body and his mind froze for a moment too, only to come back in a panic. Shoot! Shoot! But another blast from the taser took him down to his knees. He dropped the gun and fell face forward onto the floor.

Peale stood over Thursday trying to process what he was seeing. Why is the FBI trying to kill me? Why did the FBI kill Carver? He kicked the gun across the floor and got the duct tape out of the suitcase. When Thursday's ankles and arms were bound, he took the suitcase and left out the backdoor of Martha's house and climbed the wall in her backyard. On the other side of the wall, he was in the backyard of a home that he knew stayed empty most of the year. Behind azaleas and a palmetto, he emptied the suitcase, stuffing the money in his pockets. He left the taser and duct tape in the suitcase behind the palmetto and bushes. He walked through a black iron gate into the driveway and then to the street, turned and walked towards the marina with only one thing on his mind: Get the hell outta here.

37.

The podium was placed in a location on the floor of the city council chambers to optimize the space on either side of it. In front of the podium the room bustled with people moving in and out, setting up cameras, lights and other equipment around the chairs that had been set up for the media. It had been just over six hours since the explosion and the media had descended on Charleston.

Behind the podium were representatives from state and local government and first responders. The mayor stood directly behind the podium talking to a man wearing a windbreaker with "FBI" screen printed on the front left of the jacket. On the mayor's right was the Solicitor and next to him the Sheriff of Charleston County. Noticeably absent from the press conference was the Chief of Police, Charles Carlton.

Jennifer Lott was unable to find a seat that hadn't been reserved for the national and state-wide media. She could see cameras or correspondents from all of the local affiliates as well as national outlets such as Fox News, CNN, MSNBC, NBC, CBS and ABC. She also recognized two national print reporters, one from The Washington Post and another from the New York Times. Most of the newspapers that had state-wide circulation had reporters seated among the others. She worked her way between two cameras at the edge of the chairs and stood next to an older woman whose press credentials said she was from the Huffington Post. Lott was nervous, unsure of what to do. As she looked around the room at the assemblage of national and state media, she told herself You belong here. None of these people know what you know. But it wasn't the other media that made her nervous. Trying to decide what to do with the information she had was causing her mind to freeze. If I don't move quick, others will find out... But I can't make a connection between the explosion and the deaths of Khalil and Carver... Doubt and negativity worked their way into her thoughts, displacing the confidence that had pushed her to this spot at the press conference. As the mayor began to speak, Lott's mind was blank until she saw that Chief Carlton wasn't among the others around the mayor. If she was given the chance, she knew one question she could ask.

The mayor motioned to close the large, ornate double doors that led to the packed hallway outside. As the door closed there were shouts of complaints from those unable to gain entrance to the council chambers. "Shortly after nine o'clock this morning, there was an explosion on King Street near its intersection with Spring Street. The explosion destroyed a building and injured five people, one critically. At this time, thank god, there have been no deaths. An investigation is underway to determine the cause of the explosion but that investigation is not complete. As you can see, in addition to the local and state authorities assembled here, the FBI is also represented. You should not jump to any conclusions. This a local and state matter. Special Agent Rogers is here only in a consultative role and will be available to answer questions also."

~ ~ ~

The mayor continued to talk but Lott wasn't listening. Her mind was racing, triggered by the mayor downplaying the FBI's role in the investigation. The

FBI knows about Khalil and should know a terrorist group was planning something for Charleston. They also know Chief Carlton, his wife and maybe his stepdaughter have some connection to what has happened. She had learned prior to the press conference that Staci Turner was the daughter of Rasha Carlton. Are they not telling the mayor or is the mayor lying? She could feel he confidence returning. I'm bettered prepared for this press conference than anyone here. Lott focused on the questions she was going to ask.

~ ~ ~

"At this time, I'll open it up for questions." A roar of voices rose from the seated press along with arms waving in the air, hoping to get the mayor's attention. The mayor's eyes panned the crowd before stopping on a woman in the front row.

"Mandy?"

She stood and cleared her voice. "Mr. Mayor, it's Mandy Johnson, from the State."

"Yes Mandy. What is your question?"

"Are you aware that a terrorist group has claimed responsibility for this bombing and if so, is that the reason for the FBI taking part in the investigation?"

The mayor smiled ruefully and shook his head before responding. "Unfortunately, Mandy, you know as well as I that we live in an age where any group with a Twitter account can claim responsibility for anything terrible in this world within five minutes of it happening. I expect by the end of the day there will be dozens claiming they had a role in what happened. But let me also say, and this is important for everyone to remember: the investigation is ongoing and while no conclusions can be drawn at this time, early indications are that this was a gas line rupture."

Voices and arms again rose into the air.

"Yes sir, you in the blue golf shirt. CNN, I believe."

"Mayor, are you aware that there is security video that captured the explosion as it happened?"

The look on the mayor's face told Lott that he was not aware of the video. The mayor looked in the direction of the Solicitor who said nothing but slightly nodded his head.

"Like I said, the investigation is ongoing. We are looking at all sorts of evidence including security video, where that is helpful. Beyond that I really can't comment further."

"CNN had an expert in the field of munitions and explosives look at the video. It is his opinion that this was not a gas line rupture, but an explosion resulting from the detonation of a significant amount of weapons grade material. Do you have a comment?"

Until that point, the mayor had seemed prepared to deflect any question with the response "I really can't comment since the investigation is ongoing" but he was ready for someone else to take the heat.

"I think I'll let Special Agent Rogers address that. Agent?"

"Uh thank you mayor. No responsible professional would form an opinion about the cause of this explosion without considering all of the evidence. To do so would be reckless, even dangerous. In the real world, the world of consequences, that opinion of your so-called expert is worthless."

The mayor, emboldened by the agent's destruction of CNN's attempt to create "fake news", retook the podium, almost pushing the agent aside in the process.

"Thanks Jim. Next question?"

Much of the enthusiasm the media had brought to the press conference had dissipated. There were no deaths and the terrorism angle that most if not all had hoped to play up seemed to be going nowhere. There were less shouts this time and fewer arms raised. One of the arms raised however, belonged to Jennifer Lott. The mayor again scanned the faces of reporters, finding much satisfaction from the fact that more than half seemed to be losing interest. His eyes fell upon a young woman in jeans and untucked blouse, standing by the others beneath two cameras.

"Yes ma'am. What is your question?"

"I'm Jennifer Lott, from *The Sun*. I have two questions, if I may. One for you Mr. Mayor and one for Special Agent Rogers."

Only the mayor's experience handling himself in public and in front of the press kept him from displaying his opinion about a reporter from the on-line publication. A slight smile did appear as he gripped both sides of the podium and stared at Jennifer Lott.

"Of course. Go ahead."

"I couldn't help but notice Chief Carlton is not here today. Do you know where he is?"

The mayor looked over the room with a look of grave concern on his face that betrayed his opinion that he couldn't have been asked a simpler question if it had come from a student at a local elementary school.

"Ms. Lott, Chief Carlton is leading this investigation and his responsibilities as police chief prevent him from attending this news conference."

"Thank you. And Agent Rogers?"

The mayor backed away from the podium smiling contritely and gesturing with his outstretched arm for the FBI agent to step up and take a few home-run cuts at the softballs being tossed by the reporter. The agent, whose expression was serious and professional, moved behind the podium and looked at Jennifer Lott.

"Yes ma'am?"

"Agent, are you aware that three days ago a confidential informant for the FBI named Mahmoud

Kahlil was murdered in Mount Pleasant?"

Every head in the media pool seemed to turn in unison towards Jennifer Lott. The cameramen began moving around trying to get in a position that would allow them to pan from Lott to the agent or capture them both in the same frame.

The agent's expression was unchanged but for a slight squinting of the eyes as if they'd been hit with a bothersome glare. He knew he had to respond but the question was unexpected. He spoke slowly as if deciding which word to use just as it came out of his mouth.

"Confidential informants are just that. They have lives outside of their roles with the agency. If what you are saying is true, his death was most probably unrelated to anything he was doing for the FBI and certainly unrelated to what we have assembled here to discuss."

The mayor, whose face had lost all color when he heard Lott's question, looked as if he wanted to applaud the agent's answer. Instead he leaned in towards the podium as if speaking in a non-existent microphone.

"I would like to thank you all for being here today. Once the investigation is ..."

"Excuse me Mayor. I have a follow up for Agent Rogers."

The mayor looked at Lott but was no longer smiling. Without saying anything, he drifted back to his spot away from the podium and the agent resumed his squinting stare at Jennifer Lott.

"Last night, the Mount Pleasant Police Officer who was investigating the murder of Mahmoud Khalil was herself murdered here in Charleston."

The pool of reporters came to life. Some were taking notes, others took out their phones to send texts.

Agent Rogers' lips pursed momentarily before his expression returned to its stony edifice. The mayor had a feigned look of confusion on his face. The Sheriff, who had been looking straight ahead during the entire press conference, continued to do so, as if sealed off in a room by himself. Only the Solicitor visibly appeared to be taking interest in what the reporter was saying. Solicitor Baker had known of Carver's death minutes after the police had arrived at Jack Peale's apartment. He also remembered Carver. The death of a law enforcement officer would always be a top priority in his office, but it was also personal for him. He had liked Carver, her earnestness, even though it was his phone call that had led to her being fired. Maybe what he felt was guilt. Regardless, other than looking for Peale, there were no leads on the investigation into Carver's death. Until now.

"Do you have a question for me about this local matter?"

"Is your presence at this press conference actually due to the fact that the FBI believes that the murders of its confidential informant and the officer investigating his murder are somehow related to the explosion in downtown Charleston?"

Before Agent Rogers could say "no" the mayor stepped forward.

"We're going to have to end it right here for now ladies and gentlemen. Thank you for coming ..."

He was drowned out by a roar of voices from the reporters. They stood and moved forward as the mayor and Agent Rogers pushed their way through the crowd towards the door. The Mayor, at first, wore a forced smile for the cameras, but after he was jostled one time too many, he shouted "Make way!" and began forcing people aside. Jennifer Lott had moved away from the throng and watched, marveling at the frenzy her questions had caused. She didn't notice Solicitor Baker standing next to her until he spoke.

"You livened this press conference up."

Lott looked at the Solicitor but said nothing.

"Can we go somewhere and talk?"

"Sure."

"My office?"

"Let's go."

Before leaving the building, Lott had been stopped by five different national news outlets wanting an interview. She had declined them all. The local reporters that knew her would also be calling. She would turn them down too. She didn't know much more than what was revealed in the questions she asked and she wasn't going to share what she had held back until the story was published. As she followed Baker through the crowd she began to question why she had agreed to the talk. Was he going to tell her something she didn't know? Doubtful. He wants information from me.

"Have a seat – I'm sorry. What was your name again?"

"Jennifer Lott."

"And who do you work for?"

"*The Sun.*"

He looked at her pleasantly enough but said nothing as if her name and that of her employer befuddled him.

"Well, please, sit down."

She decided to ask a question to at least make it appear she was there to interview the solicitor and not the other way around.

"So, any leads on who killed Carver?"

"Cut the shit, Lott. You're here to tell me what you know, if anything."

Lott straightened in her chair. "Excuse me?"

"Those little grenades you just tossed in the press conference. What's this about an FBI informant being killed in Mt. Pleasant?"

How am I supposed to answer? Am I supposed to answer?

"And don't give me any bullshit about protecting your source ..."

My source is dead.

"I've got a dead cop and if you know something that can help, you need to tell me. Who's the informant?"

"Mahmood Kahlil."

He leaned forward. "How did you get the name?"

They stared at each other as she waited on her gut to tell her what to do.

"Carver."

He leaned back in his chair again as his mind worked on what Lott was telling him.

"What else did she tell you?"

"Not much."

"Tell me what little she said. All of it."

His bullying had stunned her at first, but she was thinking more clearly now.

"She was scared. She thought something might happen to her."

"Like what?"

"It sounded like she believed someone might kill her."

"And someone did." They again just stared at each other. "Do you know why she was at Jack Peale's apartment?"

She started to tell him the truth, but the truth was going to send him off in the wrong direction. She decided that was okay. For now. "The gun that was used to kill Mahmood Kahlil was registered to Jackson Peale."

He stood up behind his desk and picked up the

phone. "Barbara. Get Chief Carlton on the phone. Now."

Hearing the Chief's name reminded Lott of a question that had come to her mind at the press conference.

"Mr. Baker?"

He was still standing, holding the phone to his ear. "Yeah?"

"Who owns the building where the explosion occurred?"

"Some corporation or LLC."

"And who owns the corporation?"

"The Turner Family Trust. That's Chief Carlton's wife's family. Very wealthy. Probably own property all over town." He then realized the connection and hung up the phone. "Why do you ask?"

"I'm going to be writing a story about the explosion. Thought I'd reach out to the owner of the building, ask about tenants, what might be stored there —"

"I mean why did you ask that right after you heard Carlton's name?"

Lott stood quickly to hide her reaction to being caught. "Uh, no reason. Just a coincidence."

Baker stared at her. "Do you mind leaving me your phone number? In case I have more questions?"

"Of course not, as long as you will do the same."

"There's my card."

Lott wrote her number on the back of his business card and left it on the desk. A voice on the intercom gave her the chance to leave.

"Mr. Baker, Chief Carlton is on line 2."

"Ms. Lott, can you see yourself out?"

He watched her leave, knowing she had not told him everything, but unable to grasp what was being withheld. He picked up the phone.

"Chief, we need to pick up Jack Peale."

"Couldn't agree more, Mr. Solicitor. We are looking everywhere."

Charles Carlton stood over Thursday's duct taped body lying on the floor.

"Where are you now?"

"On the way to Peale's. The officer on guard isn't responding."

"Call me when you get there."

"Will do." He hung up the phone and knelt next to Thursday. Carlton held his index finger up to his lips and Thursday nodded. He then slowly peeled the duct tape off of Thursday's mouth.

Thursday whispered, "Knife. On my leg."

Carlton pulled up Thursday's pant leg and unsheathed a six-inch knife and cut the tape on Thursday's wrist and placed the knife on the floor. As Thursday freed himself from the tape around his ankles, Carlton went to the door and called downstairs. "Everything is clear up here. Stay with the body. I'm coming down." He then turned to Thursday and hissed "Disappear!"

Three minutes later, tiny Whitsett Street was again clogged with vehicles with flashing lights. Neighbors watched from their porches and postage stamp lawns as EMS and police officers moved back and forth from the street to Martha's home. Chief Carlton lingered long enough to bring a sergeant up to date on what he and two members of his entourage had found when they arrived: the body of the officer assigned to guard Peale's apartment lying on the foyer floor. They had searched the house and Peale's apartment. Both were empty.

Plummet

As his caravan moved rapidly down Calhoun Street a dull ache built pressure behind his eyes. Carlton could feel the situation slipping from his control. Time to get it back. The only outcome that allowed him, his career and his family to escape all of this unscathed was for Peale to die. Peale probably knew that now too. He didn't have a chance to question Thursday but his duct-taped body told Carlton he had run into Peale. Who else could it have been? Now Peale not only knew he was a target, he would also know it was Thursday that was trying to kill him. How long will it be before he figures out Thursday isn't FBI? How long before he puts the rest of it together? Hell, he probably already has. The burning liquid circulated in his gut again, trailing electric pain that made him wince. He rolled down the window of the SUV, closed his eyes and let the air rush over his face.

"Where to Chief?"

Good question.

38.

*P*eale had made his way to the Office and hid in the alley until Sam arrived. He had no one else to turn to. By now, every person that paid attention to the news would know that law enforcement was looking for him Even contacting Sam was a gamble. But from now on, every move Peale made would be a gamble.

As it turned out, Sam was more than eager to hide a fugitive.

"Don't tell anyone. Not even Jess."

"No. I won't. I wouldn't." Then, after a pause. "Did you really kill that cop? She looked hot on the news, I mean her picture. She looked attractive. But I guess you had to -"

"Sam. I didn't kill anyone. Listen to me. This is dangerous. The person that killed Officer Carver also wants me dead. He will be looking for me. Are you sure you want to be involved?"

"Oh, I'm sure." The look on his face told Peale that Sam had no idea what he was agreeing to.

"Then let's go to your place."

"Now?"

"Yes. Now. I've got to go somewhere to think. I've got to figure this out." Concern finally showed itself on Sam's face. He looked doubtful. "What's wrong?"

"My place, it's...well it's..."

"What? You have a roommate?"

"No."

"Then what's the problem?"

"It's not clean."

Peale cursed. "Sam, someone wants to kill me. The police want to arrest me for murder and god knows what else. I don't give a shit what your place looks like."

Thirty minutes later, Peale was following Sam up the wooden steps to the front door of a mobile home. Sam stopped at the door. "Now, remember, I wasn't expecting company."

"Sam. Open the goddamn door before someone sees me."

Before Peale's eyes adjusted to the scene inside, the odor hit him. It was offensive but not identifiable, a portmanteau of mold, rotting food, animal urine, kerosene and something sweet like a room deodorizer that was failing at its job.

"Wait here."

Peale's eyes then took in the room. The centerpiece was a card table covered by a pile of old bits of food, soda cans, Styrofoam food containers, fast food bags and paper cups that spilled onto the floor, which was covered by a carpet that squished under Peale's feet. A couch that leaned dramatically from one end to the other sat against the wall.

"Uh, let me clear a path for you ..."

Sam used the side of his foot to move garbage out of the way. Chicken wing bones bounced around as he tried to kick them towards the wall. "I'll turn on the light." A single bulb hanging from the ceiling by an extension cord cast a weak yellow light in the room. A crashing sound caused Peale to flinch and look to his right, just in time to see a large iguana slide off the top shelf of an entertainment center against the wall opposite the couch. The green lizard shuffled across the floor towards Sam, causing Peale to back against the door and grab the handle.

"Thomas! Are these your bones? Bad iguana!"

"What the fuck is that?"

"That's Thomas. He's harmless."

As if playing his part in a routine, the lizard flared the spines on its back, opened its mouth and hissed.

"Is it legal to have that thing?"

"Is it legal to kill people?"

Sam was right. Sharing a dump with a hostile reptile was his only option at the moment. He had considered calling up Maggie but didn't want to be in her debt, especially under her roof. Thinking of Maggie suddenly changed Peale's opinion of Sam's hovel and his roommate.

"Okay. No problem. But Sam, this place is a shit hole."

"I tried to warn you."

"You did. But I'm desperate." He looked around. "Where do I sleep?"

"Well, you can take the couch there or there's a bed in the back."

"Where do you sleep?"

Sam shrugged. "Wherever."

Peale walked to the hallway that led to the other rooms.

"Wait!"

"What?!"

"Don't go in the room on the left. The bedroom's on the right. You can go in there." Peale gave Sam a long questioning look. "And let me check the bathroom before you go in it."

"No problem. Any more animals?"

"None that I released." Sam's laughter at his joke faded under Peale's glare.

"Can I go to the kitchen?"

"Sure. But why? I mean, I don't really keep food."

Peale leaned and looked around Sam into the dark kitchen. "I see a refrigerator."

"It's not plugged in."

"The light. It's hanging by an extension cord from the ceiling."

"Yeah that. Well, if you want to turn on a light, you just plug it into an extension cord."

"Why?"

"Because that's the only source of electricity."

"And where is the other end of the cord plugged in?"

"Does it matter?"

Peale didn't respond. "Hot water."

"No. But I like cold showers don't you? Invigorating."

Peale told himself he wouldn't be there long enough to need a shower and the lie made him feel better.

"Do you have garbage bags?"

"No. Why?"

Peale shoved the brief case across the top of the card table knocking more garbage onto the floor. He opened the brief case and pulled out what was left of the money Staci had given him and handed a few bills to Sam. "Go buy some. And some cleaning supplies."

"Like what?"

"Just tell someone you need to clean up a shit hole of a trailer and to give you what you need."

"And buy some food – that I would eat."

"I usually just order delivery."

"But I can't take the risk that a delivery guy would recognize me. Buy some frozen dinners. You have a microwave?"

"Yeah."

"How about the freezer, does it work?"

"You got to plug it in."

"Buy some frozen dinners and canned soup. Oh, and get some bottled water."

39.

By the time Sam returned Peale had several piles of garbage throughout the trailer. After putting the garbage into bags, Sam left for the Office and Peale sat down at the card table where Sam had placed his laptop. He needed to know what was being reported on the news. The immediate stories were brief. The national news reported nothing other than an explosion of unknown origin had injured several people, that terrorism was still being considered and the investigation was underway. The local news followed the same generalizations except for one. *The Sun* mentioned the death of Carver and Khalil and the owner of the building that was destroyed in the explosion: the Turner Family Trust which benefitted two people, Rasha Carlton and Staci Turner. Peale recognized the reporter's name. *That's the same reporter that was questioning me about my gun and Khalil.* He had felt safe in Sam's trailer but reading Lott's article made him want to run. *She knows it's all connected, that I'm connected. But why didn't she mention me?*

Plummet

No connection between the deaths of Carver and Khalil and the explosion were made in the story. Meshing the two seemingly unrelated stories would make no sense to anyone reading the article. Except me. Is she trying to send me a message? Then it hit Peale. He wasn't the only one that would realize she was seeing a connection between Khalil and the explosion. Staci will know. Thursday will know. Peale sat back with a thought.. It was as if his mind had opened a door that had previously been locked. Thursday isn't FBI. Thursday killed Carver. He came to my apartment last night to kill both me and Carver. So, who does he work for? Not Staci He wanted me to give him info on what Staci was doing, same as...

The realization that Charles Carlton had probably tried to have him killed and did kill Carver made Peale stand up from his chair. His first impulse was to take off, leave town, get as far away as possible. No. You're safe right here – for now. You need to think. Stay calm and think. Peale walked into the kitchen area for no reason other than to move around as he tried to process what he knew. Why kill Carver? Hell, Carver knew it was my gun that killed Khalil and she was looking at me as the prime suspect. But so was Jennifer Lott ...

Peale went back to the computer and scrolled to the bottom of Lott's article and moved the cursor over Lott's contact e-mail at *The Sun*. He hesitated. Others may have access to her email. Others may be watching her email. No one was going to trace Sam's email. He had an onion router for reasons Peale didn't want to think about. But telling Lott that she was in danger in an email that could be read by others might put her in more danger. But he could think of no safer way to contact her. So, he decided to be cryptic and hope she could guess the sender. He typed:

Carver was a good cop. She knew what she was doing. Died much too soon.

264

He signed it Sig, guessing she could make the connection with the gun that killed Kahlil.

He clicked < SEND > and leaned back on the couch. Across the small room sitting in a folding chair was Billy Shores. Still mangled, one side of his face was swollen, a dark, reddish hole in his cheek where a bullet had passed through. But this time, he was different. He was no longer the affable ghost. He was menacing. His face spread grotesquely into a wide, damaged smile rimmed with broken, bloody teeth, his eyes dark and malevolent. "I found you."

Lott was reading emailed responses to her article, mostly claiming to know who killed Carver and Khalil and why. She read each of those carefully looking for any reason to believe its sender could be legit. But they were all bogus, just attention-seekers, nuts or someone trying to fuck with her. A few simply complimented her on the article. One criticized her, calling her article trash, saying it belonged in "one of those publications on the checkout aisle at the grocery store" which made Lott smile. Then she clicked on the newest email and read it. The sender was Iggy Tom. At first, she thought nothing of it, but after returning to her inbox, something made her click on it again. She read the email a second time. It was nothing more than a compliment to Carver but something in the wording suggested Lott should respond. Someone with a username Iggy Tom takes the time to send me an email saying something nice about Carver and signs it Sig. Why use a different name than the username? Carver had never struck her as someone with a lot of friends but that only made her realize she didn't know Carver at all. Maybe it was a friend. Or family. So why not say so? She decided to reply.

Did you know her well?

The response froze her with fear: Not really. I was with her when she died. Her first response was visceral. She jumped out of her chair and moved away from the computer as if the words on the screen were lethal. Her mind fumbled with what it could mean. Just someone fucking around, a sick joke – No! Why not come out and say it in the first email? Why risk me not responding? – Do they know where I live? Should I get out of here? And go where? – If they wanted you dead, why email you? The last thought calmed her some and she started to think more clearly. If it's not the killer, it was someone who was there when she was killed. It didn't take long for the answer to come to her. Jackson Peale. She leaned over and read the email again. Sig. That's not the name of the sender, it's the name of his gun. That's the kind of gun that killed Khalil. She stood in the middle of the apartment wondering what it could mean. If it is Peale, does that mean Peale didn't kill Carver? And if he didn't, who did? She looked at the screen and told herself she had no way of knowing Peale sent the email. But that's why he signed it *Sig*. That was enough for her. She had to go with it. She sat down at the computer and sent a response.

I'd like to meet somewhere and talk about it.

That's too risky.

For me or for you?

Both of us, now that you've written that article.

The article hadn't exactly linked the deaths of Carver and Khalil with each other or the explosion either, but the implication was there for anyone to see. And if the killings and explosion were related, the people responsible would know that she had made the connection. She typed the obvious questioned.

Did you kill Carver?

No.

Khalil?

No.

For some reason she found herself believing what she

was reading. Lott decided to follow a hunch.

What caused the explosion?

A bomb.

Her heart began pounding in her chest. She had no way of proving any of this was true but she believed it was and she knew the person sending the emails was Jackson Peale.

Were you involved in the explosion?

Involved? Yes.

How were you involved?

I was supposed to take the bomb to the target.

So the target wasn't the building on King Street?

No. I left it there on purpose.

Why?

She waited on a response but after a few minutes she knew the conversation was over, for the time being anyway. But she was now convinced of what had been only a suspicion: the killings of Carver and Khalil and the explosion were connected. How they were connected was still a mystery. She considered the possibility that Peale had been hired to menace Charles Carlton's family, but that theory didn't fit with Peale contacting her like this. Lott leaned back in the chair and reviewed what she had learned. First, the explosion was caused by a bomb. Second, the Turner's building on King Street may not have been the target. Third, Peale claims he was supposed to take the bomb to another location but left it at King Street on purpose. Lott took out a note pad and wrote the following questions:

Who wanted Peale to take the bomb to another location?

Why???

How did Peale get into the Turner building?

Lott looked back over the emailed conversation. Peale said he had left the bomb in the King Street building. So does that mean the bomb was already there? Or that he took it there?

The questions came but the answers didn't. Lott felt she was missing something obvious. Frustration crept into her mind, threatening to undo the chain of thought she was putting together.

Keep It Simple Smartass. Her mind returned to a previous thought: Peale was hired to do this to Carlton, the Turner family. For some reason she couldn't accept it. It didn't feel right. But as a theory, it worked as well as anything else she had, if not better. On the notepad she wrote Theories and underlined the word. Beside a number A1" she wrote: Jackson Peale killed Khali and Carver and blew up the King Street building because he was either (1) hired by someone to do it or (2) did it of his own accord. Except for the lack of a strong motive, it was straightforward, simple. The kind of theory law enforcement would clamp down on and not let go of. After writing down the second theory she could see the attraction of the first: Unknown person used Peale's gun to kill Khalil, unknown person killed Carver in Peale's apartment and Peale left bomb at King Street, foiling unknown person's attempt to bomb another location. The first theory pointed to Peale as the one and only suspect. Under the second, the suspect was a blank space, To Be Determined. Either Peale did it all or he has been the target of a masterful set up. She re-read each theory wondering if she was leaving something out. But nothing more came to her, only the bothersome feeling that Peale was set up. So if Peale didn't kill Carver and Khalil and foiled some attempt to bomb someone or something in Charleston, who did kill them, who wanted to set off the bomb? That's where everything goes off a cliff into nothingness. I have to keep looking. But where? Something she knew hinted at the answer, she could feel it but couldn't see it. Frustrated, she threw the notepad down and it bounced of the computer's keyboard and fell on the floor. When she reached to pick it up her eyes fell on the last question. How did Peale get into the Turner building? The answer was so obvious, coming to her as if she was reading the question for the first time. He was let in? But who let him in and were they involved also? She noticed her heart beating faster and a surge of adrenaline. She was on to something. Then there was Solicitor Baker's suspicions when she had asked about the building's owner in his office earlier that day. Does he suspect the Turner's are somehow involved in this? I don't see it. How would he know that Peale was in that building and someone had let him in? He wouldn't. But he was thinking that I was making a connection between the Turner's and the explosion, and I guess I was. If Peale isn't behind it all, Carlton and /or his family is the next best choice. Only someone in the Turner family could answer the questions she had. Neither Chief Carlton or his wife were likely to take her call so she decided on the surprise visit. Not to Chief Carlton's office, but to the Turner residence. She grabbed her keys and left the apartment.

40.

"I want you to read an article."

"Have you found out anything about Staci? Have you heard anything?"

"Not yet. But we will. Right now, I need for you to read this article."

Rasha started to throw her phone across the room but stopped and held it against her chest instead, fighting back the anger, frustration and fear that was threatening to overwhelm her. Tears rolled down her cheeks as she put the phone to her ear.

"I know you don't give a damn about Staci, but don't rub it in my face by asking me to read some goddamn article!"

"Rasha, this is important. It's about Staci."

"What do you mean?'

"The article. It connects Khalil to the bombing."

"That's impossible. Who would write something like that?"

"It's a local, online paper and doesn't make any direct connection but it's enough."

"Enough for what?"

"At the very least the press is going to be beating down the door."

"Well make sure they don't."

"Look, I know you're worried about Staci and despite what you think, I'm worried too. But we have to stay focused on everything that is happening. We will get Staci back. All those people want is money."

A cold darkness spread inside Rasha as if she already knew Staci was dead. The people that had Staci didn't want money. They wanted to be feared and they were. Ransoming Staci wouldn't enhance that fear and could even diminish it. Only cruelty would continue to feed that fear. Cruelty that would send a clear message that failure is not tolerated of anyone. Her husband didn't understand and didn't care to understand. If her daughter survived, it wouldn't be due to her husband's efforts.

"Rasha?"

Drifting away into her own thoughts, her response was barely a murmur. "What?"

"You need to read the article. Please."

She ended the call without saying goodbye.

Fifteen minutes later, after she had read the article, Jennifer Lott was knocking at her door.

At first she didn't know who the housekeeper was talking to, but as the conversation continued, the voices became louder, more persistent and eventually the name Jennifer Lott pierced through everything else that was being said. Rasha walked to the front door.

The housekeeper was blocking the entrance and seemed embarrassed when Rasha appeared next to her.

"I am so sorry Mrs. Carlton. This woman is with the paper. I told her you would not speak with her."

"It's okay Mrs. Rutledge, I can handle this."

The housekeeper gave Lott one last fierce look and disappeared into the house.

"What can I do for you?"

Lott started to fire off questions until she saw Rasha's face. What she saw surprised her. The woman had been crying and looked distraught. Guilt raced around inside her and the questions she had lined up in her mind began to break apart. She heard herself saying "I can come back later if now isn't a good time..."

"No. There is something I wanted to tell you."

Lott thought the woman had her mistaken for someone else.

"Ms. Carlton, I'm a reporter from *The Sun*. My name is Jennifer Lott ..."

"I know who you are. I read your article about the bombing, about my family."

Lott prepared herself for the verbal assault. So that's why she's crying. I dared to drag her family into the papers.

"Ms. Lott, I'm asking..." she faltered, then continued "no, I'm begging you, not to print anything else about our family in the paper."

"Ms. Carlton, one of your buildings was destroyed on King Street. It may have been a bomb. It's news. I have to report it. I have to ask questions."

The woman was shaking her head, crying again. "You don't understand. They have my daughter. They will kill her. It may already be too late..."

"Wait! Who has your daughter? What are you talking about?"

"I can't say anymore. I'm taking a chance telling you this much so I'm begging you, no more. Please."

Lott stood in the door not knowing what to make of what she was hearing. Rasha Carlton stopped crying and stood a little taller before delivering one last line before closing the door. The words froze Lott with fear.

"After that article you wrote, they may be coming after you now."

41.

The solicitor was at his desk, talking on the phone when Pete Martin walked through the door of his office. With Jackson Peale's disappearance and Charles Carlton's announcement that he was running for the congressional seat vacated by the resignation of Richard Haynes, the solicitor had decided that the investigations into Billie Carver's murder and the bombing on King Street needed to become more, in house.

Peter Martin was an investigator for the Solicitor's office and had been for more than 28 years, hired after his discharge from the Army where he was an investigator for the Army Criminal Investigative Command. Baker liked having an investigator investigating cases for him, one who wasn't employed by a sheriff or one of the police chiefs in his circuit. But it was more than just a matter of control. Peter Martin was an excellent investigator. He was smart. Experienced. He was also divorced and his one daughter was almost thirty and off on her own. The man had no hobbies that Baker knew of. As far as Baker could tell, Pete Martin woke up, investigated his cases all day and at some point went back to sleep. If he had wanted to, Martin could have retired and lived off his military and state pension while chasing a golf ball around coastal Carolina golf courses the remaining days of his life. But Peter Martin didn't play golf. He didn't fish. All he did was investigate cases and, occasionally, testify in court as a witness for the prosecution. His appearance in the solicitor's office was so commonplace that neither man acknowledged the other. Martin quietly sat in one of the chairs across the desk from the solicitor waiting for the phone call to end. He looked over at the three large, arched windows. The sky behind the windows glowed orange with the setting sun making the windows appear to be large, orange doors. To Martin, each door represented a different aspect of the case that he would soon be referring to as the "King Street Bombing." The first door represented the bombing itself, the second represented the murder of Billie Carver and the third, the murder of Mahmood Khalil. He had come to the early conclusion that all three were connected. The doors did not open to different rooms or lead to different paths. No matter which door was opened, he believed the same person – or persons – would be found standing on the other side. He didn't know the identity of those responsible at this point, but he felt sure it wasn't Jack Peale. The Solicitor wasn't convinced. In his mind, Peale was the prime suspect for both murders because he could be connected to both. Martin had to admit that, at the moment, Peale was the only common denominator for the Carver and Khalil cases. But he knew enough of Jack Peale to doubt he pulled the trigger. And nothing they had learned tied him to the bombing. According to the FBI, the explosion was caused by the ignition of acetone peroxide, most likely triggered by the paging signal from a mobile phone. An intentional act of terrorism. Even if he conceded Jack Peale was the best suspect for the two murders, there was nothing connecting him to the bombing..

He was still looking at the doors, as if waiting for them to open and reveal who stood behind them, when the Solicitor hung up the phone.

"So, we like Peale for the murders but not the bombing, right?"

He smiled. It was a sign the two men had been working too long together if the solicitor could read his thoughts. "No.

I don't like him for any of it."

"Dammit Pete, the guy in 4F was killed with Peale's gun, and Carver was killed in Peale's apartment."

"Motive?"

"He killed Carver because she was on to him for the murder at the apartment. She goes to his place to confront him, he shoots her."

"And the motive for killing a naked guy at the Shoreline that turned out to be an FBI informant?"

The Solicitor stared at Martin without saying anything at first, a look of frustration crawling over his face. "I don't have to prove motive."

"No. But if you want to convict Peale, you better be able to explain why he would want a naked FBI informant dead."

Baker stood up mumbling something Martin couldn't understand.

"And if Peale didn't kill Khalil, there was no reason for him to kill Carver."

"Okay, Sherlock, I guess you've got a better theory?"

"No. I just don't think Peale is our guy. For any of it. Honestly Dan, do you think Jack Peale killed those two people? Really? It's more likely Peale just bumbled his way into the middle of all this."

"Hey, I'm just following the evidence. And what little we got on the murders leads us to one person."

"Agreed. We need more evidence because Jack Peale didn't do it."

"Then who did?"

Pete Martin locked his fingers together and rested his elbows on the arms of the chair. "I don't know."

"Great. You want me to ignore the only suspect and do what? Nothing?"

"Well, no one is pushing you to solve these cases are they?"

"What's that got to do with it?"

"Carver has no family and the Mt. Pleasant Police Department is acting like she never worked there. We don't know who the hell Khalil was and the FBI doesn't seem to give shit. So..."

"So, what?"

"I'm not saying we don't investigate. We have to. We should. But we are probably rushing off in the wrong direction when we should be ..."

"What?"

Pete Martin glanced at the solicitor and looked away. "Nothing."

"Pete, it's been a long week. I'm tired. If you've got something to say, say it."

"Okay. I just find it odd that you never bring up the bombing. Most of our focus has been on the murders and there hasn't been much discussion about the bombing."

The solicitor shrugged. "No reason. I guess there's not much to go on there and it's really the FBI's case anyway."

"Well, I think they're all related. And I think you think they're all related too."

Solicitor Baker sat down in his chair, leaned back and looked at the ceiling. After a few seconds he rocked forward again, turned towards the desk and Pete Martin but didn't look at him. "Pete, are you ready to retire?"

The question was unexpected and slightly menacing. "No."

"Neither am I. But if we start looking into the bombing, and we aren't careful, it could cost us more than our jobs."

Pete Martin knew what was being said and found it telling that Dan Baker wouldn't come out and say that he thought the Carlton family was connected to the bombing. And the killings too. "So, what do we do?"

"Officially, Peale's our man for the killings, or we'll say, a person of interest. That will satisfy the press. We're looking for him, want the public's help finding him so we can ask him some questions. The FBI is investigating the bombing, we help there where we can but, in the end, it's a federal matter."

"And unofficially?"

Baker looked at Martin and almost said There is no >unofficially' but knew that wasn't true. "We're careful. Very careful." then added "Get in touch with Jennifer Lott. We need to talk with her."

42.

Jennifer Lott had a decision to make. She had written an article that, on the surface, appeared to be a routine piece about the bombing and two murders. Other media had published similar stories but none had put all three together in one article. And what responsible journalist would put them all together? Mentioning the murders of Khalil and Carver in the same article as the bombing was sloppy and confusing. Apart from geography, the story offered nothing to connect the three. So why had she done it? The answer was obvious. She wanted to be the first. The first to put them all together. It was her chance to show the world that the reporter from the local on-line paper could break the big story. The rush she had felt at the press conference when all eyes and cameras were on her was something she had never experienced in her career. She had wanted more of it. So she had written the article and posted it on-line for the world to see. No matter what came after, it could never be said she wasn't the first to put it all together. The article was published and dated and now part of the on-line history of the world. It had been nothing but hubris with a splash of inferiority complex thrown in the mix.

If it had been anything more than that she would still be investigating, looking for information that would show her readers how the murders of Carver and Khalil were connected to the bombing. But she wasn't. She was scared. She told herself that she may not write another sentence about the bombing, Carver's murder or the murder of

Mahmoud Khalil. Putting aside her vanity and wanting to win The Race To Report, the article had also been a stick that she used to poke at those responsible. Rasha Carlton had felt it and according to her, so had the people that now had Staci Turner, presumably the same people that were behind the bombing and the murders of Carver and Khalil. It was pathetic. One of the wealthiest, most well-known citizens of Charleston was being held by terrorists, her life in danger, threatened by the same terrorists that had detonated a bomb in downtown Charleston. But instead of rushing out in pursuit of the next article that would let the world know what was happening, Lott was hiding in her apartment with the lights out and the shades drawn, listening to the police scanner. She was afraid to leave her apartment. She was afraid to stay in her apartment. She wanted to hit the rewind button and go back in time to when she was safe, before she had posted that damn article. Ever since her talk with Rasha Carlton her instinct to survive had been sounding alarms that had drowned out all other sound. It was humbling, this realization of what she was or, more accurately, what she was not. She had to admit that she was not the courageous journalist, willing to expose herself to danger and death in pursuit of the truth behind the bombing. What that said about her she didn't like. It embarrassed her. Made her mad. Mad enough to tell herself she wasn't going to run and she wasn't going to hide. But would she pursue the story?

~ ~ ~

Within hours of her talk with Rasha Carlton, Lott had decided on a comfortable role she would play going forward, vague as it was. She told herself she should be more circumspect, more professional with what she posted. This gave her not only some satisfaction for being what she considered a more responsible journalist but also an excuse for prolonging the publication of any more articles that may get her killed. She avoided telling herself she was being careful. I'm supposed to just believe Staci Turner has been kidnaped by terrorists because Rasha Carlton said so? No responsible journalist would print that ... And with that she put aside the lead on one of the biggest stories to ever come out of Charleston. Instead, she told herself she needed to email Jack Peale and tell him about the visit to the Carlton home. His response was immediate.

Did you talk to Staci?

No. Rasha.

Does she know where Staci is?

Lott didn't know Peale's history with Staci Turner but noticed his first two questions were about her.

According to Rasha, the terrorists have her and she's in danger. Rasha was upset.

There was no response for several minutes. Had she been video conferencing with Peale, perhaps she would have seen his reaction: first, that stunned look on his face, then the expression contracting with grief, his hands gripping fistfuls of his hair, then the tears and screaming and him throwing a chair across the room and knocking over a card table. But none of that comes across on a blank screen. She just assumed he'd gone to the bathroom or lost interest. When the response finally came, Lott began to wonder what was going on with Jack Peale.

What did Rasha say exactly?

I don't remember exactly. She was crying and asked me not to publish any more articles about the bombing. Does she know where Staci is?

She didn't say. I don't think she does.

I need to talk with her. Can you take me to her.

R u crazy? U r wanted for murder. I would be breaking the law if I knew where u r and helped u.

To hell with that I need to find out what Rasha knows.

No.

There was a pause in what had been a rapid exchange. Peale's mind was clearing and he told himself that Rasha wouldn't tell him anything and her husband would lock him up. Lott was right. Contacting her would be a mistake.

Can u watch her?

What?

Watch her house, follow her. Let me know where she's going.

The realization of what was going on hit Lott like a light coming on in a dark room. Peale's involved somehow with Staci Turner. She considered what that could mean. If Peale and Staci are involved, that explains the bomb. Staci let him into the King Street building. But did she know about the bomb? Why would the terrorists have Peale deliver the bomb? The fear that had gripped her was giving way to her renewed interest in the King Street bombing. She decided to play along with Peale to see what she could find out.

I can do that. How do I contact you?

Peale gave her a phone number. Text or call but only if u see something. They could be listening.

Lott read the email twice. Who could be listening?

The feds.

Doubt tempered Lott's growing enthusiasm. Peale was beginning to sound like a government obsessed, conspiracy theorist. She remembered her conversation with Peale's former law partner and asked herself if she could trust what Peale was telling her. He could have killed Carver and even Khalil. He may have lost his mind again and created an entire scenario where terrorists and the government are to blame for it all, including the bombing that he admitted being involved in. Lott was close to cutting Peale off for good when she remembered Carver's notes and the way Carver was acting before she was killed. According to Carver, the feds were involved. That was enough confirmation for her to go along with what Peale was asking.

I was going to watch her anyway. For my next article.

It was a lie she was telling herself and Peale.

Don't write anything yet. Wait until Staci is safe. Rasha's probably waiting on a ransom demand. That could come at any time. You need to be there if she leaves.

It made sense. There wasn't a time line on this sort of thing. She was feeling better about herself too, telling Peale she was working on the next article but agreeing to hold off so she wouldn't jeopardize Rasha's efforts to free Staci Turner. Maintaining the appearance of being a journalist would be manageable for now. She just hoped it wouldn't get her killed.

Leaving now. But I won't wait forever on my next piece.

43.

The email came just after 3 a.m. There was no message in the email, only a link. Rasha hesitated before clicking, the tears welling in her eyes, because she knew who had sent the email and what it meant. Part of her wanted to delete it, pretend it didn't exist because she feared what she would see if she followed the link. It was the same part of her that wanted to continue clinging to the hope that she had kept alive since Staci had been taken, hope that she would be freed, that some alternative could be agreed upon. But a stronger part of her wouldn't allow her to delude herself any longer. That part wanted to know the truth, no matter what it brought. So she had clicked on the link.

She knew the person bound to the chair was her daughter although her head hung down over her chest and she couldn't see her face. Someone walked into the picture behind her, the face and head covered except for the eyes and nose. In his hand was a sword that somehow seemed absurd and out of place although Rasha knew what was happening. She wanted to turn away and run, run into yesterday and the weeks and months and years before that and undo whatever she had done that had brought her and her daughter to this unreal place. But she continued to watch, stoically, until another figure entered the picture, grabbed a handful of Staci's hair and jerked her head up. When she saw her daughter's face, the horror became real and wrenched her. A sound came from her like a choked scream and she began to sob. Through tears she watched as the figure with the handful of hair spoke into Staci's ear and Staci sat up straight in the chair. Makeup was smeared in streaks down her face but she was no longer crying. Her long black hair was a mess and strands stuck to her face. Rasha reached out to the screen with her fingers but drew them back as the figure with the sword pulled it back as he spoke in Arabic. Rasha stopped breathing and clutched the chair in front of her as the blade cut through the air, passing through Staci's neck and out the other side. For a moment, nothing happened, as if the sword hadn't touched her, but then the body fell to the side as far as it would go and the head kept falling to the floor. Rasha turned, walked down the stairway as if in a trance, picked up her keys and left the house.

Lott had begun her stake out of the Carlton mansion just after 9:30 p.m. There were no parking spaces within sight of the home at that hour so she had parked the car as close as she could and began the watch on foot. After midnight she was able to relocate her car to a space that gave her enough of a view to see if anyone left the Carlton home in a car. But she hadn't been sitting in the car long before she was dozing off, so she had resumed watching on foot, leaning against the railing above the wall that stood between the harbor and East Battery, across the street from the Carlton home. The wind off the harbor was cool and at times, she would take her eyes off the house and turn to face the harbor, feeling the breeze in her face and looking at the lights on Sullivan's Island. It was during one of these breaks just before 4 a.m. that she heard the sound of a car's ignition behind her. She turned around in time to see the red brake lights and then the white reverse lights on a Mercedes sedan in the Carlton driveway. She ran to her car that was parked about fifty yards away and drove it down E. Battery in time to see the taillights of the Mercedes several car lengths in front of her. She dialed Peale's number. When he answered, he didn't sound like he'd been sleeping.

"What's happening?"

"She just left in her car."

"What direction?"

"North on East Bay."

"Ok. Follow her."

"I am. What do you think I'm doing?"

"How's traffic?"

"Almost non-existent. It's 4 am."

"I'm sorry. I'm just..."

Lott wanted to ask him what Staci Turner was to him but didn't think this was the time. "What do you want me to do, just follow her?"

"For now, yeah. What she does will determine what we do."

The Mercedes continued up East Bay Street, stopping only for a couple of traffic lights. Lott was afraid she'd be noticed because there was very little traffic. Then she realized she hadn't actually seen Rasha get in the car. Someone else could be driving. Should I tell Peale? No. It's her. Keep going. Peale might lose it if I told him that.

"Ok she's turning onto the bridge."

Both cars rose with the bridge as it ascended higher and higher over the Cooper River until it reached its apex and began descending again into Mount Pleasant.

"Looks like we're going to Mt. Pleasant- hold on, she's putting on her brakes..."

The Mercedes slowed down and came to a stop in the right lane. Panic shot through Lott.

"She stopped on the bridge! What do I do!"

"Stop too dammit!"

Lott hit the brakes and she saw Rasha exit the Mercedes in front of her as Lott's car came to a stop twenty yards behind the Mercedes.. Rasha looked back in Lott's direction, turned away and straddled the low cement barrier that separated the pedestrian walkway from the car traffic.

"She's getting on the walkway."

"You've got to follow her."

"She saw me."

"It doesn't matter now. Go."

Lott got out and walked towards the pedestrian walkway. A delivery truck passed by and blared its horn. Another car came slowly by as she was straddling the cement barrier. A voice came from the car "Do you need any help?" but Lott ignored it, all of her attention focused on Rasha Carlton. She was doing something odd and unsettling. Lott had expected her to meet someone or drop something off, but that wasn't happening. Rasha Carlton was climbing the metal fencing on the river side of the walkway. She was forty yards away from Lott but the bridge was well lit and Lott could see everything. Still holding her phone, Lott started to run towards her.

"Nooo! Stop!"

Peale heard Lott screaming over the phone. "What's happening?!? Lott?!? Answer me?!?

Lott ignored the voice in her hand and continued running until Rasha stopped climbing and looked back at Lott. She slowed her pace then came to a stop, shaking her head, her eyes fixed on Rasha's.

"Don't."

Rasha's expression was flat, emotionless but Lott was close enough to see that she had been crying. As Lott started walking towards her again Rasha Carlton turned away from her and disappeared over the side. Lott stood motionless and numb, staring at the spot where she had last seen her, waiting for her to reappear, pleading with whatever had to be appeased in this world to undo what had been done. But there were no miracles to be seen, only the darkness over the water. The voice in her hand brought her back and she held the phone to her ear.

"... answer me! Lott! Goddammit –"

"She jumped.' Lott's voice was calm and quiet, almost too quiet to be heard.

"What?!? What did you say?!?"

Lott cleared her throat and tried to speak louder.

"She jumped off the bridge. Right in front of me, she–"

Peale dropped the phone and began walking numbly towards the kitchen then changed directions towards the door and collapsed to his knees, staring at the floor. He waited as the pain and anger twisted together, first in a small knot inside of him but one that grew quickly, swirling around, throwing off hot shards and growing larger still inside his chest until it erupted out of him, throwing his head back and roaring out in a scream. A scream that pierced the walls of the mobile home and cracked the darkness outside. A scream at the world, the only way he could acknowledge that if Rasha Carlton had killed herself, it meant Staci was dead too.

44.

Before walking out to greet his supporters as the newly elected congressman from South Carolina's First Congressional District, Charles Carlton had stood backstage and marveled at how he had come to this place. He remembered that night, now almost a year ago, that Rasha had told him about her and Staci's involvement with the people that wanted to blow up a synagogue in Charleston, how he had stood on the deck in the early morning darkness and made the decision not to turn them in, to let it play out, to control what was happening and its outcome in an attempt to save his marriage and his political career. His marriage had ended anyway, but not how he had feared it would, and his political career had been put into hyper drive. And if that weren't enough, he would inherit the majority of his wife's wealth, as soon as the lawyers had finished the probate process. He smiled at himself, his head dropping and shaking with disbelief at how everything had played out. Did I ever have control? Sure, I made the decision not to turn them in, but after that ... it was all luck.

~ ~ ~

He walked out onto the brightly lit stage to the cheers and shouts of the crowd that had gathered in the ballroom. He stood at a podium, smiling and waving as they clapped and cheered. Two or three times, he recognized someone special in the audience by pointing a finger, clapping himself and mouthing "thank you" for whatever that person had done in helping elect him to Congress. Upbeat music blared across the room as the people sang along with the lyrics, screamed and shouted his name. As much as he enjoyed the adulation he wanted more. This night seemed predestined to him, a moment that was going to happen no matter what else occurred in his life. It had to be more than just luck. This is my path, he told himself, as he continued smiling and waving. My decision to protect myself, to protect my career created a shortcut and opened a door that I had no way of knowing would open to me.

He now felt an impatience to begin working on the more he wanted. Whether the next step was governor or the U.S. Senate, he didn't know, but he knew he wouldn't stay in the House of Representative's any longer than he had to.

Although a Democrat, the conservative voters responded to his public image as a law enforcement officer whose wife and stepdaughter had been murdered by radical, Islamist terrorists, the same terrorists that were thought to have set off a bomb on King Street, leveling a building owned by Charles Carlton's wife and killing a passerby in the explosion. After the bombing, terror was the issue foremost in the minds of voters and candidate Carlton passionately vowed that if elected, the people of the First Congressional District would be represented by the most committed anti-terrorist congressman in Washington. His opponent's efforts to link him to the liberal democrats in Washington were mostly ignored. Some left leaning pundits complained that the election had the look and sound of a Republican primary, not a special election between candidates of opposing parties. Carlton said and did little that contradicted their criticisms. It was a conservative district and he wanted to win the election, not make a stand.

~ ~ ~

After almost a year, there had been no arrests in connection to the bombing on King Street or the deaths of Rasha Carlton and Staci Turner. The unresolved crimes left a feeling of unease in most of the city's residents, but the overall sentiment seemed to be that the failure to bring anyone to justice was the fault of the FBI and not local authorities, an idea that was implicit in Carlton's campaign. Officially, the FBI and local authorities were still investigating, but the cases had gone cold. And Congressman Carlton intended to be in charge of when those cases heated up and when they went cold again, the temperature dependent on what was best for his political aspirations.

It was past 2:30 in the morning when he arrived at the large, empty house on the Battery. After the grounds and home were cleared by his private security team, he told them to go home, get some rest and return by 8:00 am as there was a lot of work to do. When the door closed and he knew he was alone, the emptiness of the house suddenly weighed on him. He hated to be alone and he knew he wouldn't sleep. At the end of the after – election party he had talked with an attractive staffer about coming home with him for what remained of the night, but they had both agreed it probably wasn't a good idea. But standing in the foyer he reached into his pocket for his phone and considered calling her anyway. Don't do it. What would she think when she realized you didn't want sex, only company? Plus, it would be something she would have on you ... So, he walked up the stairs to his office, making as much noise as he could with his feet without actually stomping, trying to ignore the growing anticipation that someone was going to jump out from a dark corner at any moment, someone with a familiar face, the only someone he still considered a threat to his future: Jackson Peale.

It should have been easy to forget about Peale. Apparently everyone else had. But Carlton couldn't ignore the certainty that Peale was watching. Even that night, during the election victory celebration, there was a moment, while he was standing at the podium before the crowd, when he wondered if Peale was sitting in front of a TV somewhere watching him, or worse, there in the auditorium, hidden among the mass of people. And it wasn't his imagination. Four months earlier, during a fund-raising barbeque on a farm in Beaufort County, Peale had appeared out of the darkness when Carlton had stepped away to take a phone call. Later, Carlton didn't know if it was what Peale had said or the fact that Peale was stalking him that had upset him more. It was probably both.

At first he hadn't recognize the figure and said affably "Damn! You scared the hell outta me!'

But when he heard the voice and then saw the face, his mood changed.

"Sorry about that, Charles, but I don't feel like mingling with the crowd. Besides, what I have to say is private."

"Peale!"

"Things sure have turned out well for you. Congress! That's quite a jump from police chief."

"What do you want Peale?"

"Hell, Charles, I don't know what to call it. I don't believe in justice, so it can't be that. Let's see ... what would you call what I want? Well, I guess you could call it 'impossible'. Can you give me the impossible, Charles?"

"You're fucked up, Peale. You need help. I might just have you locked up ..."

"No, no, no. You and I both know that's not going to happen. You really want to fuck with me, Charles? Do you really want me to tell what I know?"

Carlton scoffed. "What you know? More like what you think you know."

"I've had a lot of time to think, Charles, a lot of time to figure things out. And this is what made more sense to me than anything else. You're responsible for all of it. That hooker in the hotel, my gun killing Khalil, those people arranging the bombing, involving Staci, making her think she had to do it to protect her mother, all the while you were pulling the strings. Tell me something, how much did you pay those people to set off a bomb in your own city, to kill Staci, to drive your wife to do what she did? How much?! Or is it a running tab? You can't put a price on having a congressman by the short hairs..."

Peale had started to lose control and had gotten louder. When people came over to check on the loud voices, Peale had slipped back into the darkness and Carlton let him go, making nothing of it when asked what the loud voices were about. He hadn't heard from him since. Peale had dropped his crazed theory like a hand grenade and run. But he was still out there, planning god-only-knows-what. There were enough fragments of truth in what Peale believed to kill Carlton's political career while it was still in the crib. He hadn't orchestrated anything but he had used their deaths – and his status as grieving husband – to get elected. If it was known that he knew his wife and stepdaughter assisted with the bombing and that he tried to cover up their involvement, he wouldn't just face political ruin, he would go to prison. The truth wasn't buried deep enough to conceal for long if anyone cared to look. And now that he was a Congressman, they would look. They would dig. They wouldn't stop. All it would take is an anonymous call from Jack Peale.

He went to the computer in his office and sent an encrypted email.

Have you made any progress?

He closed the browser and shut down the computer, not waiting on a response because there wouldn't be one for several hours. Over the past two months since he had hired Thursday to find Peale and eliminate the threat, he had learned that Thursday responded only when he was ready and never right away. It pissed Carlton off, but he was stuck with Thursday. After Peale had made his appearance and Carlton decided something had to be done, he wanted to hire someone else since Thursday hadn't exactly performed as promised the first time. But the idea of involving another person in the situation didn't seem wise. Bringing in another person is just one more person that could extort me. He had decided he was stuck with Thursday and Thursday didn't try concealing that he knew it. They only corresponded by email over an encrypted "onion" router and he would reply to Carlton only after making Carlton wait.

He walked to the deck that overlooked the backyard. The lawn glistened faintly in the moonlight. The night was still and quiet and he was suddenly tired. He laid down on a chaise lounge, stretched out and closed his eyes. How hard could it be to find Peale? Where would a guy like Peale go? He can't have much money. The daughter and ex-wife have been watched, same as the aunt in the nursing home and the dive bar he spends most of his waking hours in. But there's been no sign of him. I wonder where Thursday is right now? What if Thursday has Peale and has been holding out on me ... He could see them together sitting at a table in some shack outside the city, plotting against him. They are laughing and drinking whiskey and then Peale snorts some cocaine and laughs some more. Thursday pulls out a gun and aims it at a picture on the wall and fires wildly, laughing.

Peale stands up from his chair, swaying and walking towards Thursday. "Give me that goddamn gun. You can't shoot wurf a fuck. No ... no wonder I'm shtill ahlife." Peale rips the gun from Thursday's hand and spins around to face his target. "I'll shut the muhver fucker thoo 'is gahdamn ... eye." Eyelids droopy and body wiggling like a spaghetti noodle, Peale fires off a shot. Carlton looks closer and sees that the target is a smiling picture of himself, one of his campaign posters. The bullet has blown a hole in his eye. Peale turns back to Thursday, lets out a derisive huff and throws the gun onto the table.

"You know what we need?"

Peale takes a drink and shakes his head.

"Women!"

Peale breaks into a laugh and wipes his mouth with his sleeve.

"We got wimmen!" He looks towards a door. "Come on in here, babe!"

Carlton didn't believe what he was seeing. Rasha walks into the room wearing nothing but panties, a bra and high heels. Peale puts his arm around her and turns her towards Thursday.

"This, is a woman. And this is what you do to a woman."

Peale leans over and tries to get a mouthful of Rasha's bra cup but she pushes him away.

"Hold on, hot shot. You've got to do something for me before we get into all of that."

Peale looks up, feigning a confused look, then breaks into a wide drunken sneer. "Oh yeah. Bring him on out here!"

Dread fills Carlton as Staci walks into the room dressed just like his wife, but in her hand is a rope she holds over her shoulder. Carlton can't see what the rope is attached to, but as Staci continues into the room another figure appears at the other end. Staci jerks the rope and Carlton stumbles into view. "Where do you want him."

Thursday stands from his chair and picks up the gun. He aims it at Carlton.

"Just hold him right there."

The gunshot explodes and Carlton screams out.

"Sir! Mr. Congressman."

Carlton knew that he is still alive. He missed me? I'm still alive! I've got to get out of here…

He flung his arms and legs but they were holding him down and he cried out "Help!"

"Mr. Congressman! Wake up! It's me, Jim."

Carlton's eyes opened and he couldn't make sense of the scene. He saw a face, a face he recognized and he was outside, no longer in the shack. "They're here ... they ..." Gradually, it all slid away and he saw that he was on his back porch, the sky growing lighter with the morning sun. A member of his security team stood over him. "I heard shouting and came out here. I thought ..."

"Yeah ... Yeah. Right. Well, I'm good ... I must've dozed off." Carlton stood up stiffly. "What time is it?"

"7:15."

"Good. Uh, go downstairs. The housekeeper should be making breakfast. She'll get you some coffee, breakfast, whatever."

"Are you okay, sir?"

Carlton, let out a sound that was kind of a laugh and kind of something else. He was drenched in sweat. "Yeah. I'm fine. Now let me get a shower and I'll be down in a few minutes."

45.

The public and media interest in the King Street Bombing case had waned over the months since it happened. But the investigation had never stopped for Solicitor Baker and Peter Martin. They were still meeting on Friday evenings to go over the file, although it had bogged down some time ago.

The tidy conclusion that terrorists had simply chosen to target a wealthy Charleston family with ties to the Middle East seemed to be good enough for everyone. Charles Carlton certainly embraced it and with nothing else to hold their attention, media rushed on to more current attractions. The murder of Billie Carver was left cold, the popular explanation being that she was killed by her lover, a former lawyer that was a known alcoholic and drug addict. Mahmoud Khalil was never mentioned, forgotten, just like most other people found dead in places like the Shoreline Apartments.

"I still haven't located Jackson Peale." Peter Martin always began his report with what he referred to as the "top priorities."

"And I still haven't interviewed Charles Carlton because, well ..."

"Because he was just elected to Congress and I won't let you ask him if he was involved with the murder of a police officer, the bombing of a building in Charleston –"

"I would word-smith the questions into something less, accusatory. But I understand what you are saying.

But what I'm saying is that this investigation is at a standstill and the obvious way to get it moving is by questioning a person I can't question and another I can't find."

"What about the Mount Pleasant chief, what's his name?"

"Baskin, and we've gone over that. I talked to him early on. He's convinced Peale and Carver were involved. He has a very low opinion of Peale. He subscribes to the theory that Peale killed her. I think I remember him calling Peale a psychotic druggie, or something like that."

"There's something not right about that."

"How so?"

"One of his cops is murdered and he just writes it off as falling for the wrong guy? I'm not buying it."

"So what are you saying? Do you want me to talk to him again?"

"Was Carver really after Peale for the apartment murder? Did Baskin say?"

"From what I remember, he says he wanted her to arrest Peale for it based on the murder weapon, but that she slow played it, gave excuses not to. You know, she wanted to keep investigating. That sort of thing. He said he remembers thinking that was odd but it wasn't until she was killed that he concluded they had something going on."

"So, is he looking for Peale? Does he still think he did the apartment murder?"

"He says he has warrants for Peale's arrest for both murders and if he knew where Peale was he'd have him arrested him for both."

Baker shook his head. "Okay, so what else? Peale hasn't popped in anywhere?"

"He hasn't been back to the aunt's place and hasn't tried to contact the ex-wife or daughter."

"How can you be sure? If I were on the run I'd still try to contact my daughter."

"They have a restraining order against him. They'd call the cops if they saw a car drive by that even looked like his."

"What a piece of shit ..."

"Now, that's surprising."

"What?"

"Being so judgmental."

Baker smiled. "I may be a lawyer, but I'm also a politician."

"Yeah, well I'm not the press. I need for you to be more objective."

"Objective?"

"Yeah. Objective. We're stuck. We have to come up with some new angle or this thing goes into a deep freeze. This investigation has a sh –"

"Yeah, yeah, I know. >The investigation has a shelf life'. I recall you telling me that once or twice before. And I know that. I'm in a bad mood because I'm well aware that this investigation has a shelf life. I've got an office to run. I can't devote the time and resources that this investigation requires. It's just your amigo, and me on a Friday evening each week. I can't get sidetracked. How's that for objective?"

Martin knew the solicitor's personality, his frequent need to blow off steam. He decided to move on.

"I want to question Sam."

"Who's Sam again?"

"Works at The Office. Peale's favorite hangout."

"Right. Why do you want to do that?"

"Because if anyone has had contact with Peale, he's the most likely. From what I've gathered, the guy's a loner. Not much of a life. Nobody pays attention to him. It's not much but we don't have much."

"I don't like it."

"Well, at some point you've got to take me off the leash."

"Do you understand the shit-storm that would form if the press knows I'm investigating Charles Carlton for killing a police officer and setting off a bomb in downtown Charleston?"

"Yes. I understand. But my talking with Sam Weeks shouldn't get back to the press."

"What about Lott?"

"Haven't heard from her since last week. I dropped by her place but no one was there. Hung out for a while. Nothing. She takes her time returning my calls. She's still working. She's had a couple of stories published on *The Sun*'s website recently."

"Yeah I've seen them. Nothing on this though."

"Do you trust her?"

Baker was silent for a moment. Thinking. "I guess I trust her more than I don't. I've always gotten the sense this was personal for her. I don't know why, but I do. Besides, if she was interested in this for her own career, she would be publishing something every week."

Baker walked over to the large windows of his office and looked out over Broad Street. Peter Martin had seen him do this hundreds of times over the years they had been working together. He allowed himself to imagine that the windows were portals into which the solicitor looked into the future, searching for guidance on what decision he should make. But he knew the solicitor wasn't a mystic and that he didn't see anything beyond his office, looking instead at what his mind's eye revealed to him as all the possible consequences of questioning Sam Weeks again. And after considering all of those possibilities, he would decide. Over the years, the decision was usually the best for the situation, even if it wasn't what Peter Martin wanted to hear. Baker turned around and walked back to his desk.

"All right. Do it. But don't squeeze him. If he feels threatened, he may call the press."

"Understood."

46.

After Staci's death, I was in a bad place. Luckily Sam took care of me, letting me crash at his place for as long as I needed, which turned out to be several months. The only thing that kept me from falling into the darkness was the crazy hope that Staci was alive. I had heard about the video from the media of course. But I told myself that videos could be faked, that until her body was found and identified she could still be alive somewhere. All night I would scour the internet for news of her. It was careless, but I told myself that if the FBI hadn't knocked down Sam's door long ago, his onion router had been doing its job and would continue covering my tracks. And I guess it did. For weeks I would drop into every chat room and message board I could find relating to Islamist terrorist networks. There was plenty of discussion about the King Street bombing and Staci's death. There was even talk that Rasha had been murdered too, forcefully thrown off the bridge by the same people that had supposedly killed Staci. Well, I told myself, if what they were saying about Rasha was a lie, why couldn't Staci's death be a lie too?

Initially there was almost unanimous praise for the attack, but after a week or so, opinion began to turn. It was a missed opportunity. The target was insignificant. Charleston itself was a poor choice for an attack. As talk of the bombing began to fade, the most commonly shared opinion was that the bombing and murders were more of an isolated attack on the family of Christian Wilcox Turner, retribution for some wrong committed years before by the billionaire against the wrong person. The explanation seemed to make sense. Although several groups had taken credit for the bombing right after it happened, none were repeating their claims in the weeks that followed. Sightings of Staci at this place or another had me desperately trying to contact the people making the claim, but none responded. Sam explained that I couldn't just drop in on a chat room on the dark web and expect to be accepted. I tried anyway. But after a couple of weeks, the bombing in Charleston was no longer a topic anyone wanted to discuss. Staci had disappeared again.

So I was Sam's guest for several months longer than I thought I would be. It wasn't until Sam came home early one morning after work and told me that some investigator from the solicitor's office had dropped by the Office asking questions that I decided it was time to move on. If Peter Martin knew to ask about me at the Office, he would also be tailing Sam back to his place and stake it out. I got out of there that same night. But where to go? Whitsett Street was off the list. Even if I could have snuck in, my neighbors would be on constant alert for my return. Jess was a possibility, or so I told myself, but a part of me was confident she would turn me in. Jennifer Lott would probably take me in for a night or two but I had to assume she was being watched also. So I worked down the list in my mind to the less savory options. Maggie would let me stay as long as I met her conditions and I wasn't willing to do that for any amount of time. That left Todd Burley, if he was still around. So that last night, just before dawn, I had Sam drive me to a drive through car wash at a gas station a few hundred yards up the highway from the Fox Run Apartments, the last known residence of Todd Burley. It was after 6:00 am when Sam drove into the car wash. Half way through, I opened the door and got out with the garbage bag I had put all of my clothes in, getting soaked in the process. But if Sam was being tailed, I couldn't let him drop me off at Burley's door step. I stood against the wall inside the carwash for fifteen minutes before I went inside the convenience store, bought a twelve pack of cheap beer and walked to the Fox Run.

There was no answer when I knocked on Burley's door. I tried the knob and it was locked. Shit. Where would Burley be at 6:30 in the morning? Asleep. He may not even be home yet. Nothing to do but wait. I felt exposed hanging out alone in the parking lot, but skulking around the back of the place would look more suspicious. So I pulled up a plastic chair that was overturned in front of the apartment next door and took a seat with the beer and garbage bag next to me. Maybe I was taking a chance sitting like that in the open, but I didn't feel like I was. The place struck me as a haven for those oblivious to anyone or anything that didn't get them off or get them high. And I doubted that anyone coming or going from the Fox Run wanted to involve law enforcement in his life. The only concern is if the cops showed up, which I had to admit was a possibility. So I leaned back in the chair and kept an eye out for trouble. Everything was quiet until a guy came out of an apartment across the parking lot and got into a Jeep Cherokee, which was the nicest ride in the lot. A minute later, out came a woman in jeans and halter top. She stood in front of the door looking around like she was expecting to find a ride or something. When she saw me, she started in my direction. Halfway across the lot she starts talking.

"Heyyyy luvvverrr."

I looked away from her, toward the highway, hoping she would get the message.

"You lookin' to party? You look lonely, you need a friend? Huh? I'm your friend."

I turned and looked at her. She was standing six feet in

front of me, one hand on her hip and the other adjusting her halter top. She was Southeast Asian, probably a Filipina.

"I'm just waiting on someone."

"Let's go inside. Hey, what you have in bag?"

She used this as an excuse to put a hand on my shoulder, lean over and with the other hand open the bag. "Ohhh! You a party animull! Tammy party with you all day if you like." She straddled my lap and rested her arms on my shoulders, then, in a much quieter voice, gave me the hard sell.

"You wan' my juicy pussy for your big cock? You put your big cock anywhere in Tammy. You —"

"That sounds tempting but could you help me with something?"

"Yeah baby. Twenty dolla and Tammy help you with all of it."

"No. That's not what I meant. But I will pay you. Do you know the guy that lives here?"

"Todd?"

"Yeah. Have you seen him?"

"Todd no fun no more. Got mean, ugly girlfriend. Said nasty things to me." She made a pouty face to indicate how much this hurt her.

"Are they here?"

"No. Girlfriend took him to her house. Said he don't live here again. Fat, ugly woman. Look like a pig."

Did she mean Maggie? There's no way, not even for a lowlife like Burley.

"He doesn't live here?"

She shook her head as she licked her lips and spread the top of my shirt apart. She didn't seem to be fazed by the dampness of my clothes. "But I live here. You come to Tammy's. We party all day and all night."

"I've got a better idea. Which one do you live in?"

She pointed across the parking lot to the door she had

come out of a few minutes earlier.

"Well baby doll, let's go talk business."

She continued with her hooker talk after we got inside her apartment until I convinced her that I didn't want sex, just a place to crash for a few days.

"This no hotel. It's my place. I work here."

"I'll pay you. How much do you charge if a guy stays the night?"

She twisted her mouth, put her finger to her chin and looked off across the room, as if she was adding up the various costs of such an arrangement.

"Five hundred."

"What? You get 500 bucks a night?" I immediately realized that she might be insulted by my incredulous tone. She was.

"Get out! You no fuck, you no pay, you go!"

"Hold on. Wait. Wait." She was grabbing at my arm as I jerked it away. "I'm sorry. You have to work, I understand that." She stopped grabbing. "How about this: I pay you $200 per night and you can keep seeing your customers? I'll leave when you're working."

She was still mad but I could tell my offer appealed to her. Again, she took on the same expression although I can't imagine what she was thinking about. Four hundred dollars a night had to be more than she was making in a full day of work. Maybe she was working out the logistics of getting me out and the johns in.

"Okay. But if you want sex, it extra."

"Deal."

I looked around the room. I was surprised by how neat it was. There was a funky smell of mold and incense but there was no clutter, no trash. A queen bed with a thin, brown spread sat in the middle of the room against a wall. The bed had been made even though I know her customer had just left. There was a table with a lamp and clock radio next to the bed. Next to the far wall was a round table and two chairs. A small refrigerator was in the corner behind the table. A cheap light with a paper cone around the bulb hung from the ceiling over the table. On the other side of the room was a door that I guessed was the bathroom and next to it a small area that set back far enough that she could hang her clothes from a bar. Under the hanging clothes was a stack of plastic drawers. I was impressed.

"How long have you been here?"

The question seemed to make her sad and irritable.

"Where the money? You pay it now."

I reached in my pocket and pulled off enough money for the first night.

"Here." She took the money and went into the bathroom, shutting the door behind her. Only then did I wonder if she knew I meant I would stay the day and night for $200. She must have stashed the money in the bathroom because she came back out without me hearing the toilet or sink being used.

"I been here two years, three months." She was walking across the room to the refrigerator when she said this. I just nodded and didn't say anything else about it since it seemed to be a touchy subject. An awkwardness settled in as she opened a water bottle she had taken from the fridge. We stood in silence as she drank her water. Just as I was about to say something, her phone rang.

She picked up the phone and looked at the screen. "Hello, Mike. You come see Tammy today?"

And she went into her hooker talk again and arranged a for Mike to come by around 12:00 that day.

"How long should I stay gone?"

"Mike won't take more than hour. You stay in chair outside and I come get you when he leave."

Three times that day I sat in the chair. Not literally, but that's what I called it when she needed to work. When she hung up the phone after a call I'd say "do you need for me to go sit in the chair?" I would sit part of the time, but I'd usually just walk around the place. Once I walked down the highway to the convenience store where Sam had dropped me off. But it didn't matter if I was sitting or walking, I would always be thinking. I thought about Megan and different scenarios where I could work my way back into her life. And Staci, of course, which would lead back to Carlton and the bombing. Later that first afternoon, I was sitting in the chair in front of Todd Burley's old apartment, trying to find a common thread that passed through everything that happened from the night I went out with Burley until Rasha jumped off the bridge into the Cooper River.

Burley finds me at the Post Office ... Staci pays him to spike my drink and take me to the Paradise ... I spend the night with a hooker at motel in North Charleston ... the hooker takes my clothes and gun ... Staci pays me five grand to find her boyfriend ... Carlton asks me to keep him updated on my progress ... I visit the Islamic Center in Columbia ... Maggie tells me the boyfriend has been all over the middle east and is back in Charleston ... I get an anonymous text with an address for the Shoreline Apartments ... I find Mahmoud Khalil dead ... meanwhile Staci and I become lovers ... Carlton wants me to keep him informed on Staci and Khalil ... Thursday pops into the picture wanting the same thing, saying he's FBI ...

I stood up and walked the length of the apartments under the canopy, going over all of it again, which made me realize what a fool I'd been. It also revived the lingering guilt that Carver was dead because of me. But I didn't let that distract me. My mind was focused on following the thread that tied all of this together. If Staci had me drugged, then she arranged for the hooker to steal my gun ... So Staci wanted Khalil dead and needed my gun to do it ... all of that was to frame me for Khalil's murder? Then she asks me to help her with the bombing? And now she's dead. And Rasha is dead too... If there was a thread running through it all, it was too small for me to see. The only fact that was certain was that Carlton was the only person that seemed to have benefitted from any of this, if you could say that a man who had lost his wife had benefitted from anything. He was now a Congressman and probably the only beneficiary of the Turner wealth. He had gone from police chief and a police chief's salary to a congressman and a multi-millionaire. Was it possible that he manipulated all of this after all? I had accused him of it that night at the fund raiser and I had believed it at the time. But that had been nothing but ravings, fueled by the pain of losing Staci and the anger at what she'd done to me. I was just blindly lashing out. But now, looking at it again, I might have just wandered into the truth without knowing it. Carlton was either a master manipulator or lucky as hell. And then there was the hit on me and Carver. Who else would have ordered that? Not Staci. She needed me for the bomb. Carlton was the only possibility I could think of and Thursday was his hit man.

I went back to the plastic chair again, sat down and leaned forward, resting my chin in my palm, my elbow on my knee, oblivious to everything around me. If I kept it simple I could say that Staci framed me for Khalil's death and tried to blow me up. That's simple enough. Carlton wanted to stop it so he wasn't working with her. Thursday is his hit man so he wasn't working with her. Staci ends up dead. Rasha ends up dead. That works doesn't it? So why do I think I'm missing something? I went deeper and deeper, zoning in on everything I knew in its simplest expression. What was missing? What was wrong? Then it hit me, the reason I was having trouble accepting such a simple explanation for everything that happened. Staci actually believed I killed Khalil. I had been assuming she had killed him. That means Khalil's killer is still out there.

But that isn't what bothers me. What bothers me is why? Why would someone other than Staci kill him? And frame me for it?

Later that evening inside Tammy's apartment I sat in a chair at the small table under the light and thought of what to do next. Tammy was sitting on the bed painting her nails after a shower. She only wore a towel and her hair was wet and shiny, smoothly combed back so that it hung down past where the towel was wrapped around her back. There was something beautiful and peaceful about her now. Only then did I realize I hadn't seen Billy Shores or heard from Batista since moving in with her. It was something of a relief, but I knew they were still there, inside me, ready to reappear anytime I go on a bender or my life gets too fucked up. My own personal ghosts, sent to my world by some misfiring neurons as a warning that I had strayed into forbidden places. Maybe I should keep Tammy around as an antidote.

These were my thoughts as I fell asleep watching Tammy. It seemed like only seconds had passed when I was waking up the next morning on top of the covers. Tammy was already awake, the business woman again, completely focused on selling her body for sex.

"I make money today. You have to leave. Come back late tonight. Got four men calling me." I was lying in bed and she was standing over me, irritated and impatient, like the guys were lined up outside the door already.

"Fine. But I need to take a shower."

"Shy-wuh?! That take too long. You go now."

"Fuck that. I'm taking a goddamn shower."

She walked over to where I kept my clothes and the few other things I owned in a large plastic bag, grabbed it, carried it to the door, opened the door and threw the bag into the parking lot.

"Nice."

"Get out. Don't come back."

I would have just taken a shower then left, picking up the bag from the parking lot on my way but for the fact it held – unbeknownst to Tammy – the remainder of Staci's money, still several thousand dollars. While I was outside picking up the bag, I heard the door shut behind me. Part of me wanted to leave, but I needed more time and I wasn't likely to find a safer place. I pulled out $1,000 from the bag and knocked on the door.

"You go or I call the cops."

"Tammy, I'll pay you $1,000 if you let me stay just four more days." My only chance was to appeal to her business logic. That was more than she was likely to make hooking over the same time period with the added bonus that she didn't have to work if she didn't want to.

"You go get money, I let you in."

"I'm holding it right now." She pulled the thin curtain back from the window and I held the money up, spreading it so she could see the bills. The curtain fell and the door opened. As I walked back in she was reaching for the money. I held it over my head so she couldn't reach it.

"Hold on, not so fast."

"You lie to me, muthafucka!" She was acting wilder than usual so I handed her the cash.

"There." She snatched the money from my hand and counted the bills. I sat down on the bed while she counted. "Now, I need to talk with you about doing something for me –"

"This don't include sex. Sex extra." She was waving the money as she spoke.

"No. It's not sex but I'm sure you are equally good at what I'm going to ask you to do. And I'll pay you another $500 to do it."

I had been thinking of a way to get in Carlton's home, to confront him, record our conversation. It was lame but I couldn't go on like this. I had to try something to clear myself. What was the worst that could happen? He wasn't going to turn me in. I knew too much. And I doubt he'd try to kill me in his own house. That's why I needed Tammy's help.

She agreed before I told her anything about the plan. We went over the details a few times until I was sure she understood. We would take a cab to the Battery where we would be dropped off, then walk to Carlton's home where Tammy would start an altercation with his security team which would hopefully give me a chance to slip inside, undetected. That's as far as I had gotten with my plan. It was my hope that whatever happened after that would clear me enough to go back to my life.

48.

harles Carlton stood next to a window that provided a twilight view of King Street and beyond from the Palmetto Suite of the Omni Hotel. It was just past 6:30 p.m. and he was waiting on the drink he had just ordered when a tall, attractive blonde woman entered the room smiling and walking his way.

"Mr. Congressman, thank you so much for making time for me –"

"Hold on. It's not 'Congressman' until I'm sworn in. Please, call me Charles."

"Well, just for tonight then. Charles, I'm Katherine Zimmer. Did someone offer you a drink?"

"Yes. Thank you. What can I do for you, Katherine."

"This is just an introduction really. I am with The Resolute Corporation. Are you familiar with the company?"

"No, I'm afraid not."

"Well, this little get together is meant to change that. Oh, here are our drinks." The small man in the white jacket that had taken Carlton's order returned with his drink and another that Katherine Zimmer took. "Go ahead and bring the hors d'oeuvres out Tommy. Charles, let's have a seat over here."

Carlton sat down in a chair by a lit gas fireplace. Katherine Zimmer sat across from him on a sofa. She crossed her well-toned, bare legs and leaned back. Her blouse parted at her chest, as if part of an overall orchestration of subtle shifts of clothing meant to draw attention to some of Katherine Zimmer's barely obscured attractions. "Charles, Congressman Davis suggested that I reach out to you. He has been a reliable friend to Resolute over the years."

"Of course. I've relied on him quite a bit over the years myself. Good man."

"Yes. He is a good man. Washington can be overwhelming. Clarence has helped me in so many ways. And I wanted to return the favor to him by doing the same for you."

Carlton thought he knew where this was going but wanted to push back. "What do you mean exactly."

"I want you to know that you can rely on me for anything. Whether it is Charleston, Washington, Baghdad, wherever. You call, I'm coming."

She made it sound so classy, so normal, like she was offering interior decorating tips for an apartment in Georgetown. Well, she must know I'm rich. She can't buy me with money ...

"What exactly does Resolute do?"

"I'm glad you asked. We provide solutions to armed conflict implementation."

Carlton's wide, silent smile spread across his face. "Meaning?"

"We provide contract forces for armed conflicts."

"Okay. Just for the US I hope."

"No worries there. Resolute's founder and CEO is fiercely patriotic." She looked behind Carlton. "Tommy, just put those on the table there." The small, quiet man put the tray softly on the table next to Carlton.

"And who is the CEO?"

"Roger Stone. He's a former Marine. Retired as a Lt. Colonel. He started Resolute 13 years ago. Last year we had revenue of $4.3 billion."

"Impressive. But what does this have to do with me, if

you don't mind my bluntness."

Katherine Zimmer was smart, young and beautiful. But Carlton wasn't going to sleep with her. Giving favors and owing favors were two different things. He wanted to be owed favors. He didn't want to owe them and if he did, the price would be a hell of a lot higher than sex with a beautiful woman. He had seen the political benefits of being independent of national party platforms during the campaign and he wanted to maintain that independence as much as possible in Washington. Rasha's money gave him that opportunity. It was up to him not to squander it.

"Charles, budget cuts are coming. Not during your first term but they are an inevitability. Do you look forward to explaining to your constituents the cuts that will have to be made in their Social Security and Medicare? Not many in Congress do. So Congress, being Congress will look for other options – no offense."

"None taken."

"They will look at military spending. And that's where we come in. Do you know how much of the annual military spending is a result of bureaucratic waste?"

"No idea."

"The Pentagon itself found $125 billion. But it's hard for a government bureaucracy to eliminate wasteful spending. It's easier for a corporation and much of the country's defense needs can be contracted out to private companies like Resolute, saving billions every year. That's an easy sell to voters when it's time to cut the budget."

"Make sense. So far. But why me, why now? You said yourself this won't happen in my term."

"We aren't waiting for the last minute. Charles, Resolute is positioning itself to be the best option for the United States when it comes to providing a superior armed forces product."

A superior armed forces product? Is that what she just

said? Carlton stood and drank what was left of his drink. "Well Katherine, you've given me a lot to think about. I look forward to working with you."

"Charles, we were looking for a commitment from you tonight."

The wide, silent smile spread across his face again, but this time there was something facetious at its edges. "Katherine, I cannot commit to support Resolute tonight, on anything. I intend to look at all sides of an issue before deciding. I mean, even if I thought private military contracts was the way to go, another company may offer the same services for less than you can." She walked over to him, took the glass from his hand and leaned over to place it on a side table. When she leaned over Carlton had a clear view inside her blouse, and there was much to see. She stood again moving closer to him as she did. "Why don't you stay so we can talk about it some more. I'm available all night for you." She reached up and lightly touched his arm.

"That sounds really ... uhm ... nice. But I've got another engagement that I'm already late for ..."

He started towards the door. "You've been wonderful and I meant it when I said I look forward to working with you."

"Charles, are you sure you won't stay?"

Damn, she's persistent. He half-turned as he entered the foyer. "Thanks again. I'll see you soon."

He was feeling good about escaping the snares of his first encounter with a lobbyist when he heard her voice behind him say "Bates". Thinking it had nothing to do with him, he continued walking to the door when a figure entered the foyer from his right. It stopped and turned to face him. When Carlton first saw the face he didn't make the connection, only dumbly wondered why Thursday had decided to track him down then and there. "What..." As the words started to come out of his mouth Carlton was seized with the sensation that a chain had suddenly clasped around his neck, the other end held in the grip of Katherine Zimmer.

Carlton took a seat on the same couch he had been sitting in just a few moments earlier. This time however, he and Katherine Zimmer were joined by Thursday who sat at the other end of the couch. Carlton stared at Thursday for a few moments before turning to Zimmer.

"So you know each other?"

"Charles, I have a confession to make. I was hoping it would have been more obvious and we could avoid this, but I see I will have to lay it out for you."

Carlton's face flushed with anger and he stopped himself from saying what he felt. *Who in the hell is this bitch and what in the fuck is her connection to...* The anger inside him suddenly flipped when he realized Thursday worked for Resolute, leaving him stunned for a moment.

"In a way, Resolute's most valuable product is strategic planning. But it's not just a product we sell to our customer's. It's a skill we employ to ensure our long-term survival. One aspect of strategic planning focuses on identifying reliable friends in government."

Carlton thought of Clarence Davis. *Does he know? Did he keep this from me?*

"We have to be assured that our friends will be there when we need them."

"And that's what you want from me? Friendship? You've got a fucked-up notion of what the word means."

Katherine Zimmer smiled. "Of course, I'm using the Washington meaning of the word, Charles. And it's not what we want from you. It's what we expect from you and, if necessary, what we will demand from you."

Carlton stood up. *I'm not taking any more of this shit.*

"It's time I left."

"Please, Charles, sit down. I don't want you leaving

without a clear understanding of our relationship."

"Relationship!"

"Charles, we've been involved with you since the beginning. Well, from nearly the beginning."

"Yeah, yeah, I know. Your boy Bates here – who sucks by the way -"

"It's more than that, Charles. Much more."

He felt the chain again around his neck. Felt it wrapping around his arms, his waist, his legs. The weight lowered him to the couch again.

"Now your wife and stepdaughter's prior associations had nothing to do with us, of course. But that association and what they had planned, provided an opportunity for you- and us."

"Oh, I see. You are going to tell me that everything that happened was orchestrated by Resolute? That I owe you somehow? Bullshit."

"Not everything, Charles. We can't control the outcome of elections. That was you. But we created the opportunity for you to run."

He had to think for a moment. He was angry and tired. Not at his best. What opportunity? The memory of Richard Haynes' fall from grace slowly came to him. "You set up Richard Haynes?"

"It wasn't hard. He had a history with male prostitutes. We saw an opportunity and made it happen. Made your future happen. Made our future happen."

"Wait a minute. Richard Haynes would have been your prototype for a congressman. You couldn't have invented a more reliable asshole for the kind of legislation you want passed."

"That's true to a point. But he wasn't very reliable, Charles. Actually, he was a greedy prick. Wanted us to funnel money to an offshore account he has. That's not what we do."

Carlton found himself believing what she said. Not all of it. But he could see them taking down Haynes. Zimmer continued talking.

"Clarence Davis is reliable. A good friend, like I said. After you hired Bates, he told us more about you and it was decided to put everything in motion."

So Clarence did know. Sonuvabitch. "So why were you watching Khalil?"

"Routine. He was a sometime informant for the FBI. Involved himself with people and places we are interested in, our clients are interested in, our friends are interested in."

"Terror groups?"

"It's not that simple. If you just label an organization a >terrorist group' you can underestimate it's potential. And the term has become too political, too facile."

Good god, what is she babbling about. "So why were you watching Khalil? Were you watching Staci too?" He feared Staci's connections to that world were deeper than he knew. Maybe Zimmer could confirm that.

"Your stepdaughter was ancillary. We were just following Khalil. A guy like that can connect dots all over the globe."

"So, you didn't kill him?"

Zimmer looked at Thursday for the first time indicating it was time for him to join the conversation. He sat up and cleared his throat.

"Khalil acted as a go-between. He already knew Staci and your wife. When Staci and Rasha were contacted about paying 'their debt,' Staci reached out to Khalil to help. With what exactly, I don't know. But she knew he was connected with this particular group. So it made sense to have someone you trust help out. At some point she found out he was an informant. By the time I got involved, Staci had already found Jackson Peale."

325

"Are you telling me Peale killed Khalil?"

Zimmer cut back in. "We have a good idea who killed Khalil."

There was a pause as Carlton waited for her answer and she waited for Carlton to comment.

"Are you going to say who?"

Zimmer and Thursday exchanged looks. "Let's just call them 'competing theories.' But that doesn't matter. What matters is what law enforcement thinks. What they can prove. They need to think Staci killed Khalil. Tie this thing off, once and for all."

"How is that going to happen?"

"Who can say otherwise?"

Carlton knew what was coming. He didn't disagree with it. Hell, he'd been saying the same thing. Even tried it himself.

"Finding them could be a problem."

"Set up a meeting with Jennifer Lott. Tell her it's an interview. Let's see what happens."

After returning home from his encounter with Katherine Zimmer, Carlton went upstairs to his office with a bottle of scotch and fell into a chair. He poured himself a drink and found Jennifer Lott's phone number in his contacts. He stared at the name and number while he took a drink from the glass. *Three more deaths. Damnit. I've got to be more careful. This can't continue.*

He dialed the number and waited. Voicemail.

"Ms. Lott, this is Charles Carlton. I think now is a good time for the interview you asked me about awhile back. Give me a call and we'll set something up."

He put the phone down and took another drink. *Will she call back? If she knows something, she may be too scared. Nothing to do but wait. She's a reporter. A newly elected congressman just called her about an interview. If she hasn't called back in an hour, I'll assume she's scared.*

He stood up and carried his drink to the French doors that opened onto the deck but didn't go outside. Nothing could be seen in the darkness outside but he looked anyway, his thoughts on what had to be done. Baskin should be easy. He's predictable. Probably has the same routine every day. Peale will be the problem. He knows I'm after him and he's hiding. What if we can't find him?

Peale had not talked with Lott since the night Rasha died. When he saw her name on the phone screen, he hesitated answering. It might not be her. Could be law enforcement. Tammy was in the bathroom and he walked over to the door.

"Tammy, answer this for me."

"Why?"

"Just do it. If it's a woman named Jennifer, give it to me. If it's anybody else hang up."

Tammy gave a look like Peale was asking her to run to the store for groceries but took the phone and answered.

"Hello?" Peale could hear a woman's voice talking.

"Who is this?"

Tammy tossed the phone to Peale. "It's your Jennifer."

"Lott?"

"Who was that?"

"It's a long story. I didn't expect to hear from you." He was still suspicious about why she was calling. Only Lott and Sam knew his new number. But neither had any reason to contact him as far as he knew.

"Look. I just got a call from Carlton wanting an interview. It freaked me out. I didn't know who else to call."

All suspicion about Lott and why she would call vanished immediately when Peale heard what Lott said.

"This is perfect." He was talking to himself as much as he was talking to Lott.

"Perfect? Not if I get killed!"

"No, no, no. That won't happen. Listen to me. He

doesn't know you know anything. He probably just wants to see if you will respond. If you don't, he'll assume you know something. The safe bet is to call him back quickly and set it up."

"I do know something and I'm not some spy that can pull off that kind of shit,"

Lott was scared, he understood that, but he wouldn't get another chance like this. Lott had to call Carlton.

"Lott, what reporter in her right mind would not want to interview Charles Carlton? Jump on this. Get the interview and as a bonus he'll no longer think you are a threat. Don't call, and your name will be right under mine on his hit list. Do you want to hide the rest of your life?"

"Maybe I should call the police ..."

"He is the police!" Peale was almost shouting and Tammy gave him a look.

She knew Peale was right. If she didn't call Carlton back, it would be suspicious. She had to do it.

"Okay. I'll do it"

"Call me back with the time and place." When she didn't respond right away, Peale softened his tone. "Lott, you can do this."

"Why do you want to know when and where it is?"

"Because I'm going to be there."

"How is that supposed to be safe?"

"Not there with you. I'll be close by. After you're finished and you've left, I'm going to drop in on him. See if I can get him to talk."

"What? That's not going to work."

"It may not, but this is the only chance I'll have. I'll have my phone on so you can hear everything."

"This is crazy. It won't work. You won't be able to get to him, and if you do, he won't admit anything."

"Leave that to me. Will you do it?"

"I said I would. But I'm going to be gone when you show

up. I don't want him connecting us."

No problem. Now hang up and call him."

Carlton suggested that they meet at his home at 9 p.m. the following night Lott called Peale and gave him the place and time. It was short notice, but Peale didn't have a choice. He didn't have a plan other than just showing up and confronting Carlton. Lott was right. Carlton wasn't going to just admit everything. I've got to flush him out and I've got less than twenty-four hours to figure out how.

Lott hoped Peale could pull it off. She did. But that's all there was. Hope. She still didn't believe he could do it. At least he was trying something. As far as she knew only her, Peale and Carlton knew the truth about what had happened on King Street. Then there was Carver's murder. Peale wanted that cleared up too. As far as law enforcement and the public were concerned, Peale was the only suspect for that crime.

Not that anyone was very concerned anymore. As the months went by and the story spun by Carlton on the campaign trail took hold in the public's imagination, Carver's death became less the death of a law enforcement officer in the line of duty and more the predictable end for any woman foolish enough to involve herself with a mentally fucked-up drug addict like Jackson Peale. Even Lott began to question her motivation for telling the story. She was a journalist, she told herself, and the story hadn't been told. And it was a hell of a story, a story no other journalist had a clue existed. There didn't need to be further motivation for her. The story would be the biggest of her career. But here was more to it than public and professional notoriety. Carver's death couldn't be written off as some doomed romance gone the way of the gun. Carver was a pain to deal with but she was a good person. She deserved better.

But Carlton wouldn't just sit down and tell her how it

all went down.. When she had written the article that made the loose connections between Khalil, Carver, the bombing and Rasha Carlton, most considered it borderline tabloid journalism. But Carlton didn't and neither did his wife. Had Rasha Carlton not called her she would have never really been convinced that Carlton knew what had happened. She would have suspected he knew, but she wouldn't have known for sure. Rasha was a distraught woman when they had talked at her home. She knew what had happened, who had done it and why. And if she knew, her husband knew. After her death, Lott was not only convinced Charles Carlton could be brought down if the facts were ever revealed, it also convinced her that if she pursued the story further, she would probably end up dead also.

So she had put it aside, went back to reporting on the mundane happenings around Charleston – the opening of a new restaurant by a "celebrity" chef, the efforts of a group of organized, downtown residents to ban dining on the sidewalks and another group's demand that city council pass an ordinance that prohibited the sale of alcohol after midnight. She intentionally did not draw attention to herself by not publishing anything about the bombing or the Carltons again.

But that was about to change apparently and at the invitation of Charles Carlton himself. She was scared and she knew she wouldn't be able to hide that from Carlton. What he would do when he saw that fear scared her even more.

48.

Sam arrived at the Pelican just after 8:00 p.m., knocking on the door of the apartment. Tammy came out of the bathroom when she heard the knock.

"That's Sam. Are you ready?"

"Don't I look ready?"

She was wearing her trademark tight blue jeans, heels and halter top. Her long black hair was brushed smooth and straight.

"What if you have to run?" I was looking at the heels.

"Run? You no say run. When do I run?"

"Never mind."

Sam's eyes lit up when he saw Tammy and he gave me a knowing smile.

"Sam this is Tammy. Tammy, Sam."

"Hey, Sam."

Sam stammered a "Hi." As chatty as he can be at times, the sight of a real, live sexy woman can really tie him up.

"Let's get going. Lott will be there at 9:00."

As Sam drove us back to Charleston, I looked around, looking for a tail. "Did anybody follow you on the drive out?"

"Not that I noticed. I mean, I was looking but didn't see anything."

That wasn't good. Part of my plan was to have whoever was watching Sam follow us to Carlton's, to witness whatever happened. But what I wanted to do didn't depend on witnesses. Carrying out the plan would just be riskier if it were only me and Lott. It was a longshot that someone would still be following Sam anyway.

"So you want me to just drop you off at the Battery and leave?"

"That's it."

"You want me to pick you up later? I got the whole night off."

"No. I'll meet up at the Office later."

"Is that safe?"

"Maybe. Maybe not. I'll make that call when the time comes."

"What about her?" Sam jerked his head towards the backseat where Tammy sat.

"She knows what to do. She'll be fine."

"Did you drive by Carlton's on the way?"

"Yeah. Two guys out front, dressed the way you said they'd be. I didn't see anybody else."

"Okay."

"How much longer. This car stink back here." Tammy had been quiet until then. For a hooker living in a shit hole apartment, she didn't like messes, filth or bad odors. She always kept her place neat and clean. She wouldn't last fifteen seconds at Sam's place. I smiled and glanced at Sam. A worried look had taken hold of his face, as if his fantasy of wild sex with Tammy was dissipating in his mind..

"Just a few more minutes, Tammy, then it's show time."

49.

L ott had to walk several blocks from where she parked to the Carlton home. Walking along the waterfront she passed people walking the other direction, on an after dinner walk perhaps, enjoying the cool fall air and the salt-tinged breeze off the battery. But Lott was too focused on finding the house with security guards to notice any of that. Not that it was hard to find, even in the dark. Most of the homes were well lit and when she did reach the Carlton home she stopped and let herself marvel for a moment before crossing the street. The home was beautiful. Lott guessed it had to be more than a hundred years old. Three stories, with open, inviting porches on the first two floors that contrasted with the porch-less third floor, that sat high enough from the street to convey a sense of the unsurmountable distance that existed between the passerby and the home's occupants. A brick drive ran along the side of the house to her right. In the drive was a dark SUV, blocking the entrance. A short, wrought iron fence, suggesting a barrier rather than creating one, ran between the remainder of the tiny front yard and the sidewalk. Two men in dark suits stood leisurely on the front porch. She walked across the street. As soon as she stepped her foot on the driveway, both men were coming down the steps in her direction.

"Hold it right there, mam."

"I, I have an appointment."

"Identification please."

She fumbled with her purse that was hanging by a strap over her shoulder and pulled out her press credentials. One of the men examined the document with a flashlight while the other turned and spoke to someone in a microphone she couldn't see.

"Okay, Ms. Lott, come with us."

Flashlight led the way while microphone followed behind her. Walking up the steps to the front door Jennifer Lott became aware of how improbable this meeting was. Carlton didn't need her interview. He could have his pick of interviews, print, TV or internet. But he agreed to an interview with me after Peale tells me to call him. She felt her heart rate increasing and her ears began to ring. She wanted to turn around and run but she couldn't. Her legs were heavy and sluggish and she was trying to ignore her body's physical response to her fear. Don't be stupid. It's an interview with the congressman-elect. If you're going to be a journalist, you can't give in to irrational fears. She breathed deeply at the top of the steps as flashlight opened the door and she walked in. As the door closed behind her, a man she hadn't seen before approached her. He had a crewcut and boyish face and wore a suit like the others. He smiled and held out his hand.

"Ms. Lott, my name is Thursday. The Congressman is waiting for you."

50.

fter Sam dropped us off at the park, Tammy and I made the short walk to the Carlton House. I had been to the Carlton home twice before with Staci, but only briefly. The second time she had shown me a key that was behind a brick in a wall that bordered the lot next door. She had told me she wanted me to know where it was in case I ever needed to let myself in. She didn't say why I would need to do that, she just let the suggestion hang in the air with all the other mysteries that hovered around her. This was the only time I had used it. If it wasn't there, I was going to have a problem making a surprise entrance.

Tammy and I stopped on the sidewalk when we had a view of the Carlton House.

"See the drive on the far side."

Tammy raised herself on her toes and grabbed my arm for balance. "Yes."

"I've got to go down that driveway to the back of the house. You need to distract those two on the front steps, get them to move to the other side of the house."

"They chase me."

"Right. Now go to it."

Tammy sashayed her bell-shaped ass down the sidewalk in front of Carlton's home and turned into the drive. The guys on the front porch started down the steps and I started walking. As I passed the house I could hear Tammy cranking up.

"I see, Chief Carlton."

"No, you won't."

"Yes. He owe me money."

"Alright, honey, get off the property or we're calling the police."

"Call the police. I tell them he fuck me, don't pay. He should go to jail."

"Look ..."

I walked beyond the driveway and stopped. I stood next to a brick column that was built at the end of the wall between Carlton's property and his neighbor's. I looked over my right shoulder and checked on Tammy's progress.

"You touch me, I scream rape so loud they hear me in Hilton Head." A couple walking down the sidewalk stopped to watch the show.

One of the guys tried to quickly grab her arm and she darted to the far corner of the house, away from me. When both turned to chase her I went around the column into the drive and hurried to the backyard. I could hear Tammy screaming as they dragged her to the street. If they didn't let her go, I had given her pepper spray to help her escape. I was hoping she got the chance to use it.

I stayed in the dark as much as possible away from the light of the house. It took me a while to find the brick in the dark wall but when I did, the key was there. It must have been Staci's secret. Hell, maybe Rasha's too. I took the key and looked up at the deck that extended from Carlton's third floor office. I was guessing that Carlton would want the interview to take place there. A few steps rose from the back yard to the deck on the first floor, then another flight to the second-floor deck. The key should open the door on the second-floor deck because Staci had told me to use it on that door. What I didn't know was whether or not it opened all of the doors or just the one. Staci's bedroom was on the second floor so it was possible she just wanted me using the most direct route and not wandering all over the house.

I climbed the stairs to the second floor and saw that there were no stairs to the deck above me on the third floor. That was a problem. If Carlton and Lott were in his office on the third floor, that meant I would have to climb a flight of stairs inside the house, increasing the chance I would be heard before I was seen. I put the key in the deadbolt and turned it, feeling the bolt slide back into the door. I grasped the door knob and turned, feeling the door give way in my hand. There were no squeaks and I let out the breath I had been holding. The door was mostly paned glass on the upper half, but there was no view inside because of the closed, louvered blinds. Any view of what was behind the door was blocked unless I opened the door. I pushed it open slowly and looked in. The immediate room was dark but there was a small lamp lighting a hallway in front of me. I kept still for a moment and listened. There were voices upstairs, a woman's and a man's. I wasn't sure but the man's voice sounded like Carlton. That's them. They're upstairs like I thought. I pushed the door open harder than I should have because it almost immediately slammed into a table or something that scraped across the floor, making a sound that could be heard all over the house. I froze. The house was quiet. Then I heard footsteps coming down the steps. I waited, not moving, blood pounding in my ears. As the footsteps reached the bottom of the steps a flashlight came on in the hallway. The beam quickly traced the wall and landed on me. Not the entrance I wanted to make.

"Peale! Why am I not surprised? Come on up and join us."

Thursday flipped a switch that turned on an overhead light. He turned off the flashlight he was holding in his left hand and motioned me forward with the gun he was holding in his right. "Come on."

Upstairs, Jennifer Lott sat in a chair, her cheeks and eyes wet with tears. I felt bad involving her in this but I needed to know Carlton would be here if my plan was going to work. My plan. My plan was fucked. Carlton stood by his desk, a bemused look on his face.

Thursday put the gun into my spine and frisked me, finding the taser and duct tape in my jacket pockets. When Lott saw them her eyes widened and she jerked her head towards me.

"You used me! You sonuvabitch! You used me!"

Carlton was laughing now. "Goddammit, Peale. You are one crazy motherfucker. I don't know what you thought you were going to do, but I'm glad you decided to drop in."

Thursday pushed me in the direction of Lott. I couldn't help but look at her. Her eyes were swirling with hate and fear.

"I'm sorry. I didn't —"

She looked away.

"Well, this worked out well. I can take care of two problems at once. Thanks, Peale. Thank you, thank you, thank you." He walked over and picked up the taser and held it up for Thursday. "Is this what he got you with?"

Carlton was smiling.

"I ought to shove it up his ass."

"No. You are here to kill them. We don't have time for torture. Plus, I don't want shit all over my office floor. Come to think of it, I don't want blood on my office floor either. Take them out on the deck."

Carlton opened the French doors that led to the back deck. My mind was racing as Thursday directed Lott and me with the gun. What should I do? Try to take Thursday? No. Not yet. You've got time to think of something ..."

Outside we faced the low, white, columned railing of the deck. Behind it was darkness, and somewhere out in the darkness, down below, was the yard. My mind quickly weighed the options — broken bones or a bullet?

I'll jump. Fuck it, I'll jump.

Just before I took off, something grabbed my hand. I looked down and saw Lott's arm, her hand clasped around mine. I looked at her face. Tears glistened in her eyes and her lower lip was pushed up and quivering, holding in the crying she wanted to do. I hadn't thought of her and guilt crawled all over my insides.

"Turn around."

She released my hand and we turned to face Thursday. Carlton came out on the deck and closed the doors behind him.

Jumping is the only chance. But how can I get Lott to jump too? She's rigid with fear.

Thursday raised the gun, pointing it at me first, then moving it to Lott, then back to me again. The guy never stopped being a dick.

"Quit playing games and kill them."

"What do I do with the bodies?"

Carlton looked at Thursday with a >what the fuck?' expression.

"You're the hired killer. Getting rid of the bodies comes with the damn contract."

I can pick up Lott and run towards the railing. He'll have time to shoot. I'll probably get hit but it won't stop me. I can get to the rail and go over, giving Lott a chance. That's what I'll do. It's my fault she's here anyway –

I was so focused, running through my mind the exact motions I would take to pick up Lott, run across the deck and somehow get us over the rail that what I saw happening behind Thursday and Carlton didn't register at first. But as Thursday and Carlton turned, I knew I wouldn't be jumping over the rail with Lott.

51.

Peter Martin had kept irregular contact with Jennifer Lott during the time he had been investigating the King Street bombing. Not that she was giving him any information, but she knew more than she had told him and he felt it was only a matter of time before she decided to give him the rest of what she knew. She was scared but of what or who he wasn't sure. He could guess. The list was short. But he didn't like guessing. He preferred knowing. His pretense for calling was to ask if she had heard from Peale. She never answered when he called but would eventually call back. He wondered about that and concluded she needed time to prepare herself for the conversation, like she didn't trust what would come out of her mouth if she just answered the phone and started talking. Lott seemed smart enough, but Peter Martin sensed a lack of confidence. None of that mattered other than confirming what he had always thought: she knew more than she had told him and was being cautious about what she said. He had continued to call and ask about Peale and Lott had routinely called him back to say she hadn't. Until last night, when she had called unexpectedly. She told him that Carlton wanted to meet with her for an interview and that Peale was going to be there. According to Lott, Peale wanted to know the time and place. But she was scared of Carlton and of what Peale might do.

Having worked in the Solicitor's Office for almost thirty years, Peter Martin knew Jackson Peale. He had always thought Peale was a gifted lawyer, one of the best he had encountered. But, like most everyone else in the local legal community, he had watched from a distance the decline and ultimate destruction of his career. He knew Peale was still around, on the periphery of the Charleston legal world, doing private investigations or something of the sort, but he hadn't seen Peale or talked to him in years. His opinion of Peale was not much different from anyone else who no longer had any reason to involve Peale in his life. Peale was an addict with severe, untreated mental health issues, both of which made him unpredictable, unstable and potentially dangerous. Now he was the only suspect in the death of a law enforcement officer. Martin couldn't believe Peale would actually show up at Carlton's home, but on the off chance he would, he told Lott that he would be there. She asked him if he had a gun. He told her he did and she said to bring it.

He had followed Lott in his car and on foot until he was near the Carlton home, staying some distance away, but close enough to see whatever happened in the front of the house. And what he had seen was much more than he had expected. Jennifer Lott goes inside the home with what appeared to be security guards ... the guards return to their post outside the front door ... A small woman creates a scene in the front of the house with the security guards ... a man on the sidewalk quickly sneaks up the driveway when the guards are distracted ... he can't see the man's face but it has to be Peale ... The security guards bring the woman back to the street and send her on her way ... They return to their post on the front steps for a few minutes before leaving the house in a SUV ... as he is waiting and watching the same woman returns and goes to the front door, opens it and walks inside ... Martin crosses the street, walks to the front door and goes in ... standing in the foyer, he can hear things happening upstairs ... a woman's scream, a man's shout, another scream, what sounds like suppressed gun fire and the sound of something or someone falling and rolling on the floor ... Martin runs up the stairs ... a wild scene greets him on the back deck ... the congressman and another man rolling on the floor coughing , swearing and moaning ... the small woman standing over them with a gun pointed at both ... another woman crouches down next to the motionless body of Jackson Peale ... the woman next to Peale looks up at Martin ... it's Jennifer Lott ...

It took a lot of convincing but the Asian woman finally gave Martin the gun she had trained on Carlton and the other man. Carlton had immediately demanded that Martin call for back up, which he did. But by the time they had arrived, Lott had told him enough that Martin instructed the officers to place Carlton and the other man under arrest. The unknown man went quietly but Carlton was raising hell, threatening everyone he saw. Even the paramedics working on Peale, who had been shot twice, was unconscious and bleeding. When EMS took him away Martin told himself that Peale probably wouldn't survive.

52.

Solicitor Barnes was slouched on the sofa at home, half watching an NBA game when his mobile started vibrating, then ringing loudly. His daughter, annoyed at the volume, looked up at him from her iPad at the other end of the sofa. Not wanting to talk to just anyone at 10:37 p.m., he held up the phone to see who was calling.

"Dad! Mute it!"

The phone vibrated and blasted the preset ring tone again, an obnoxious clanging noise that everyone his daughter knew changed as soon as they bought the phone. "Dad!"

He now had the phone within the limited range of distance from his face that he could make out the name without reading glasses. Pete Martin.

"Pete?"

"Do you think Judge Taylor can come down and sign a stack of arrest warrants?"

"Now?"

"Yes. Now."

"Why now? C hold on. What's this about? Warrants on who?"

"Let's see ... Congressman-elect Carlton, you know, the former Police Chief of Charleston. And ..."

Barnes was struggling to lift himself from the sofa while holding the phone to his head. "Hold on, Pete – what the hell are you talking about?"

"Oh and there's a John Doe. Won't give me a name, no

Plummet

ID—"

"Goddammit Pete! Slow down! What are you talking about!"

Barnes' daughter looked up at her dad with disapproval before going back to her online world.. Barnes saw the expression and moved to his bedroom where he could talk freely without a pre-teen audience. There he listened and after hearing what Peter Martin had to say, he was changing his clothes and making his way to the Charleston City Jail.

53.

I was awake when a nurse brought in my lunch and the news that a visitor had come by to see me that morning. She said the visitor was a young woman but she would have to check on the name. My first thought, or hope, was that Wendy had let Megan visit. But that wasn't likely. They had to know what had happened at Carlton's home. I had seen some of the coverage on TV. But what I saw on TV probably just confirmed in Wendy's mind that she was right in keeping Megan away. Maybe she was. The only other visitor had been Pete Martin. He had filled me in on the legal fallout from the other night. Carlton was being held on obstruction of justice charges and kidnaping. Thursday was charged with assault and battery of a high and aggravated nature, kidnaping and possession of a weapon during the commission of a crime. More charges were coming. Lott had told him Thursday killed Carver, so they were running ballistics test on his weapon to see if it was a match. I assured him it would be.

Later that afternoon an attractive Filipina in a pink halter top, tight blue jeans and heels came by to visit. For some reason, I hadn't expected to see her again. Realizing it was Tammy and not Megan that had been by earlier to see me made me emotional. Not in a sad way but what I was feeling after everything that had happened was complicated. And I was pretty doped up. But I was genuinely happy to see her and I also remembered what she had done.

"I think you are amazing." My voice was cracking, tears wetted my eyes.

"Shut up."

"You saved my life."

She made a noise that suggested I was being melodramatic and walked closer to the bed. That was Tammy. She wasn't going for any emotional bullshit.

"Where does it hurt?"

"Everywhere." She made one of her faces that could convey so much without saying a word. I read this one to be somewhere between Apoor little thing" and "tough shit." If I thought she was being serious I would have told her to cut it out. Instead, I laughed, and it hurt.

"Serves you right for laughing at me. Why you laugh at me?"

"Your expressions. They're hilarious."

"If you think I'm joking, I leave. I go make money."

"No, no, no. Stay. I'm sorry. I'm glad you came. Sit down." She walked to the chair in the corner, threw her bag on a table and plopped into the chair with an attitude of someone that had something better to do.

"How long have I been here?"

"Three days. I think."

"What have you been doing since..." I didn't know what to say. "... since that night."

She shrugged and looked away. "Just working." The image of a her as a superhero – Wonder Hooker – popped in my mind, swooping in to save me and Lott from death and returning to her life as a hooker the next day. I wasn't laughing to make fun of her, although that's how she took it. She stood up and reached for her purse.

"I'm leaving."

"Stop. Please. It's the medication. It makes me loopy."

"You act drunk."

"If I wasn't on the meds I'd be screaming in pain. This

is better."

She sat back down. "I can't stay long. I gotta work."

That sobered me up, the thought of Tammy doing all that she had done for me, now returning to life as a hooker at the Fox Run. What I said next just blurted out of me.

"Move in with me."

Her first expression was one of surprise, but she caught herself. "You don't have a place. You live with me, remember?"

"I've got a place that I can go back to now. I want you to come with me. No charge."

She was suspicious. "Oh, you want sex. You pay for sex. I pay you rent."

"No, I don't want sex and you don't have to pay rent. I just want to help." That came out wrong. Tammy was too proud to admit she needed help. What I wanted to say is that she could stop being a hooker, do something else with her life. She didn't see it that way.

"Why I need your help. You need my help. I been helping you!"

"You have, more than I can ever repay. I'm just offering you a chance to get out of the Fox Run."

The idea must have appealed to her because she did that thing again where she puts her finger and thumb on her chin and looks away, as if pondering the proposal.

"Where I meet clients?"

She wasn't getting it. Maybe it was me that wasn't getting it. Maybe she was fine with her life, with her profession. I didn't think so. Although the idea of running a brothel South of Broad appealed to me, she would have to stop hooking if she moved in with me. I could see this wouldn't be an easy sell.

"We'll talk about it later. Will you help me when it's time for me to go home."

"You pay?"

"Yes, dammit, I'll pay." If I expected her to give up her current job, I'd better have something to replace it with.

On the day I was released, Tammy showed up and actually pushed my wheelchair out the door. Waiting for us on the curb was Pete Martin.

"You need a ride?"

"Sure. As long as you're taking me to my place and not someplace owned by the County."

"Your place. For now anyway."

He opened the back door to his nondescript sedan and they helped me in. When Tammy got in the front, Pete looked at her, then at me.

"She's coming too. My home health nurse."

"Right."

On the ride to Whitsett Street, Pete filled me in on how the cases against Carlton and Thursday looked. Thursday was being charged with Carver's murder since ballistics matched his gun with the bullets that killed her. Neither Thursday or Carlton were talking and both had lawyers, out of town guys from D.C.

"It's going to be a hell of a fight, but I think we have solid cases on what we've charged them with so far."

I wanted to ask about the terrorists, about Staci. But that was dangerous territory for me. To involve Carlton with any of that could suck me right back in too. Hell, I actually had my hands on the bomb. When it came to the bombing on King Street, I was as guilty as anyone. I suddenly felt the need to get out of Martin's car. I looked up and caught Martin looking at me in the rear-view mirror. What came out of his mouth made me think he was reading my mind.

"I don't think we can connect Carlton to the bombing. If anyone else was involved, the proof died with Staci Turner and Rasha Carlton."

Was he giving me a pass or fucking with me? Whichever it was I was silent for the rest of the trip.

Martin let us out on the sidewalk in front of Martha's home. Tammy was barely tall enough for me to lean on for the walk up the steps to Martha's house. I thanked Pete again for the ride and we turned towards the steps.

"Aren't you going to ask me about your gun?"

I stopped and looked at him. "Yeah. Do I get it back?"

"You aren't supposed to own or possess a firearm, remember? So, no, you won't get it back."

What was he going to say next? That I was still a suspect for Khalil's murder? Will this never end?

"You know, we still don't know who killed that guy at the Shoreline." He stared at me for a few seconds, time enough to let all of what that statement could mean sink in. "You couldn't help us with that, could you?"

"I told Carver everything that I know about that."

"We'll probably need to talk with you about it again, anyway. When we go over everything else. But we'll give you time to heal up some. Get your strength back."

He looked down the street as if deciding on something in his mind.

"Hell, I doubt we will ever know what happened at the Shoreline." He looked back at me. "Will we?"

I shrugged, turned from him and with Tammy's help, hobbled into Martha's house.

54.

Once Jennifer Lott recuperated from her ordeal at the Carlton house, she decided to start work on what she could now publish about the King Street Bombing, Carver's murder and Charles Carlton. She had to be careful. She was the victim and witness to the only charges that had been filed against Carlton and Bates. When she called Pete Martin, he asked her not to publish anything. Not yet anyway.

"It won't go over well and could potentially damage the case. You are no longer just a reporter. You – along with Jack Peale – are our witnesses."

"So I just have to sit back while all the other media cover what is happening?"

"Yes."

She knew what he was saying was right. She had all but told herself the same thing before she called him. But that didn't make it any easier to accept.

"You'll have a story once it's over. Once there's a conviction. It's not going away."

"What about the Shoreline killing, what's his name, Mahmoud Kahlil? Is that off limits too?"

Martin had hoped that that case would stay forgotten, but Dan Baker didn't want to leave any of the cases connected to Charles Carlton unresolved. He had instructed his staff to seek an indictment against Jackson Peale for the murder of Mahmoud Khalil. When he told Jennifer Lott, she couldn't believe what she was hearing.

"Are you kidding. Look, as far as I'm concerned, I

never want to see the guy again. He uses people, thinks about nothing but what he wants and doesn't care who gets hurt or shafted in the process-"

"Ok. I get it. Is there a >but' in there somewhere?"

"But, he didn't kill Khalil."

"His gun did."

"Did you know I talked to the people that lived in the building where Khalil's body was found? Six or seven. Not one heard gunshots."

"So."

"Carver told me she responded to a 911 call where someone reported gunshots. An anonymous call."

This was news to Martin. He hadn't looked at the Shoreline case that closely. All of his attention had been focused on the bombing. If what Lott was saying was correct, it may need to be revisited.

"Carver thought the killer used a silencer –"

"Suppressor."

"– right, that's the word she used. Otherwise, the 9mm would have been heard by someone. Especially six shots."

"Do you have the names of the people you talked to?"

"I can find them."

"Do that. I need to delay this indictment proceeding. A string of witnesses testifying they heard nothing would be more than enough for a good defense attorney to prove reasonable doubt."

"Especially since you are prosecuting someone else for another murder that we know prefers using a silencer, I mean, suppressor, when he commits murder."

"You'd make a pretty good detective Lott."

It made her feel good to hear it. She was beginning to feel like she had before any of this started, although she suspected she'd never return completely.

"Thanks. But I'll stick with the media."

55.

I don't ever remember wanting to kill myself, even during the worst, the darkest times I experienced after losing everything. But there was this one day, just before I got help, I went to the marina and had my 22' Carolina skiff put in the water. It was September, the weather was beautiful and the water was like glass, the sky a dome of blue over a bottle green sea. When I cranked the boat and pointed the bow towards the mouth of Charleston Harbor, I can remember having only a vague intention of escaping, of following the horizon to some other place laying just out of sight, beyond that line where sky meets sea, where...where what? Where another life could be lived, freed of my personal history? That wasn't possible and somewhere deep within me, I knew that. Had I been chasing after another life, I might have seen the absurdity of it, turned the boat around and put myself back on shore. But I wasn't chasing anything. I was escaping. There was no destination, only the intention to be somewhere else. There was nothing more to the idea than that. Just get in the boat and go.

Normally, taking a small skiff off shore is a bad idea, but like I said, on that day, the sea was calm, almost still, as if quieted for me and my pointless journey. Looking back, I can see where some would say it was a trap, laid out for me, by whatever has the power to do that sort of thing in this world. But I don't believe in that. The stillness of the water was just a coincidence. Had there been heavier seas, this would have been just one less event in my life.

At the Charleston jetty I opened the throttle and felt the

thrill of skimming across the open ocean in such a small boat. The sensation felt almost forbidden. I kept going, towards the horizon, for I don't know how long, but with every passing minute the heavy darkness inside me seemed forced to the surface where it fell away in pieces until I literally felt lighter. As the feeling of lightness increased a giddiness overcame me and I started to laugh I laughed into the sound of the wind rushing past my face until the tears came and clouded my sight and I could feel them blowing out the corners of my eyes. When I realized I was no longer laughing but crying I throttled down, allowing the engine to idle as I fell into the seat and sobbed. I remember not knowing why I was crying and then feeling panic at the thought of where I was. I stood up and wiped my eyes. The blue of the water around me was stunning and terrifying. I was so low to the water, there was no sight of land. Looking over the side, the water was clear until, at some point, the blue darkness rose from the depths. It looked menacing, that darkness, as if it shrouded dangers stirring just out of sight. The first swell seemed to arrive just as the terror did or maybe that is a false memory. No matter. The swells were real. The first one lifted the bow of the boat and rolled beneath the hull, dropping the bow and lifting the stern in a dramatic see-sawing motion before dropping the stern again as it continued on its journey. The next one arrived soon after and I scrambled for the controls at the center of the boat, turning it towards the setting sun and what I hoped was the direction of shore. The ride back took much longer in the swells and I had a growing fear that my little flat bottom boat wouldn't make it back if the swells grew larger. Water began coming over the bow and the stern and on one particularly large swell, the boat was dropped, its hull slammed so violently I was bounced from my seat into the floor of the boat. In my memory, the sky darkened, and in that darkness, just as it does in all darkness, hid the demon that wants to destroy each one of us. I could feel it at my back, beneath my boat, closing in. My escape had become a fight to survive. Only the simple thought of staying in the boat and keeping it moving towards shore kept me going. So I was chased back to shore, beaching my boat miles away from Charleston, but on solid earth again, walking away from another encounter with what should have killed me.

I don't think there's a reason I've survived other than what little will power I sometimes have and a lot of luck. Anyway, according to Pete Martin I've survived again, this time indictment and jail for Khalil's murder. But that had nothing to do with me or luck. That was Carver and Lott. I tried calling Lott to thank her, but she won't return my calls. Another on the list that won't. Megan and Wendy are still on that list too.

So now it's just me in my apartment with my new neighbor living in Martha's house. Tammy promised me she would stop hooking, but I'm not sure she's given it up completely. I haven't seen any other "visible means of income." My neighbors are getting more and more curious and concerned. She told me that if I wanted to be sure she wasn't doing it, she could move in with me. I think I'll just take her word for it. At least for now. I'm going to enjoy the quiet for a while.

Thank you for reading.
Please review this book. Reviews help others find
Absolutely Amazing eBooks and inspire us to keep
providing these marvelous tales.

If you would like to be put on our email list to receive
updates on new releases, contests, and promotions, please
go to AbsolutelyAmazingEbooks.com and sign up.

About the Author

Born in 1965 South Carolina, the author was compelled through the public school system of South Carolina, accumulating through the years, sufficient course credits and test-taking skills that he was admitted to the University of South Carolina in 1984 and its law school in1989 where he earned, respectively, a BA degree in English and a *Juris Doctor*. Today, he is a lawyer in Anderson, South Carolina, where he resides with his family.

This is his first novel.

ABSOLUTELY AMAZING eBOOKS

AbsolutelyAmazingEbooks.com
or AA-eBooks.com

www.ingramcontent.com/pod-product-compliance
Lightning Source LLC
Chambersburg PA
CBHW060933030726
47503CB00003B/581